Burial of Hearts

Shania Sarup, a 17-year-old enthusiast of all things art, finds inspiration in history, literature and the world around her. Her works are influenced by nature, people and emotions, reflecting the beauty she sees in the simplest aspects of life.

Aspiring to be a lawyer and part-time writer, Shania finds the most joy in sharing her unique perspective with others. She can be found either curled up with a book on a rainy day or playing movie soundtracks on the piano.

Burial of Hearts marks her second book, following her debut collection of poems titled *Along the Lines of Youth*.

Connect with Shania on Instagram: @artandpoemsbyshania

Burial of Hearts

SHANIA SARUP

RUPA

Published by
Rupa Publications India Pvt. Ltd 2024
7/16, Ansari Road, Daryaganj
New Delhi 110002

Sales centres:
Bengaluru Chennai
Hyderabad Jaipur Kathmandu
Kolkata Mumbai Prayagraj

Copyright © Shania Sarup 2024

This is a work of fiction. All situations, incidents, dialogue and characters, with the exception of some well-known historical and public figures mentioned in this novel, are products of the author's imagination and are not to be construed as real. They are not intended to depict actual events or people or to change the entirely fictional nature of the work. In all other respects, any resemblance to persons living or dead is entirely coincidental.

All rights reserved.
No part of this publication may be reproduced, transmitted or stored in a retrieval system, in any form or by any means, electronic, mechanical, photocopying, recording or otherwise, without the prior permission of the publisher.

P-ISBN: 978-93-6156-032-3
E-ISBN: 978-93-6156-656-1

First impression 2024

10 9 8 7 6 5 4 3 2 1

The moral right of the author has been asserted.

Printed in India

This book is sold subject to the condition that it shall not, by way of trade or otherwise, be lent, resold, hired out or otherwise circulated, without the publisher's prior consent, in any form of binding or cover other than that in which it is published.

For Mama,
who forever inspires me
and truly is my entire world.

This book would never have
been possible without you.

Silana

Silana Haydn was ecstatic. She had vaguely noticed the unmistakable outline of a rectangular package perched on her bedside table in the morning light filtering through her curtains and wasted no time clambering out from beneath her covers. Though her extremities had hardly adjusted to the change in temperature, it didn't matter, and she enthusiastically flung her curtains open. The sun beat down on her lidded eyes and she quickly spun around, staring at the adjacent wall and away from her glass-paned window.

Once her eyes had recovered from the effulgent aftershock, Silana's gaze fell on the package lying on the mahogany table. She sauntered over and was met with a wax-sealed, yellowed parchment envelope with scribbles in her native Polish; it read 'To Silana—Happy Birthday, my darling daughter'. She kept it aside, resolving to open it later, and picked up the package, her hands quivering ever so slightly as she tentatively opened its crinkled saffron reams. Her mother was careful about preserving wrappings—wastage was not tolerated. Silana cautiously pried the tape from the delicate packaging and peered inside—a broad grin stretched across her flushed face.

With trembling hands, she picked up the two books that were placed squarely on top of each other. The first was a rust-coloured leatherbound book with a tiny clasp and sprawling red letters on the front that read 'Writers of the Ages: Stories of Success'. Running her finger along the textured spine, Silana shifted her focus to the other book, which had been beckoning her from beneath the shadowy remnants of the wrappings. Placing the first book aside, she fished out the second—a relatively large, burnt-sienna leatherbound journal with a similar clasp as the other one. Inscribed on the cover were the words 'Silana's Memories' in italic golden font. She could hardly contain her excitement as she flipped through the blank parchments, careful not to crease them.

Silana couldn't get carried away so easily yet—she had to read the note impatiently waiting for her on her desk, bathed in the golden beams of the morning sun. She reached to grasp it, her fingers skimming over the textured, raw-edged wax seal, which delineated an owl, its talons grasping a book. Eager to explore its contents, Silana hastily opened it; her eyes widened at the hefty sum of 100 Reichsmarks that she found inside. Sifting through the banknotes, she noticed a bright trifold paper. *That must be the note.* And it was. She opened it and squinted. Her father must have penned this in a hurry, for she could hardly understand a word. Even as she adjusted her glasses, the words appeared as unfamiliar as Greek and Latin. But soon enough, the embers of an idea began glowing in her mind.

Silana placed the note on her desk and rushed to get ready. After brushing and bathing, she put on an indicolite knee-length dress with a lively, swirling floral pattern. She looked in the mirror, her green eyes flashing with excitement as she studied her reflection. Perfect, she thought. Now she must take extra care not to get her outfit dirty. She left the bathroom and, on the way out of her room, grabbed the letter.

Silana flew down the spiral staircase that encircled a low-hanging chandelier, subsequently entering the foyer to discover her entire family beaming, with birthday-themed pennants strung up, alongside the remnants of the family's breakfast and a white three-tier cake as the new centrepiece of the expansive dining table. 'Happy Birthday, Silana!' they chorused, and the girl grinned heartily from ear to ear. She sprinted to tackle her elder brother, Sebastien, first in the line of fire, then her younger sister, Sunne and finally her parents.

'I can't believe you're 15 already, ma chérie. Where did all the time go?' her mother remarked in her delicate French accent.

'Mother, I'm not even that old yet. Sebastien will be 18 in a few months' time!'

'Yes, I suppose you have a point. How fast the sands of time slip through our fingers, yes?'

'I do suppose you've had an opportunity to appreciate the gift your mother and I picked out?' Silana's gaze landed on the beaming face of her father. His thick Polish accent had always fascinated her, as did the wooden tobacco pipe he always seemed to carry around.

'I did indeed. Father, they were simply spectacular—just what I needed to pen my daily happenings. But most unfortunately I didn't really have the chance to read the note in the rush to get ready. It would be so lovely to hear it in your voice. Would you mind?'

'Not in the slightest.'

Silana handed him the note. He cleared his throat and began—

Dearest Silana,

A very merry 15th birthday to the most remarkable child I could ever have asked for. You radiate exuberance and positivity, and your passion for writing and your marvellous works append a spark to the pages of my life. It's been a pleasure watching you blossom over these past 15 years, and I wouldn't miss even a moment with you for the world.

All my love,
Lukas Haydn

His heavy Polish accent lingered in the air, with everyone in awe of how easily he could captivate a room. Silana, full of pride, hugged her father tightly, and he chuckled warmly.

'Why don't you write so beautifully for us, Father?'

'Now Sunne, we don't compare. Silana is a budding author. I write to increase her indulgence in the beauty of language and perhaps spark some inspiration, yes?'

Sunne, two years junior to Silana, was far from satisfied with this disclosure. But her father was in a good mood today and even she knew not to try his temper. Bright days such as these were unnervingly scarce.

'Sil, you haven't forgotten about the cake, have you now? We'd better cut it soon; the roses on top are calling out to me, I swear it,' Sebastien teasingly interjected as the family erupted into laughter.

'He's right. Someone bring the candles!' her father guffawed.

Sunne determinedly sped to the kitchen. The group watched her peel back and hand a matchbox and some candles to her elder sister.

Silana muttered a few obscure words of thanks and gingerly placed 15 candles in a circular pattern on the cake. She pulled out a match and was about to strike it when it was snatched away by Sebastien. 'Here, let me handle this. Truth be told, I don't trust your ability to light a match.'

Silana opened her mouth to protest but paused when her father shot her a warning glance. She slumped and dejectedly shook her head as Sebastien deftly lit the candles one by one. For a brief moment, Silana was enraptured by the saffron flames; then, her attention was redirected to the lilting harmony of her family singing 'Happy Birthday' once more. Her mother urged her to blow out the candles.

'Make a wish, dear!' her father prompted. And she did. But alas, her wish wasn't to be.

As much as she loved it, dinner that evening was an exhausting affair for Silana; the party had continued beyond midnight and into the wee hours of the morning. She excused herself, bidding goodbye to her guests and family, and trudged up the stairs.

Silana had had the most fantastic day with her kith and kin. Her friends had been invited for lunch, which had been a grand feast. Her morning had been just as eventful—after the celebration with her family, she had sat down to reply to the letters her cousins and aunt had sent. Her father had been unnervingly silent all the while, which had put Silana off a bit, but she was mostly caught up in the exciting happenings of the day.

Silana had one final agenda in mind—documenting her day. She entered her pitch-dark room and flicked on a tiny kerosene lamp. As the shadows scrambled to hide, Silana sat at her desk and flipped through the empty pages of her new journal. She sighed as thoughts swirled through her mind. Should she address the diary to an imaginary confidante or simply keep it for documentation? Deciding on the latter, she dipped her beloved quill in ink and began writing.

5 April 1939

What a wonderful day to turn 15, indeed. Today was arguably one of the pleasantest days since Papa began working at his new posting. Just imagine— all of us together for the first time since Sebastien's birthday! This idyllic Sunday started perfectly, the sun casting its alluring golden rays upon Kraków and with it the melodious chirping of passing birds

Her train of thought was derailed as Sunne burst in, panting. Silana hastily shut her journal and stood up, dropping her quill.

'Dear God, Sunne, you startled me.'

'Silana, you didn't think your special day was over, did you?' Her sweaty hand grabbed Silana's stiff one. 'Follow me, Papa and Mama are calling you!'

The mere mention of her father prompted Silana to chase after her sister down the spiral staircase back into the foyer, where her parents stood waiting. Her father scooped her into a hug, the impact knocking his moon-shaped glasses to the floor.

'Your mother and I thoroughly deliberated on this gift. But we realized that making you happy was most important, no matter the cost.'

Silana grinned from ear to ear and glanced at her mother. She looked like she wanted to say something, but her gentle smile hid any clue of her true intentions. Sunne grabbed Silana's hand and led her to the backyard, their parents trailing behind. Both pairs subconsciously locked arms. Silana fantasized she was in a fairy tale, being led by her trusty associates to a carriage. And what a carriage it was indeed. In the middle of the sprawling greenery of the backyard stood the most beautiful thing Silana had ever laid her eyes on—a marvellous bicycle.

Silana rushed to inspect it, and it was everything she had dreamed it to be. A glazed, shiny coat of white made the bike glow alluringly even in the dim light of the moon. A delicate woven wood basket was placed in front of its handlebar. Silana couldn't form words, squealing as she rushed to hug her parents.

'You needn't borrow Sebastien's bike any more,' her father beamed. The family gathered around the bike and admired its streamlined design. The night ended in merry laughter and many glasses of champagne. Silana soon felt heady enough to retire to bed. She wobbled up the stairs, holding on to Sunne tightly. The colours of the night blurred together, and as soon as Silana's head hit the pillow, she was whisked away to the familiar land of Nod.

Tara

Tara never strayed from routine. She was a firm believer in order—a stark contrast to her younger sister, Tanisha, who preferred to leave things to the wind. Dear Lord, why did her hair have to be so incorrigible? Tara yelped as another one of her nicer brushes tugged at her hair, frizzy as ever due to the humid weather. As one of her staff worked carefully to wrestle the brush out of her hair, Tara lost herself to the thoughts of the day ahead of her. She fiddled with the cap of her most prized lipstick, opening and closing it incessantly, the subtle clicks serving as a welcome white noise. After her hair was done and the attendant left, she began to apply her makeup.

Her father, the Maharaja of Bramsadha, Tanisha and she had quite a few meetings with cabinet ministers that day, followed closely by an outing with a few ladies of the court. Mercifully, they were the ones she liked; her father wouldn't be around to force her to entertain all of them—he was leaving in the afternoon to take care of some business related to the war. Tara didn't bother herself too much with such matters. She usually attended to the more pressing ones—the colour of the lehenga she would be wearing that day, which jewellery would match it best and what shoe would best accessorize it. She glided eyeliner across her lid, marvelling at the precision with which she was able to do so. Smiling to herself, the Princess of Bramsadha carefully applied her lipstick and kept a close watch on the door to make sure no one would disturb her at this time of morning. She hated nothing more than when the palace staff would intrude upon her private time when she had specifically requested them not to do so. They were all so terribly inconsiderate. Well, with the exception of Aarti.

Tara was near her wits' end with the ongoing insurgency. Their family had not really been affected by the British Raj; however, she had heard the common people were staging plenty of protests and were resisting quite fervently. Her role as royal had been limited to working in the community alongside Tanisha, who was studying for a degree in finance, much to her family's reluctance. Tara used to attend cabinet meetings to show support for her father, but now, due to the absence of their mother, the burden of the situation had fallen mostly upon the young princess—much to her irritation. She had truly believed nothing could go wrong for her until it actually did. Now, all of 23, Tara had to shoulder the responsibility of the kingdom alongside her grieving father—quite a convoluted situation.

She refused to let her thoughts bother her any longer and rose from her dressing table, leaving the mess she had created from fiddling through blushes and liners behind for one of the lowlier schmucks to clean up. Admiring her sparkling indicolite lehenga in the full-length mirror—hand-sewn and embedded with crystals—she did a half-twirl in the gift her father had gotten her. She took a second more to admire herself in the mirror. She was undoubtedly beautiful—she had timeless features—a spitting image of her late mother.

Her eyes were a soft brown, in contrast to her younger sister's uncommon chartreuse eyes—Tara quite openly envied them though Tanisha seemed least bothered. She had a Greek nose—effortlessly straight. Her hair, however, was exactly the opposite—springy, ringlet-ridden and prone to the ill effects of humidity. When well done, it framed her face with the elegance of a classical portrait, and Tara was meticulous in managing it—well, meticulous in supervising others to manage it. Just as she was about to add the finishing touch—a beautiful tiara, courtesy of the British—there was an urgent knock at her door. Tanisha, without waiting for permission to enter, came gallivanting into the room looking irritatingly happy and much less dolled up than her older sister, much to Tara's annoyance.

'Tara! Good morning! It's such a lovely day…pleasantly sunny outside. Mind if I draw the curtains?'

Tara did mind but hardly had any opportunity to protest as her sister flung open the exorbitantly expensive curtains. The harsh summer sun streamed in through the expansive windows overlooking the palace garden. Tara groaned and flopped down into the chair facing her dressing table, too tired to even protest.

'Tani, let me at least do your makeup. I simply cannot have you looking like a sleep-deprived monkey beside me.'

Her younger sister was averse to makeup of any sort, often refusing her sister's 'expert' help in that regard.

'Papa is downstairs for breakfast and asked me to alert you that the ministers will be here shortly. He wants to brief us regarding what to say.'

Their father, ever the organizer. Tanisha rambled on

about her plans for the day and Tara revelled secretly in her presence—her sister was usually the most ideal source of entertainment, considering the alternative was to finish dressing alone. The sisters were a fabulous juxtaposition— one would rarely talk and loved to listen, and the other preferred exactly the opposite. The two headed down to one of the many dining rooms of the palace for breakfast. The one their father preferred most was the rose state dining room. It had been designed by their mother shortly before Tara's conception. They made a quick stop at Tanisha's suite as Tara was insistent that she 'accessorize' a little more, much to her sister's reluctance.

Aarti had laid out a wonderful breakfast spread for both the princesses and the maharaja. She playfully chastised Tara's tardiness as her bemused father bore witness, 'Tara ji, mujhe bhi kaam karna hai iss ghar ke liye. Main hamesha aapke liye nahin ruk sakti hoon. Samjhi? Aapka chai aur dosa thanda ho raha hain! Khaa lijiye. (Miss Tara, I too need to finish my chores. I can't always be waiting for you. Do you understand? Your tea and dosas are getting cold! Please eat.)'

Aarti, the 60-something grey-haired lady of the household was now the closest thing that Tara and Tanisha had to a mother. All her sarcastic quips and guilt-tripping anecdotes were taken with a pinch of salt—after all, she cared deeply for the sisters and had stood by them through thick and thin. Aarti had been around longer than anyone could remember and the sisters had been practically brought up by her. She was a devout Christian, her devotion as fierce as her management tactics. She made sure to provide Tara with a long, hard look with her acclaimed 'angry-yet-disappointed-eyes', a term creatively coined by Tanisha.

'Maaf karo, didi. Phir nahin hoga. (I'm sorry, didi. It won't happen again.)'

Aarti gave a final huff of mock disapproval, all too familiar to Tara, as the latter settled next to her father, with Tanisha choosing to sit opposite them. The morning sun bathed the rose state dining room in a golden glow, accentuating its soft pink walls and airy ambience. Gold-framed portraits of a few family members and relatives—both close and distant—lined the walls while ornate patterns adorned the high ceiling. It mesmerized all who saw it for the first time. The room was designed to infuse antiquities with the colour pink—their mother's favourite elements. Ancient clocks and intricate wooden tables dotted the space, with a grandfather clock nestled in the far-right corner of the room. Crystal chandeliers that hung low reinforced the elegance of the room, juxtaposed against its pastoral surroundings.

The Maharaja, in an orange kurta and a white turban wrapped royally around his head, had already begun eating, tearing the flimsy dosa bit by bit, dipping it in chutney and sambar before savouring it. Normally the three would have engaged in some semblance of a conversation; however, the anxiety in the room that day was palpable. The sisters knew exactly why it was so—a few 'important' ministers would be coming and visiting the family today, by order of the British. These were routine visits, nothing of terribly large concern to them but they had heard stories about what had been done to some other princely states such as theirs. Those foreigners had no right to divide and conquer these lands as their own. Thus far, their kingdom had co-operated with the British, but that alliance seemed to have been dissipating over the past few meetings. It had been advised that the sisters attend this one to familiarize themselves with the situation.

Tara decided not to engage her father in conversation as the latter was evidently tense and engaged in a winning battle with the now-decimated dosa. Her father was one of the most selfless men Tara knew, never wanting to burden people with his worries. Regardless, she sensed he simply wanted to mull over the situation today; thus, to quell the silence, she engaged her sister in conversation. They chattered quietly about the happenings in the palace for a few minutes—some of their staff had been killed in protests, the gardener's wife had given birth to a baby, Aarti had reprimanded both Tara and Tanisha in the last two days (a sign she was in a bad mood). The morning breeze carried their conversation away through the open windows and the earthy scent of the soil, exacerbated by the lingering dew, soon lulled them into silence. Eating breakfast with this view had always been so beautiful, especially when their mother used to sit across from them in the now-empty velvet chair.

Tara had a particular fondness for the sprawling greenery and the mountains that dotted the distant landscape. Occasionally, she wished that she was a part of the stillness—no duties or obligations—simply serenity and peace. Tanisha, on the other hand, was considerably more restless—fidgeting with her dupatta, twiddling her thumbs and occasionally tapping her foot on the floor, only to earn her a warning glare from Tara. She longed for activity and resented confinement.

These sentiments only fostered her hatred for these few breakfasts.

The growing void in their conversations was driving Tanisha to her wits' end. Though Tanisha's spirited demeanour was all but wasted when it came to her family, she was indebted to them for offering her a haven to pursue her passion for mathematics. Tanisha's pursuit of education and her work ethic to achieve the same was admired across her close family. She had been working to achieve a degree in finance, with the intention of implementing reforms in their country when she had the opportunity to—if she had the opportunity to. Tara was the current heir to the throne and there was also the touchy subject of marriage and the complications that arose with that arrangement.

But those were issues future Tanisha and Tara would have to face. Presently, the two exchanged knowing glances, the younger beckoning the other to strike up a discussion. But their 'no, you do it' exchanges were quite a fruitless endeavour.

'Good morning to you two girls.'

Tara, relieved her father was back in his usual good mood, smiled and stood up to warmly embrace him, Tanisha following suit.

'How did you sleep, Papa?'

'Very well, my darling.'

'Are you ready for the cabinet meeting?'

'At least, that is what Om told me.'

Om ji had been their family's *darbaari* (chamberlain) since the Maharaja had learnt to walk. Along with Aarti, he was a constant in their lives.

The girls chuckled. 'Maybe next time we'll help him pick a colour with a little less, ahem, emphasis.' The bright orange stung Tara's eyes as she spoke. 'Although the seams are very well done and so is the turban.'

'My daughter, the artist. Although you must excuse Om ji—his age might be affecting his eyesight. He told me it was a dull orange.'

'Dull?' This time it was Tanisha's turn to guffaw. 'You may be right indeed.'

Tara missed laughing like this. It had only been two years since their mother had passed; however, the wound was still quite fresh and stung even more due to the sheer suddenness of it all. Moments like this took her back to the past. Their mother had been 40; Tara had just celebrated her 21st birthday and Tanisha had been fresh out of school. They had just returned from a family trip to the beach palace after reconnecting with their uncles, aunts and cousins and relishing the warmth of the summer sun—they had not a care in the world for anyone but each other.

Their mother, the Maharani, fell sick just a few weeks after that trip. The doctors suggested it might be something she had eaten, but her condition deteriorated with each passing day. After the Maharani was confined to bed, she spent her days painting small pictures—mostly the items in the room and whatever she could see of the gardens through the windows. The Maharaja had insisted she be moved to the grandest bedroom in the palace, with a view that put the finest paintings to shame and a quiet yet evident luxury reflected in the silk sheets, Greek vases and Chinese curtains. Her daughters and husband brought different varieties of flowers every day for her to paint. Once that bored her (the free-spirited woman got restless spending her days fixated on a single subject) she started painting memories.

The Maharani often wondered why she hadn't started with that in the first place. She conversed with all the palace residents, from her immediate family to Aarti, the other attendants and even the sweepers. She probed for their happiest remembrances, asking them for a brief description of the incidents and subsequently painting the memories and gifting the paintings to the people who shared them. Her idea, though noble, was short-lived. She only managed a few of these more personal paintings before becoming too weak to even lift a brush and put it on canvas. The Maharaja had the finest doctors from across India sent in to treat her. Some suspected dysentery, others the pox, all eventually arriving at the conclusion that this affliction was not responding to treatment or medication of any sort, much to the family's distress. The girls spent hours holding their mother's hands, comforting her as much as they were each other. The Maharani used to complain that their hands were too cold, prompting them to giggle and fervently rub their palms together. That was before she lost the ability to speak altogether.

The day their mother died was more or less a blur for Tara. She had been woken up abruptly by a teary-eyed Aarti and knew instantly; she rushed to bang on her sister's door, and they hastened to their mother. An assemblage of stoic-looking men in gleaming white coats circled the French bed where her mother lay, her frail form covered with a white sheet. Tara shoved her way through the white coats, reaching the bedside and lifting the sheet from the mound she assumed to be her mother's head to find her eyes closed, lips slightly parted and skin as white as the sheets she had been confined under. Her father stood on the opposite end of the bed, ordering his daughter to retreat, but by that point, Tara had already sped away through the same line of doctors. Nightgown trailing behind her, stumbling all throughout, Tara made it back to her room and exploded into a storm of pent-up tears and rage. It would be several hours before she left the room, the occasion in question being the cremation of her mother. She grasped Tanisha's hand tightly as her father set ablaze the heap of sticks and wood that they once called the Maharani of Bramsadha. Days seemed to slip by quicker from then on, but the sands of time remained tainted with their mother's blood. The Maharaja rarely spoke about his deceased wife to his children, the subject being too frighteningly painful. They had all made a silent pact that day to hold on to each other, no matter the costs.

Tanisha drew her elder sister's attention back to the matter at hand, snapping her fingers a few times right in her face, startling her.

'Are you done?' Tanisha was persistent. 'The meeting is in a few minutes and you've barely touched your food. Enjoy dealing with Aarti later.'

'She's right, Tara. Please, do hurry or eat after the meeting.'

Tara stood and carefully smoothed out her lehenga—God forbid she somehow wrinkled it. The tiara slipped from her head. She readjusted it as her father and Tanisha rushed out of the room. This was certainly not an outfit for running. The princess walked slowly behind them, befuddled at how flippantly her family disregarded grace, hands folded in front of her as she maintained a careful pace all the way from the dining room to the throne room—undoubtedly the grandest and most extravagant room in the palace, if not the kingdom. The Kashmiri carpets that lined the marble floors were the best and only ones of their kind, as were all the chairs and furniture—some a gift from the British, others cherished heirlooms passed down through generations. The walls were nothing less than works of art, a plethora of pillars all intricately carved with scenes from Indian mythology and great victories of legendary leaders. The ceilings were similarly gilded with gold and reflected beautiful designs, all accentuated by the miniature arches formed by the pillars in the room. The ministers had already settled down and were anticipating the arrival of the royal family. They rose to greet the Maharaja and his daughters, taking their respective seats after the family had settled down.

Tanisha whispered to Tara as the ministers bowed their heads in deference to them, 'On the way here, Papa told me that he has a special something planned for both of us, and he will reveal it after this meeting!'

The meeting seemed to drag on for hours; Tara nearly fell asleep, nestled in the comfort of her velvet-lined chair. It took the prospect of this alleged surprise and the dreams of what it may entail to help her keep her eyes open. As a minister in a disgusting lime-green kurta was saying something about the gall of the British and their expansionistic ideals, Tara nodded along intently as her mind rushed through possibilities. *Another car? That couldn't be it...she had just gotten one a month ago. Perhaps the snakeskin bag he had promised her? Or...it can't be...truly? Had her father gotten her jewellery? Diamonds?* Her heart picked up pace, the beat echoing in her ears and drowning out the sound of the lime minister still droning on in an oddly high-pitched voice about the 'pretentious colonizers'. *Perhaps a necklace. Maybe another bracelet. Earrings!* Oh how she wished for earrings—finally, she would have something positive to give those snooty court ladies to gossip about.

Seated beside Tara, Tanisha seemed to be listening quite intently to the discussion, even making a few suggestions. But for Tara, the hours ticked by more slowly than they ever had before, the court still hung upon the decision to cooperate more proactively with the British. The situation hardly concerned Tara as she waited impatiently for the ministers to salute her father one by one as they left the room. It was beyond excruciating. She was even (to her surprise) able to resist making a sour face at the Minister of Slime, lest she be held in contempt by her father. When the throne room had finally cleared, the Maharaja ushered the girls back to his quarters. The residential wing of the palace was essentially half lived-in by the three of them, guaranteeing privacy.

Tara's excitement was reaching a crescendo at the secrecy of it all! Her father beckoned them inside his private sitting room—one of Tara's favourite rooms in the house—much to her excitement. This particular room spoke of a more subdued luxury, the blinding white walls found in most other rooms replaced with those of black marble. The numerous windows allowed ample daylight to seep in though it was quickly absorbed by the expansive darkness of the walls, which had a foreboding aura about them. The room was themed to appear a careful yet sophisticated blend of black and gold, the latter manifesting through the furniture.

The two sisters took their seats on a sofa across their father. Tara scanned the room for some indication of a jewellery box, a pouch even, confused upon noticing the absence of either. 'Papa, what is this surprise you've had Tanisha inform me of?' In her excitement, she had switched from English to her native Hindi, something their mother had encouraged them to do in private settings.

'Girls, you have to listen very closely to what I have to say. Now, this may come as a shock to the both of you, but I've recently been in contact with some associates from Poland.' *How could Polish diamonds possibly shock them?* 'The ongoing war ravaging Europe has had an adverse effect on the Jewish children of Poland; they've been displaced from their homeland and torn away from their families, suffering through what I can only describe as a living hell on earth.' *Again, what did this have to do with her diamonds?*

'I have thus agreed on behalf of our family to host these children in our summer palace at Balganga until this war ends. I plan on building residential quarters on the land and using the main house as a makeshift school and health centre to retain some semblance of normalcy for these children. The idea certainly isn't perfect, but I trust you both will assist me in taking care of them. They have nowhere else to turn to and with the power vested in us, I do feel it is our responsibility to take care of these children until the storm passes.'

Silana

The atmosphere in the classroom was gloomy; as the biology teacher droned on about the class' recent performance, the distance between Silana's eyelids shortened with every passing minute. Periodic nudges from Anna Eichendorf, seated beside her, were the only thing keeping her from falling asleep on the uneven desk. While the enthusiastic students in front of Silana scribbled away on either comically large notebooks or loose sheets of paper, her thoughts slipped away from academia to reflect upon the rest of her day—she allowed herself this liberty considering this was the last period.

The festivities of last night had resulted in the pounding headache she was now experiencing. Silana glanced around sleepily, noticing the classroom to be unusually empty. She wondered who all were absent but this thought blended into the many she was trying to process with hardly five hours of sleep. Silana felt feverish, but glancing at the clock, had a sudden incentive to pay close attention for the remaining seven minutes of class.

'…and the test, as you know, shall account for a third of your grade.' Silana's eyes widened and she turned to Anna, who had been paying attention, unlike her.

'For those who haven't been studying as diligently as they should, I do wish you all the very best.'

As Mr Diesing shot a glare in her direction, Silana averted her eyes from his gaze. He started calling out the names of the students to distribute the papers. Silana, upon hearing her name, hurried to his desk.

'I'm not satisfied with your work, Silana, though not particularly surprised,' Mr Diesing remarked gruffly, holding out her test. He glowered at her before carrying on. Silana's heart raced as she hesitantly glanced at the wrinkled paper in her hands, rushing back to her desk and smoothing it out gently to discover a giant 'D' codified in cruel red ink. She inhaled deeply and didn't realize she was holding her breath until a friendly tap on the shoulder startled her. She turned around.

'How terribly did you do this time?'

'More so than I'd care to discuss.'

Sigrid Fellenbaum peered at Silana intently, her hazel eyes darkening with concern and enhancing her doe-like features. Dirty blonde hair cascaded down her shoulders and Sigrid swept it away before leaning in closer. 'In any case, I'm quite certain this assignment doesn't matter as much… well, at least in the grand scheme of things.'

'Now it'd do us both well to forget this blessed assignment. Would you be able to join Anna and me for tea today?'

Sigrid smiled and nodded before a thunderous knock on Silana's desk startled them both. Silana slowly turned around, feeling the harsh stare of Mr Diesing on her.

'In your current position, Ms Haydn, I would concentrate on educational matters rather than irrelevant banter. Or perhaps, you would like to share this important topic of conversation with the rest of your peers?'

Silana's mumbled apology was drowned by the school bell that rang in the distance, freeing the class stifled by the lesson's tedium. Silana hastily grabbed her weather-beaten schoolbag and dashed out before her teacher could make any more implicitly snide remarks. She waited outside the doorway for her two closest friends, Anna Eichendorf and Sigrid Fellenbaum, to navigate the mass exodus of exuberant children. The three once again made their way through the hallways, bursting at the seams with students, to the much-awaited declaration of the positions for the student council. Silana had stood for president against her long-time competitor, Hannah Tomaszewski. She and her friends rushed to the expansive pin-board designated for announcements, spotting a solitary piece of white paper on the board that the students had crowded around.

Silana pushed past them and ran her finger along the list of names. She had won; however, there was a glaring 'DISQUALIFIED' stamped across Hannah's name. She squinted, unsure why this was so. Silana noticed that a few other names had been crudely struck through. She looked around, confused, until her eyes landed upon a teacher nearby attempting to control the surging wave of children. Elbowing through the crowd, Silana asked, 'Miss Bartkowski, there seems to be some mistake. How is it possible to have such widespread disqualifications at such short notice?'

'Have you no sense, dear? Those children are Jewish. You must know that they can no longer hold positions of authority in our school, as mandated by the board.'

Though some girls around her squealed in excitement

and she received several pats on the back, Silana couldn't help but feel like this was nothing to celebrate.

A cool breeze enveloped Silana as she left school, with Sigrid and Anna on either side of her. Gravel crunched under the trio's feet as they made their way home, heading towards the main road. They navigated a winding path through a densely forested area, the spring sun glowing gently. They would have taken the tram, but they were all too familiar with the ban placed on Jews from doing so. As a sign of support for Anna, Sigrid and Silana walked the distance to and from school with her every day, even though they were advised against it.

Silana indulged in intermittent conversations with them but her mind was some place else. Her friends had evidently not paid much attention to the list of the names of elected members, nor had they noticed the fact that every promising candidate of Jewish descent had been either disqualified or not been elected at all. That day in class, she had observed that quite a few of her peers were absent; stiffening, she realized that almost all were Jewish.

She wondered how her father would react to the cursed piece of paper shoved indifferently in her backpack. It'd been months since he'd last 'overreacted', leaving a scarlet handprint across her face. Her mother had hidden her away until the bruises healed, tending to her incessantly. Her father seemed to have forgotten about the event almost as quickly as it occurred. The cycle had then repeated itself but he'd learnt from his previous mistake and hit her in a place where it had not been particularly noticeable—her back or her upper arms. Lost in thought, her friends chattered on while Silana absently nodded. Soon enough, her two-storey house loomed in the distance, the burnt-sienna exterior becoming more prominent as they approached. Silana felt an unpleasant yet familiar knot forming in her stomach.

I'm going to be sick, she thought while walking up the driveway and through the well-manicured lawn. Her hand felt heavy as she grabbed the bronze wolf-shaped door handle. She pounded on the mahogany door three times.

'Coming!' cried Sunne—her homework could wait. She leapt from the dining table and sped across the hall to greet the trio.

'Thank you, Sunne,' they chorused as they entered and Silana locked the door behind them. She gathered that her father wasn't home after peering at the coat rack—his was missing. Anna and Sigrid carefully made their way up the creaky staircase while Silana dashed past, urging them to quicken their pace. The privacy of Silana's bedroom prompted them to exchange gossip about Sigrid's recent love interest and Anna's upcoming birthday. However, this rapidly transitioned into complaining about Mr Diesing.

'How can he be so cruel to his own students? Fancy that—hardly 15 students in his class yet he finds a reason to deride each one of them, unquestionably eroding their self-esteem in the process.'

'I heard he's been quite caught up in this recent Nazi business.'

The girls fell silent. The topic had been bound to come up sooner or later, it being the most prevalent one nowadays. One couldn't enter any public space without hearing the term being discussed in hushed whispers. The residents of their small town were split down the middle, with a significant Jewish population. Anti-Semitism had been rampant, especially in the epicentre of town where old Mrs Goldman's house had been vandalized by children who claimed to follow the Nazi ideology. They weren't disciplined, rather they were praised, and this incident had only widened the rift between the communities. Additionally, news had travelled from neighbouring countries about the treatment of Jews. Silana had never supported the concept of anti-Semitism, having been raised strictly as a Catholic herself. She had ascertained through religion that one should care for everyone equally, whether they be a friend or foe. She found comfort in it and was conflicted as to why an ideology meant to heal humankind was doing it so much harm.

'You do realize that Hannah might have been deported, don't you, Silana?' Anna's sharp words caused Silana to reel backwards. She was shocked by the bland, matter-of-fact way her friend was relaying this information. 'Sil, I'm being realistic. You know what a stir Friedrich's deportation caused. Poor soul, walking across the street to buy bread before he was rounded up. It is quite frightening.'

'Quite an optimistic way of thinking, I must say, Anna.'

'Sil, as much as I love you, you really do live in your own private bubble.'

'I—'

'Let me finish, for once. Had you noticed the absence of your peers until today, when it literally slapped you in the face with big red letters? Last week, the couple living across you was snatched from their homes in the dead of night along with their month-old baby. No one knows what became of them. We just passed their house, hardly 10 minutes ago, and it's already been stripped bare of anything not bolted down. I speculate they may not return for a long time, perhaps never.'

Silana remained silent, partly due to shock but mostly due to a chilling realization.

'Sil, all I'm saying is we live in perilous times. You and I have been sheltered because of where we were born. Sigrid too. I am truly afraid because...well...you know I'm Jewish. My father's political connections will only keep us safe for so long...which leads me to something I must tell you both.'

Sigrid and Silana leant in closer.

'My parents and I are leaving for Switzerland, either next week or the one after. My father has had to pull quite a few strings to arrange safe passage for us. It shan't be all that bad; we're staying with Grandma in Gstaad and riding out the worst of it. Father predicts we'll return before spring next year.' Anna stopped, taking a breath, and allowing her friends to digest the news. 'I may not be able to write, but I shall try my very best to.'

'Oh Anna,' the girls choked back tears and embraced Anna, whose eyes were glassy as well. Her voice quivered. 'In any case, I believe while we all are still here, we should do something, anything, to stand up for them.'

'Who?'

'The Jews, Silana. My God, you are daft. You heard what Ms Bartkowski said this morning. "Jews can no longer hold positions of authority in our school." Half the students in our class are Jewish, including me. I can confide in you because you are my sisters and I know you both will remain by my side if worse comes to worst. Many others aren't as lucky. I have heard that most people knew the Gestapo were coming that night your neighbours were taken away and actively tried to conceal that information from that couple.'

'What are you saying, Anna?'

'Sigrid, I wouldn't be telling you all this if I didn't trust you and Silana with my life. My brother has started spreading messages in school through discreet means that discuss Nazi activities in Poland and the consistent violence against Jews. Let us do something similar while there is still time. They've already mandated my family and me to sew this star into our clothing and I truly fear how far they may take this.' Silana put her hand on Anna's but Anna shook it off. 'Silana, when is your father coming home?'

'In around an hour. Why—'

'Because you know exactly what he thinks of me. If he found out any of this, God knows what he may do. I don't care what happens to me—'

'I do understand the position my father is in and the lengths he is willing to go to consolidate it. But, I will never compromise my commitment to the humane treatment of others. You two are more family to me than he will ever be. Now, how do you propose we go about this, Anna?'

Anna laughed. 'I admire your enthusiasm, Sil, but we did just get home from school. I have a lot to tell you two about.'

The next half an hour was spent in random banter. 'Oh Anna, what do you think of Hans' new haircut? It's quite abhorrent, you must admit. Maybe he can borrow one of your hats.' The girls' teasing about Anna's 'boyfriend's' new haircut earned them disdainful looks and playful swatting. Soon they eventually moved on to more universal matters.

'He's moving to our school? That is ridiculous.'

'Yes, well, apparently, she went to his house yesterday.'

'No, they aren't dating.'

'Really?'

'Well, I ought to ask them instead. We can't believe every piece of gossip, you know.'

'I propose we continue this over ice cream. The occasion does call for it.'

As the girls headed out, Silana scribbled a quick (but neat) note addressed to her father, promising a quick return. As they crossed the street to reach the main road, Silana passed by the house of the Jewish couple who had been deported to God knew where. She heard it more clearly this time—their screams lingering in the depths of her mind. The simple one-storey house had once boasted gleaming white exteriors and a beautiful front porch. Now, the once-pearly walls were a deathly shade of grey and the paint half-burnt.

The house seemed soulless, as though there was a void that would never be filled. Silana remembered the laughter of the parents punctuated by the crying of their child (whose laughter could also be heard sometimes) and wondered if the house would ever experience such wholeness again. She peered inside through the half-open door and felt as though she were looking at a corpse. The sleek wooden flooring lay in miserable tatters as did the neat tiling of the roof. The word 'JUDE' and crude renderings of the Star of David glared menacingly at the trio. Silana didn't realize that she had been staring, fixated with fear, at what remained of the house until Sigrid linked arms with her and pulled her in the other direction. Silana huffed and stole a final glance at the house, which looked back blankly.

Ice cream was a brief indulgence that soon gave way to more serious matters. Once back in the familiar comfort of Silana's room, the girls began strategizing; they were determined to do something about Anna's predicament.

'I suggest we begin by subtly catching people's attention—not too loudly.'

'It's like marketing. How big a banner do we need?'

'Banner? That's too full throttle for a first time!'

'What do you suggest then?'

'Distributing flyers,' Sigrid suggested. 'They're far more portable and will easily fit in our schoolbags. Plus, I assume it may be quite a task to trace them back to the three of us.'

'Agreed. But we really must start small—a short message. And not in school—the dwindling numbers could lead to us being detected in the premature stages of this plan.'

'So, the neighbourhood, then? We could stick the posters on street lights, telephone booths and any other noticeable area.'

'Not my neighbourhood!' Silana was adamant about her father not finding out, even though she fully agreed with the sentiment.

'Sil, we know. How about mine?'

'Are you willing to take that risk, Anna?'

Anna sighed. 'This is perhaps me being pessimistic but I have a sinking feeling the war may not end very soon. There are too many intricacies and several motivations to make this a forever war.' Her voice became a hint more subdued. 'As you know, I'll be gone very shortly. I cannot say for sure when I'll return and I refuse to leave my neighbours in the lurch. There's a family with three children just across from us, an old couple beside us and a new one about to move in.' Her pace quickened. 'After we do a few trials, we can definitely expand into the not-so-Jewish friendly neighbourhoods—not that there are many left. But the most critical aspect must be to never ever get caught. And should that unfortunate circumstance befall any of us, never betray each other.'

Silana and Sigrid nodded their heads and locked their eyes in silent agreement. Anna grabbed each of their hands and squeezed them reassuringly. Silana knew exactly what kind of sacrifices Anna expected her to make for this cause. She was ready and, frankly, beyond willing to make them. Her most immediate concern was that she would be doing so at the expense of her family.

Just then, Silana picked up the faint sound of muted but ponderous footsteps near her bedroom door. She craned her neck to check through the gap between the door and floor and saw the dim outline of two large feet. Her heart was in her mouth. Her stomach felt like a bottomless void, with her thoughts racing and skin prickling. Sigrid and Anna too fell silent as they noticed what she was peering at.

I'll play it cool. Silana clambered out of bed and rushed to the door, swinging it open with a large smile plastered on her face. She was greeted by her brother, wide-eyed with surprise, standing a little distance away from the doorframe.

'Is he home?'

'Not yet.'

Silana motioned for him to enter, and he did, stepping inside hesitantly to be greeted by the terrified looks of the other girls. Silana shut the door (conscious not to bolt it; she remembered what had transpired last time) and pleaded, 'Sebastien, I'm terribly sorry. Please, please don't tell Father. None of this ever happened. Sigrid, Anna, I suggest you—'

'SILANA. Relax.'

She took a shaky breath.

'You know, Jakub was deported yesterday.'

'But he's your best friend. Father offered him protection! How—'

'We're still trying to make sense of the whole ordeal, Father and I. Apparently his father fell out with some of the higher-ups, what with all the, let's say, controversial articles he was editing. But as of now, we have no idea where the entire family will be taken, let alone when they will return. I had heard stories, Silana, but didn't believe them. Now this war has reached our doorstep and this can befall anybody we love, no matter how close we keep them.'

He turned to Silana. 'I want to help. Now, the idea to start putting up posters in a familiar area is particularly daft, and not just because you three proposed it. Firstly, not only would the suspect list be narrowed down quite easily, but if we happened to be caught, Father would flay us alive. His associates outnumber even the children of this area, and his cronies would rarely hesitate to tell Lukas Haydn of his children's misdemeanours. School is, truthfully, quite a viable space to begin spreading our message. Just the other day poor Hans Rommel was being pelted with shoes and rocks after we were handed back our maths papers. He does always come first, so there was no surprise once he did. What was different this time was that our teacher himself accused him of cheating. "That's what Jews such as yourself are known to do, aren't you?" The rest of our class, green with envy, took his nonsensical ravings to heart and believed their own version of events, twisted by jealousy. Hans' only crime was being Jewish.'

The girls were dumbstruck.

'I propose we start with a message that isn't outrageous, but is personal. One that strikes a chord with everyone and anyone associated with someone Jewish who has suffered a similar fate to Jakub. Silana, you're the maestro of language, are you not?' He grasped her shoulders. 'Think of Anna, channel the anger brimming from your loss and spill it out on to paper.' He let go of her. 'It's getting quite late and Father will be home soon. Today has been exhausting. I suggest we mull over things tomorrow.'

As Sebastien left the room, the girls started packing up and Anna remarked how mature he'd become. Silana had noticed that too. Aside from the occasional snide remarks here and there, the lines on Sebastien's forehead had become considerably more wrinkly these past few months. The darkness between his brows occasionally leapt out at her like a panther, but most people were too enraptured by his carefree indigo eyes to notice. Silana bid farewell to her friends and decided to take a walk, with the intention of clearing her head before her father came home and inevitably saw the abhorrent grade she had received. She intended to take a five-minute stroll across the property, which briefly intersected with the nearby forest. Silana knew the path like the back of her hand and the early twilight offered some remaining sunlight. She quickly grabbed a black coat and a scraggly woollen cap, telling Sebastien to inform Father of her whereabouts in case he arrived home before her.

Gravel crunched under Silana's feet as she slowly made her way across the narrow, leaf-strewn path. It was relatively isolated and she hardly ever ran into her neighbours. Usually, she would encounter old Mrs Goldman walking her three dogs, including that ravenous chihuahua of hers. A gentle breeze brushed against Silana's cheeks, relaxing her, and she took a deep breath. Rebelliousness was never really a trait she associated with herself. Her biggest pride was staying out of trouble—for the most part—and validating herself through the praise and appreciation her parents bestowed upon her.

Silana continued, subconsciously picking up pace and making deliberate attempts to step on the crunchiest leaves. She stopped in her tracks when she spotted a squirrel; she gawked at it and it eyed her back with matched curiosity. She regretted not carrying pistachios. 'Next time,' she promised, carrying on. Sunne wouldn't have forgotten to carry a wide variety of nuts for every nearby mammal to consume.

Sunne, how busy she'd been lately. The war had taken its toll on Silana's beloved younger sister as well. Before all of it, they used to write and direct their own plays—much to the amusement and apparent delight of their parents—and these were performed on an almost weekly basis. It was one of the reasons Silana loved theatre. However, both she and Sunne had grown more aware and more mature in recent months. Though Silana was grateful she would never embarrass herself like that in front of her family again, she felt as though she had been almost robbed of some of her childhood innocence and playful youth. She could hardly remember the last time she flouted a curfew or had gotten into some sort of trouble not related to a poor grade.

Silana felt tense as she quickened her pace further, her fists, tucked away in her coat pockets, clenched ever so slightly. The encroaching darkness crept across the thicket, chasing her as she strolled on, the shadows lengthening. What if they were to be caught? How would her father, the role model of all citizens and Christians in the city, digest the fact that his children had become the very plague he sought to eradicate? It'd be much more than just a temporary source of pain or humiliation. Her mother? Well, in case their father ever found out, Silana had accepted that Mother would not be of much help. Yvonne Haydn would dutifully tend to her children's wounds, but never to what was causing them.

The century-old oaks around Silana bore silent witness to her ponderings and she was careful to notice each one. Something about their ancient appearance and uneven bark made Silana want to drop everything and sit right there, sketching them while seeking their sage wisdom. She wished the breeze would blow her away too, as she observed it picking up the scattered leaves, dead and with no hint of purpose, carrying them to the viridescence of the forest. Blending with their fallen counterparts, though alone, displaced and scared, they acquired a new purpose.

Silana looked wistfully behind as the ribbon-like trail carefully led her out of the forest and towards civilization. When she reached the clearing and her house loomed in the distance, Silana felt a terrible mix of both eagerness and dread. How would she explain the grade to her father? He had sat across the dining table, sacrificing his Sunday evening, to prepare his daughter for the test. She was afraid not of failing herself but of failing her father. Lukas Haydn had sacrificed a tremendous amount to reach the position he was in today—a successful businessman with a loving wife and three children he was able to provide the best of everything for—he was everything a man aspired to be. Added to it was the fact that their family was one of the most well-known and politically affluent families in all of Poland.

Silana's thoughts meandered as she approached her front door. She grasped the heavy metal door-knocker and pounded it three times. Yvonne answered in hardly 30 seconds, tightly embracing her daughter, and lingering in the embrace for much longer than Silana did. 'We missed you, my love. Come, your father has just arrived! He's been waiting in the living room for you.'

Silana insisted she'd only been gone five minutes but a hurried peek at the clock hanging admonishingly on the adjacent wall confirmed that she'd been out for approximately 20. She removed her coat frantically, flung it on the coat rack and rushed to greet her father, who was browsing lazily through the day's newspapers while sipping on steaming coffee. He looked up at his red-faced daughter, his half-moon glasses reflecting the lustreless glow of the overhead chandelier. Silana sat down across him, heart pounding in her ears.

'Good evening, Sil.'

'God evening, Father.'

'I trust you've had a productive day, considering you've had time for a stroll?'

'Yes, I have. I'm terribly sorry, I somehow lost track of time and—'

'It's all right, Sil. Mistakes do happen.'

Silana was stunned. Her father was rarely ever one to possess a cheerful disposition; something wonderful must have transpired at work. Drawing from experience, she was prompted to enquire about his day. Lukas Haydn set down the copious amounts of newspapers he was skimming through, took a long sip of his coffee and began recounting the events of the day, unfolding the narrative from its very inception—his wonderfully prepared breakfast—up until the present moment. He described the promotion of one of his closest political allies in excruciating detail, elaborating on the ceremony and what this would mean for his company. He even joked—JOKED—about the appearance of one of his senior associates in attendance. 'He looked more like a silvery, anxious penguin than my associate,' he chortled. Silana and Yvonne, who was readying dinner in the kitchen but could hear the conversation, were both astonished by what had put him in such a good mood.

A hint of jealousy crept into Silana's mind—if only his children could make him this joyous every day—but she pushed it to the back of her mind, reprimanding herself. Now was hardly the time to be negative. He described a major commission he had facilitated at work and Silana nodded along enthusiastically, although unsure what exactly it entailed. As he continued, Silana tried to push the nagging thought of that dreadful piece of paper languishing in eerie anticipation within the recesses of her schoolbag out of her mind. He ended triumphantly, 'It's one of the largest we've ever agreed upon in the history of our company. I'm sure I have set quite a precedent for Sebastien to follow once he assumes the mantle of our family business. Now, my dearest daughter, do tell me about your day.'

'Well, nothing too exceptional. School was average at best. Anna, Sigrid and I had a quick ice cream stop.'

The light in his eyes dimmed. 'Silana—'

'Yes, I do recall your advice regarding Anna. Sigrid and I are trying to distance ourselves from her, truly. It certainly isn't easy but I promise that we're taking it one step at a time and making quite ascertainable progress.'

'Good. You do realize, my girl, that we live in troubled times. Not every loved one can be trusted, even those closest to you. I have, albeit painfully, realized this. I only want what's best for you and your siblings and I will do everything in my power to ensure that we remain in peace.'

Silana smiled. Her father wasn't an affectionate man; his declarations of protection were his way of comforting them, akin to a hug.

'Dinner!' Yvonne's voice snapped Silana and her father back to reality—they both had a tendency to get lost in their thoughts several times a day. Sunne and Sebastien bounded down the stairs, taking the seats that were assigned to them. One thing about Lukas Haydn—he was not a big fan of change. Lukas had insisted that Yvonne and the children choose their seats during their initial meals and they had stuck to it.

Intermittent banter evolved into full-fledged conversation once food was served, accompanied by unrelenting compliments. The air was imbued with a tantalizing aroma that brightened the entire atmosphere and transported Silana into a land of utter bliss. The Haydn family partook in a remarkably enjoyable repast, their laughter and delightful conversation flowing as if oblivious to raging turmoil brewing just on their doorstep—an atmosphere buoyed by the pleasant mood of their patriarch. The family was encouraged to keep thoughts of peril aside until their plates were clean and their stomachs bursting.

The test result had almost completely slipped Silana's mind until she returned to her room to pack her bag for the following day, where she found it lying staunchly on her desk. *It could certainly wait one more day, the world isn't going to end*, she convinced herself. She'd come this far already; what was the point of ruining a perfectly good day at its finale? Her father's moods were ever-changing, leaving her uncertain if another joyous day such as this would grace her family again.

Tara

Tara was beyond mortified. Not only would she not be getting any diamonds but she would also now have to share her summer home with some aggrieved refugees. She sat in stunned silence as her father continued, all of a sudden seemingly hell-bent on some noble quest to help these children.

'The sufferings they have had to endure are far beyond what we could ever imagine.'

Tara shifted uncomfortably on the couch, her lehenga bunching beneath her. Tanisha, on the other hand, nodded along eagerly. 'Father, I wholeheartedly support this initiative of yours.' *Ugh. Tanisha. Ever the one to bow and scrape.* 'How do you want us to assist you with this?'

The Maharaja smiled. 'Girls, I would like for you to make the children feel welcome. Give them a home here because they have lost theirs. I can only hope that they will imbibe the values your mother and I have taught you. You have the ability to make a home for them in this country until they are able to return to theirs. I would like you both to continue your duties as usual but please make frequent visits to the children.'

He then dropped the most painful bombshell. 'The first batch of children will be arriving in three days' time.'

The first? How many batches of children would there be?

Tara left in a considerable huff after the Maharaja dismissed them, suggesting they pack for at least a few days. She pulled her sister into her room.

'Tani, truthfully, was this the "big surprise" Papa had planned for us?' Tara asked with an expression of genuine confusion etched upon her face.

'Tara, are you all right?' Tanisha mentally braced herself for another temper tantrum as she sat the heiress down on the bed and followed suit.

'The way you worded it, I really thought he would be giving us diamonds or something equivalent.'

Tanisha snorted. 'Wow, you really are spoilt.'

In mock offence, Tara lightly jabbed her sister's side.

'You can't even deny it!'

'You know, Tani, the more I think about it, it isn't even the failed prospect of diamonds that bothers me. It's the change associated with all of this.' Tara's rigid belief in order came from the turmoil she had experienced after their mother's passing and the upheaval it had brought. She had always had a soft spot for routines and schedules, but it had been exacerbated by her newfound fear of unpredictability.

'I empathize with you, Tara. I really do.' Tanisha lay beside Tara, both staring up at the gleaming chandelier that hung as a cloud above Tara's bed, glittering in the serotinal majesty of the sun. 'But I also empathize with the children who now can't sleep in their beds, eat home-cooked food or grow up looking out of the windows of their bedrooms at the bittersweet beauty of the world beyond, feeling both a poignant sorrow and a longing for the freedom they cannot yet experience.'

Tara turned her head to the side. 'Wow! That was profound. Have you ever considered writing speeches for Papa?'

Tanisha chuckled. 'No thank you. I'll be too busy implementing them.'

Tara giggled in agreement. 'If only the Minister of Slime had your level of confidence.'

'Who now?'

Tara spent the next 10 minutes explaining her one-sided rivalry with the talkative minister who had an unusually high-pitched voice and a non-existent fashion sense.

'So this vendetta is only because of his fashion sense?'

'And his voice. I promise you, listen to him more closely next time, and you'll see that this hatred is not unfounded in the slightest.'

Tanisha rolled her eyes, sliding off the bed and on to her feet. 'As fun as this was, I suggest we get to packing.'

'I'll be packing later; I have a meeting with a few ladies of the court now.'

'Sounds painful. I wish you luck!'

Tanisha sauntered out of the room, closing the door behind her while thoughts of what gossip to satisfy the bejewelled court ladies with swirled around in Tara's mind. Tara spent the rest of the evening with the ladies and not just because she had to—she loved being the centre of any and all attention. The princess engaged in conversation with them as they joined her for tea on the terrace, cloaked in a thin veneer of politeness. Unfortunately, the setting sun disrupted the charade, forcing Tara to commence her packing. She visited Tanisha before doing so, finding an irritable Aarti who informed her that her sister had finished long ago and was now frolicking with her own friends. These friends weren't even political allies but childhood friends and classmates from Tanisha's old school.

Tara fumed as she packed. As the heir, she was supposed to have it easier; however, in every situation, it was quite the contrary. While Tara slaved away, listening to ministers more aged than the walls themselves or entertaining her father's guests, the Maharaja drooled over Tanisha and her 'intelligent and promising' future. All Tanisha ever had to do was further her education with a measly degree, and suddenly she was all he could talk about. Meanwhile Tara, who had also been eager to pursue a degree in philosophy, had been denied that because she had more 'pressing responsibilities', according to her dear father. The cruel and unrelenting hypocrisy manifested as a stinging pain in her eyes as she packed—or rather, laid her clothes on the bed to be packed for her. She chose her least fancy and most lightweight clothing as per her father's order. He had warned them in advance that there would be lots of movement involved, as well as long durations spent in the sun. Her absolute nightmare was coming alive.

It took her an hour altogether, and by the time she had finished laying out whatever she needed to survive the trip, dusk had fully settled, enveloping her room in a lilac sheath. Sunsets in her kingdom had always been so beautiful. She went to her balcony, her hands recoiling at the sharp coolness of its railing. Tara looked up at the infinite twilight sky where stars dotted across like holes in a container, letting the light of the heavens stream through. Clouds periodically covered a steadily disappearing sun, the moon not far behind. The wind gently riffled her hair, which had come undone as a result of her partially frenzied packing.

Tara knew she gained nothing by harbouring resentment towards her sister. A few hours alone to regain her senses was all she usually needed. *Everything will change once I become the queen*, she reminded herself. She would convince her father not to bother finding a suitor for her; he was getting quite worked up about the matter. *All in due time, dear father.*

Tara had spent years cooped up in the palace while Tanisha had been able to venture beyond its grandeur, all in preparation for her destiny to guide and advise her future husband. Tara may have been spoilt, but she was by no means stupid. She had a knack for languages and history, the former of which she could speak five. Legions of the most prolific private tutors and lecturers from all corners of the world had taught her all she needed to know about the business of ruling, keeping in mind that she wouldn't be the primary representative of the future royalty. Tara looked at the gardens. She hated how the men of the court viewed her as merely an accessory to the future king. Tara despised the idea of a union that was purely meant for politics. A small part of the princess, behind the glamour of her title, wanted to break free of her duties. But that was absurd. She had a duty to her people, and she was determined to fulfil it.

Closing the balcony door and making her way back into the room, she noticed that the carriage clock read 7.17 p.m.—nearly time for dinner. She worried her father would be pontificating about those Polish children they would be giving asylum to. This was worse than the time he had taken her and Tanisha to an orphanage for blind children. She wrinkled her nose slightly, remembering the godawful smell that had been so pervasive. In case the Maharaja tried in any way to bring up the topic of the children, Tara had three subjects of conversation she had mentally prepared beforehand, aiming to divert his focus—thanks to the ladies of the court and their insatiable thirst for gossip.

Dinners were affairs where each of them recapped their day for the others to provide input. Tara had never been much of a talker—a trait shared by her father; both were perfectly content with Tanisha hijacking two-thirds of the entire discussion. This evening was no different; Tanisha jabbered on through the entrée and half of the main course. Tara tried in vain to be cautious of her meal intake—as of late, a few of her outfits weren't quite fitting her like they used to—but their chefs had prepared assorted vegetables and butter chicken, her favourites. She was certain her father had planned this meal as a pitiful gesture to appease her for the upcoming events, but she didn't seem to care. She spooned the tender meat into her mouth till her stomach nearly burst, her vision blurring with the soft glow of the candles placed at regular intervals across the Prussian blue tablecloth. Tara dragged herself up to her room once dinner concluded, eyes heavy, wishing the distant chattering of the palace attendants would cease.

Another dreamless night transitioned into another dreamless day for the princess. She had a few duties that didn't take long, leaving her to spend most of the day wandering aimlessly around the gardens. Carrying a few books with her, she headed towards its centre—a rose garden, which had been constructed to commemorate her birth. Sealed off from the rest of the gardens and not easily accessible, one would have to know exactly where they were going in order to find it, just as her mother had intended. One of her first wishes upon becoming pregnant had been commissioning this garden as a getaway for her prince or princess. Tara, in honour of her mother, made sure to visit the garden once a day, whether with purpose or without. In the midst of the rose garden, with the flowers forming concentric circles, stood a wooden bench that Tara placed herself and her books upon, reserving two hours for reading at that very spot. A concerned Aarti would sometimes bring her tea, insisting she return inside the palace before it became dark. Today was unsurprisingly no different.

'Tara ji, vaapas jaldi upar aao! Aapke papa bula rahe hain. (Miss Tara, come back up quickly! Your father is calling you.)'

Aarti had never learnt to speak English and had given up trying for the sake of the convenience of the sisters. Tara knew Aarti's gimmick well enough. Her father, upon questioning, revealed that he never directed Aarti to summon Tara. Nevertheless, he forbid Tara from returning to the garden in front of a triumphant Aarti, on the pretext of it being too late.

At dinner that night, the dreaded subject of the children finally came up. Tara supposed she had put it off long enough.

'You both have packed for a week, yes?'

The girls nodded. *A week? How ghastly.*

'The children are arriving in two days. We shall leave

for the summer palace tomorrow and welcome the children when they arrive the day after.'

Tara remained determinedly silent for the rest of the meal while her sister yapped on about the events of her day. Tanisha's nonchalance was really starting to get on Tara's nerves. She felt both the pre-existing irritation and the heat creeping up her legs and swimming around in her head, creating a familiar unpleasant sensation. Of course, her dear father wouldn't care to notice her deliberate silence, always too enraptured by his younger daughter and some impressive tale of her studies and attaining her degree. Tara wondered why she even bothered with the two of them in the first place.

All this will change once I am in charge. She meant no threat or harm to her family but just the establishment of a new dynamic to tip the scales in her favour. She, of course, loved her sister and was truly proud of her. Being one of the only women working towards a degree was a tremendously daunting task. This pride, though, was soon swept away as she remembered sacrificing her summer home. The thought of spending an entire week away from the main palace gnawed at her slowly but secretly. To her utter disbelief, neither her father nor her sister recognized the drastic shift in her mood, putting quite a damper on Tara's motivation to continue simmering in it. And she did so—throughout the night, boiling over with unrest.

Another nearly sleepless night was followed by a day where time seemed to slip through the princess' fingers like sand. She was finishing up her packing, running to and fro from her closet to her bathroom to one of the several bags she had laid across the floor.

'Tara ji, aap kab tak wahan rehne waale ho? (Miss Tara, how long are you going to stay there?)'

She didn't have time to entertain Aarti's unwarranted sarcasm. After some needless arguing, Aarti forced her to take out 'essentials', including a pair of shoes for each day (which meant she would have to repeat—God forbid any of her friends saw her; she'd be the court's new jester), multiple outfits and an entire bag full of toiletries.

'What if the children taint these clothes?' Tara whined as Aarti unpacked the bag furiously, muttering to herself. The princess would have carried the claw-footed tub to Balganga if it had not been for the piping system and bolts that rooted it in place.

'Aarti, you're a miracle-worker!'

She'd reduced Tara's baggage count from seven to three. Aarti revelled in a brief round of applause before summoning some houseboys to load the luggage into the motor car that would be leaving in the late afternoon. They would be travelling in their mother's favourite one (for luck, the Maharaja claimed)—a 1930 Buick Series 40 Phaeton. It was pearly white with scarlet leather seats and gleamed quietly in the harsh afternoon sun. The family set off with a squadron of staff, Aarti included, under the pretext of going for a holiday. This was indeed considered routine for the royals, the Maharaja having quite an indelible penchant for vacationing at their smaller palace in Balganga.

The staff left behind to take care of the main palace waved farewell to the procession of cars as they left. Tanisha and Tara were both seated in the back, their father up in front with an ancient driver. Sukhdev ji had been the official family driver for even longer than Aarti had been around. Both their presences were so routine that the entire squadron of staff considered them parental figures and often sought their guidance. Sukhdev ji was usually never inclined towards conversation, preferring mainly to speak with his eyes. Tara noticed the excited sparkle in Sukhdev ji's eyes as the Maharaja conversed with him regarding the children's arrival. The car navigated its way through awestruck residents, shrieking vendors and scraggly hagglers who had lined the roads. Tara looked at the awed passers-by, careful not to make eye contact for too long.

'Girls, I'd advise you to rest for some time. The drive to Balganga will take four hours and we will not be making any stops.'

Tara agreed. 'I'm going to try to sleep for as long as possible. Wake me up once we reach.'

One of the many talents the young princess possessed was the ability to fall asleep in the most uncomfortable of outfits and situations. The Maharaja had advised the girls to wear minimal jewellery and cotton clothes but Tara wanted to look presentable upon their arrival at the summer palace. Wearing earrings that dangled to her collarbone may have been a mistake but not one she regretted. She had compromised by wearing her smallest tiara—it was the only one she had brought—Tara had tried to pack a different one for each day but Aarti had scolded her and forced her to take just one. She deftly removed her diamond-studded necklace and placed it in a purse that had just enough room for it.

Tara rested her head against the back of the seat and tried to let the surrounding chatter and the intermittent rocking of the car lull her into sleep. Perhaps it would have been a bit easier if not for the debilitating heat. She drifted in and out of sleep as the royal procession navigated winding roads etched into great mountains through scenic valleys, bobbing like a ship navigating stormy waters as they made their way through the lush surroundings. The frequency of houses dwindled, as did the cacophony of civilization.

As they traversed the unmetalled roads uphill, the houses became increasingly more precarious in their positioning. When the girls were younger, they used to point features of these houses out to each other. During monsoon, these houses would be surrounded by murky puddles that reflected the storms the processions had to brave. Tara used to imagine what it would be like to live in those houses, away from the cradle of luxury she was accustomed to, aghast at how anyone could be punished by fate to such an extent.

The environment at Balganga was equally quiet, allowing Tara half an hour of restless sleep before the royals and their entourage finally arrived at the summer palace. It was considerably less grand than the one at Bramsadha but extravagant nonetheless. Tara's ancestors may have even been more affluent than the princess herself, as was reflected in the gleaming marble entrance, the sprawling acres the palace looked upon and the fleet of staff at the royals' beck and call. Tanisha shook her sister awake, the latter's tiara slipping out of her hair and clattering to the floor of the car.

Still dazed, the sisters made their way into the palace as Tara pleaded with their father. 'We're both exhausted.

Tanisha even stopped talking at one point! The situation is bleak.' Tara stumbled as Tanisha elbowed her. 'Be careful! If I trip on this and tear it, you're paying for it.'

Mostly to avoid being caught in the crossfire of his daughters' bickering, the Maharaja waved them both off to their rooms to rest before assembling for tea in one of the many sitting areas of the palace. 'I'll send Aarti to give you 10 minutes' notice.'

Their summer palace had fewer storeys than the main palace, as it was more, as her father put it, 'open to nature'. Upon finding a worm under her sheets, Tara spiralled into a fury, directing her ire towards any staff member who approached her. She ordered them to make the entire bed once more and sweep the room again while they were at it. Her father chose to focus on his work and ignore her frenzy. To let off steam, the fuming princess knocked on Tanisha's door. Her sister, still smarting from their earlier exchange, allowed Tara to sleep on a deliberately uncomfortable chaise in the bedroom. The sisters hardly even had the time to consider unpacking before Aarti roused them.

'Your father wants to see you in the green room.'

The green room was one of the sitting rooms in the house, decked from floor to ceiling in all shades of green, where the Maharaja was waiting with chai that he had asked to be laid out for his daughters. They each took seats at the table across from him, as was routine.

'Now, to discuss the matter of the children.' *This again.* 'As you both know, the first batch will be arriving tomorrow. If all goes well, I shall offer to harbour more of them until the war ends. Although, judging by how things are panning out on the world stage, I can see no logical end in sight—just one that ends in a bloodbath.'

Tara was taken aback. Her father was never one to be intentionally morbid unless the circumstances were grave enough to necessitate it.

'We have 20 acres of land attached to this property. I've decided to use some of it to build living quarters for the children.'

'That should be quite expensive. How did you manage to get the British to invest in sheltering these children?' Tanisha chimed in. *Of course she would question the expenses somehow, the brazen know-it-all.*

'Thank you for bringing that up, Tani. I have to discuss that and another thing with you.'

Oh, how desperately Tara wanted to wipe that conceited smile right off her sister's face.

'The British government had nothing to do with this plan or anything remotely connected to the children. In fact, they would not give me permission to harbour them in the first place. At least, not on their watch.'

'So what you're saying is—'

'Yes, it is exactly what you think. But first, I do hope you haven't informed anyone about the children.'

'Papa, if you intend on keeping this a secret, I guarantee it'll be quite a lofty goal. I don't assume you'll spend your entire life making rounds and begging our staff not to release that information.'

'You just leave that to me. The British absolutely cannot know about these children for as long as we can keep the information safely within these walls. They have refused to fund me in the past and are strongly against these Polish children seeking refuge in India.'

'So how do you plan to fund the relocation of these children? Unless...' Tara did not like where this was going.

'Unless you plan to fund these children out of your own pocket,' Tanisha concluded.

'Exactly. We must use some of our generational wealth to build homes for these children, take care of their education, their shelter and any additional amenities they may require. That does, in turn, mean that we shall have to cut down on some staff and make a few sacrifices. For instance, I have put our other summer home on the market. I already have a prospective buyer—a business tycoon based in Bombay.'

This is a nightmare. This is a nightmare, Tara repeated to herself. She may have only visited that particular property a few times, what with its distance from Bramsadha, but she loved to show it off to the ladies of the court! Those cursed children and their infinite needs were wrenching every fraction of her identity from her grasp.

'What does that mean for us?'

'I would hope that you girls will adapt to the situation, for there shall indeed be fewer butlers that may directly affect your current lifestyle. Perhaps Aarti could teach you both to make the bed.'

Make the bed? She was an heiress! Tara could not possibly be expected to fulfil her royal duties and perform menial household tasks simultaneously. Her kingdom would need her, but that wouldn't be possible if the princess were being treated like a working-class schmuck. Tara clasped her hands tightly together, failing to realize till her fingers turned glaringly pale and caught a worried Tanisha's attention, who nudged them apart.

'I further expect you to treat the children as if they are our own citizens. Most of them had to forsake their ties to their native Poland and our objective is to make them feel as at home here as you both have felt your entire lives.'

There he went again, preaching about the importance of 'citizenship' and 'being a gracious host'. Tara could very well manage the hosting aspect, but only for a few hours! That is what the court ladies had trained her for. She was hardly willing to devote that amount of effort to victims of a war that had no end in sight. Additionally, Tara and Tanisha were the only palace residents able to speak Polish, having learnt the language as children. Tara was grateful for being exposed to such a vast variety of languages and cultures as a child, certain that would come in handy if she'd ever need to romance a wealthy, foreign gentleman, but the task presented to her under these circumstances seemed quite the antithesis of that.

'The children's living and schooling areas have already been constructed. For now, they'll be using the lawn for recreational activities, but if we decide to take in some more, I may decide to build them a makeshift park.' *As if they didn't have enough already.* 'All right. You girls rest for a bit and then I shall give you both a tour of their accommodation.'

Tara left in yet another huff, this one considerably more huffy than the last. The princess was drained and had also learnt from one of her staff that the insufferable drilling noises they kept hearing were workers finishing up the children's accommodation. The noise impacted Tara's sleep once more.

Those children were a plague—pervasive, terrifying and never-ending. Tara chose to burden her sister with her worries.

'They are single-handedly taking over our entire life. What if they decide to never leave our property? The British will certainly not intervene and our father will end up having wasted all of our wealth on those squatters.' She spat the last word out.

'Tara, they're children. They're not money-hungry lunatics hell-bent on seizing our wealth at the first opportunity. Don't act daft. Papa's initiative is not for the weak-hearted and it is our duty not just as princesses but as his daughters to support him through thick and thin.' Tanisha shifted closer to her sister, taking her hand in hers. 'You need to understand that he has a different way of showing us love. In your case, it's overprotectiveness and in mine, it's overwhelming support.'

'Why's mine so much worse?'

'Because, and this is just my theory, you remind him too much of Mother. His heart can't withstand losing another one of us and especially you, being the heir to the throne.'

Tara chuckled, trying to coerce the tears back in. 'You know Tani, I reckon you're much better suited to the throne than I am. You are a chatterbox but none of your chatter is meaningless. You have wisdom far beyond what I could ever hope to achieve.'

'Yes, well, I have experience dealing with you on a daily basis.'

Tara feigned offence as her sister cackled. 'There was no need for that…'

'And yet, somehow, there absolutely was!'

Silana

A mild breeze blew as Silana trudged to school. It had been pouring just a few moments ago and her backpack was soaked from the premature showers. She could almost make out the scolding face of her father in the overhead clouds—cast in hues of grim disapproval and sneering up towards the heavens. Silana sighed. Father somehow found his way into every nook and cranny of her mind—sometimes in moments of imagination, more often in ones of fear. She saw her father's face in the nearby foliage too, before reaching her school.

Sigrid and Anna were waiting outside their classroom, the former's normally inscrutable countenance now filled with sorrow. It was Anna's last day, Silana remembered. She rushed to the girl and embraced her, nearly sending them tumbling into their peers nearby.

'It's one last of everything now. The last time I see you first, the last time we part and then convene in this wretched school.'

'It's never the last time, Anna,' Silana said defiantly. 'Never. If you long hard enough for the next time, it is bound to happen, some way or the other.'

The school bell tolled in the distance as the trio embraced once more. Their classes that day passed in a haze, each girl more focussed on what the other two were thinking.

Anna's fingers, empowered by her anxiety, were a blur of movement as she fiddled with every conceivable thing she could—from her laces all the way up to the buttons of her coat. Sigrid noticed Anna's face, marred with worry, and nudged Silana, the two sharing a silent look.

Lunchtime arrived quickly and Silana was shocked by how absorbed in her thoughts she had become; she had hardly looked at the clock, which was usually a regular habit for her. The three girls rushed out of the dingy classroom and towards their spot—a mossy undergrowth situated below an adolescent oak tree at some distance from the school's quadrangle. They didn't even bother with their lunches— they had too much to discuss. The disconnect from their studies facilitated a rather lively conversation about Anna's desired explorations in Switzerland.

'I shall go skiing in the Alps, definitely.'

'Perhaps you will meet a very nice mountain boy—Peter to your Heidi!'

Anna doubled over, laughing her terribly contagious laugh. Their banter eventually grew more serious as they discussed what to do with their posters. For the past few weeks, Silana, Sigrid, Anna and Sebastien had all brainstormed and worked together on these 'rebel' posters, meant to be informative, in their spare time. Their first attempt had gained an immense amount of traction within the school—it had been Sebastien's idea to hide them under desks. This daring stunt created an uproar amongst the teachers and some of the more radical students but most had taken their passionate words to heart. The three of them realized this whenever they overheard snippets of conversation while passing through the hallways. However, there had been a major hitch in their plan when a Jewish boy was implicated for the posters. Somewhat fortunate was the fact that the school took action against him independently and there was to be no involvement of the Gestapo if he cooperated. The group felt terrible about what had befallen their young acquaintance and decided to extend their operations outside the school. They began with unfamiliar neighbourhoods, awkwardly sticking posters with weak adhesive on street lights.

Though they may have left a trail of confusion in their wake regarding the perpetrators, their call for action through awareness did resonate with some people, though unbeknownst to them. The fact that their base of operation was in the lion's den itself—Silana's house—meant that the two siblings had taken the initiative and diligently kept their father from finding out what they were a part of. Once they had all gotten a hang of how (and where) exactly to quickly install a plethora of these posters, they became increasingly better at it. Anna had suggested that they move sporadically across neighbourhoods so that there wouldn't be a definite pattern or any symmetry to their movements, striking every two to three or sometimes even four days so that there wouldn't be any cohesion in that aspect either.

Their initiative had made such an impact that security was tightened around areas suspected to be hit next, but the group always managed to stay one step ahead. They frequented a few neighbourhoods a lot less often nowadays, gripped by the fear that they would be recognized, as there had indeed been a few mishaps along the way. With

Anna gone, Silana wasn't sure how they would continue. The former had been an integral part of the entire idea, considering it was her brainchild.

'Continue, please. I implore you. We are doing meaningful work here, something impactful. It had to be done and I'm surprised it was us who first realized this. But for heaven's sake, do be careful. You remember what happened the other night.'

Sigrid had almost been noticed by an old Polish gentleman settling into bed when she knocked over a mailbox and startled the man.

'Never compromise your well-being for our cause. Those who participate in such things are never truly safe.'

Anna sighed. 'Besides our political escapades, I have so much to thank you for. Sigrid, you were my first friend in this school before Silana joined. We were indeed ostracized at first, but there is no one I'd rather have lunch with. Silana, you are the perfect blend of talent and kindness, and I will never stop admiring what you have done for both me and our project. You both have cared for and loved me through times I didn't share the sentiment myself. I will miss you dearly but also have a feeling that this is not where our friendship will end. What say we meet once this war is over?'

'Well, that isn't foreseeably soon,' Silana said.

'In 10 years?' Sigrid proposed.

'In 20 years?' Silana added.

'That's far too long. I'll hardly want glimpses of my once-bright youth when I'm 40; I'll be old and grey and bitter!'

'Aren't you already, Sil?'

Anna dodged clumsily as Silana swatted at her.

'I'm serious, Anna. All we need is a time, place and luck on our side. Luck…that only God can give.'

'Only God,' Anna echoed.

'I've always wanted to go to Paris, you know…'

'We're not meeting on top of the Eiffel Tower, Silana. You'll fall off, and Sigrid and I have never been enthusiasts of high towers.'

'That's disappointing. I have another idea! There's a small café across Arc de Triumph—Un Jour Rosé. I went there two summers ago. Mother, Sunne and I stopped there quite briefly while Father and Sebastien were at a convention. If it's still there, that's where we'll meet. Their pain au chocolat isn't something I'll forget any time soon.'

'So it's settled then. Silana's café it is,' Sigrid affirmed as the distant cry of the school bell signalled the end of the lunch period.

Silana felt a knot form in her stomach, twisting and tightening as she ran towards her school, looking back once more to see the oak tree bidding her farewell. She had double maths and biology and was certainly not looking forward to it. In class, Anna sat between her two friends, who intermittently wrote words of comfort and encouragement on bits of paper but were cautious not to mention any details of either her future absence or its reason. Silana's words were considerably less covert as she was attempting to actually understand the subject matter as well. Her grade in the last biology test had shaken Silana to her very core and she wanted to make up for such disgrace, lest her father lay a hand on her as he had done on the day she had disclosed her marks to him.

Anna wondered what would become of her friend, who was hastily scribbling on two sets of notebooks. She knew that Silana never complained when things were going badly. She usually found creative ways around tasks and hardly ever talked about her stifling home environment. Anna hoped that Silana would forever retain that optimism, not just because of how much it had gotten her through, but because it encouraged others to keep theirs up too.

Silana eyed the clock every two minutes—the class dragged on and it seemed like a century before the bell wailed one final time. She felt a familiar sensation in her stomach—a painful blend of trepidation and fear, similar to the one she felt around her father. 'Evil butterflies', she called them, for they were generally a bad omen. Silana pushed this awful thought to the very back of her mind. *Now is not the time for doubt*, she affirmed as she and Sigrid slowly followed Anna out of the class after staying back for a few minutes to avoid the overwhelming human traffic.

Anna would have gone to Silana's house one last time, but her parents had demanded she return at the earliest since things for Anna's family had been getting worse as the days wore on. A drunk sailor had let slip incidents of passport-snatching a few days prior while haranguing her father, who felt threatened and spooked enough to leave a few days ahead of schedule, much to the dismay of her friends; they also felt slightly relieved as the top priority was Anna's safety.

The girls walked arm in arm towards the main road, exchanging gossip as usual, until they reached the stretch where their paths diverged. The girls stood in silence, exchanged looks and quietly embraced each other. Silana was no longer trying to fight the tears; she let them flow freely down her cheeks, wetting her glasses and obscuring her vision almost entirely. Seeing Silana, who generally didn't cry easily, break down so suddenly stirred something in Sigrid, causing her to sob softly and shed briny tears.

Anna was taken aback by their sudden outburst and attempted to console them with a mixture of 'shhhs' and intermittent words of comfort. 'I just don't know if we'll ever meet again,' Anna sobbed. 'Everything inside me is telling me to believe you, but something is telling me not to.'

'It all depends on whether you accept the "something" or not,' replied Silana. 'Trust me, somehow, we will meet again. Do you really believe that this war can keep me away from you two?'

'It better not.'

Anna laughed that contagious laugh of hers a final time before spinning around and jogging towards her home. Her friends silently watched as her auburn hair, tied in a delicate ponytail, caught the sunlight, reflecting it to give her an almost halo effect until she melded into the bustling chaos of pedestrians. Sigrid turned to Silana, face still wet and eyes puffy and scarlet, as if expecting Silana to do something. Silana noticed her expectant look and realized something jarring—both of them were the introverts of the group; Anna had been the foil to their regular silences with her penchant for long-drawn-out conversations. The absence of Anna's constant chatter only added to the growing void in Silana's heart, now more palpable than ever.

'Let's pick up this week's issue,' Silana suggested. Though

their posters were meant to incentivize people and initiate a call to action, the group had also been taking inspiration from a real-time, uncensored news source—a rebel tabloid based a few towns away. At one point, Sigrid had been caught with a stack of posters—they had since learnt not to travel with too many at a time. It was only through good fortune that the couple who caught Sigrid red-handed were associated with this rebel outlet. The four friends read the newspaper on consecutive days—the issue arrived on a Wednesday, so Silana and Sebastien would read it by Thursday and then pass it on to Anna who would give it to Sigrid by Friday. It was then her job to dispose of the newspaper as soon as she was done. Sigrid usually either burned it in her family's large fireplace or soaked it to an inconceivable extent and then ripped it to shreds and flushed it.

As they made their way to the couple's house, both girls were silent, though not awkwardly. Silana found this fact strangely comforting—after all, you can make conversation with almost everyone but it takes a special kind of person to be comfortable in silence with. They were soon handed the newspaper, wished luck as usual, and after a few hesitant goodbyes, they parted to head home.

Silana decided to once again tread the familiar narrow winding trail near her home, which took her to the outskirts of the forest. Until a few months ago she used to accompany her father as he led her through the trail, often stopping to comment on the varying shades of the leaves as they fell around him, almost as if drawn to him. It reminded Silana of the way people would flock to her father at every opportunity—at social events, in the cinema, sometimes even at the poolside. It seemed as though his magnetic attraction extended even to inanimate objects.

Silana sat on one of the benches, taking comfort in the fact that her father wouldn't be home for a few more hours. However, she was quickly jolted out of her idyllic haze. She noticed Sunne running towards her, frantic, with an ashen look. As the words escaped her lips, Silana's world grew red.

'Your posters—Father knows. He knows.'

Tara

The camps were quite the opposite of what Tara had envisioned. They were essentially wooden cabins outside the palace—at quite some distance—serving as living accommodation, while the common areas of the palace functioned as educational and recreational spaces. Workers were still drilling away at loose planks of wood, tending to the bathrooms and making final rounds of the cabins. There weren't enough bedrooms in the palace to provide lodging for the children, so they would be used for the teachers and staff.

'Is it not inconvenient for the children to walk 10 minutes every day to reach the palace?'

'I have an explanation for that, Tani,' the Maharaja replied. 'In case of surprise visits from the British, as has happened in the past, I would like to give no indication that we are housing the children close to us. If they are in the palace or roaming around, capturing them would be easier. With them staying at some distance, our guards will be able to give us a 10-minute warning.'

Tani nodded in understanding.

'The children will dine with us in the great hall. I have received word that 22 of them will be arriving in the first batch. If we choose to expand, I shall commission the construction of a functional canteen near their cabins as well.'

The cabins were primarily made of wood and stone. Tara marvelled at her father's ability to successfully have two cabins—one for boys and one for girls—constructed at such short notice. The cabins had working electricity and running water, with the two bathrooms situated behind them. Bunk beds and drawers lined the walls of the cabins—around 25 in total, Tara counted.

'I've hired tutors who speak both English and Polish, and a few who know Hindi as well, to tutor these children and help them communicate with the staff. I want them to feel as at home as possible.'

The tour continued. Tara was regretting wearing a half-decent outfit for it. Truth be told, the family would probably end up as peasants—better she started learning to live like one. She focussed on trying to salvage the hems of her white lehenga as it brushed against the muddy, dew-ridden forest floor. How she hated nature and its quaint little atrocities. Her shoes had been spoilt beyond saving, and the princess was stewing over the fact she would have to walk another 10 minutes back to the palace. The grass surrounding the cabin was uneven and scraggly, and the land around it was dotted with various shrubs and towering trees, though the areas near the cabin had been cleared to accommodate them. Tara couldn't fathom sleeping in any of those beds, with mattresses and pillows as firm as bricks, blankets as thin as a singular hair strand and the prospect of insects invading her space at any given moment. So taken aback was she by the circumstances that she forgot about the root cause of all the fuss.

'I have been informed that the children are apprehensive

about their new life here in India. They have journeyed long and far to reach us, away from everything they hold dear and familiar. Most have been orphaned. I expect we shall be accommodating these children for at least a few years, if not longer.'

A few years? Tara was on the verge of sinking into the mud and grime and letting it claim her, white lehenga and all.

'They shall be arriving tomorrow evening. For now, I suggest we return, have an early dinner and retire to bed soon.'

The palace, situated on a low hill, often experienced a significant temperature drop at night. Tara's tolerance for the cold was abysmally low. At her father's insistence, they dined on one of the terraces to revel in the view of the city below, freckled with subtle lights. The princess ended up partaking in the meal wrapped in three layers of blankets and shawls. The night brought with it a dreadful storm, branches flying and clattering against the windows while furious gusts of wind howled outside. The new moon only added to the eeriness of the empty sky. Even the stars could not burn bright enough to be discerned from the impenetrable storm clouds that loomed over them.

The adrenaline and worry about the day to come formed a dangerous cocktail in the pit of Tara's stomach. Sleep had all but mocked the princess that night. She aimed to delay breakfast for as long as humanly possible, opting to finish one of her new books instead—that would certainly keep her busy for a good few hours. After finishing the novel, she lay staring blankly at the ceiling, eyes unfocussed, for another half hour before she gathered the energy to face the day.

Perhaps she could feign illness. Tara considered it before an angsty Aarti pounded on her door, no doubt to lecture her about the importance of punctuality. She couldn't even take pleasure in the one thing she loved most—getting ready for the day. Tara felt like a heap of fabric in her cotton attire, as pale and bland as wet rice. Her jewellery and tiara, at the very least, added accents of glamour to an outfit that otherwise made her resemble a field of cotton. She twirled, allowing the thick fabric to absorb some of the breeze she let in through her open window, before going down to the dining table.

'There has been a change of plans. The children will be coming a few hours earlier than expected.'

Tara, who had just been about to shove a dosa drenched in chutney into her mouth, looked up. 'But that means they'll be here in two hours, or three, maximum.'

'Exactly!' Her father beamed.

Her sister, frustratingly enough, looked equally ecstatic. 'Papa told me during our morning walk! Isn't it wonderful?'

Morning walk? How come her father had never bothered to offer his elder child a similar activity?

Breakfast was a tense affair, the chatter dying down relatively quickly as the girls noticed a shift in their father's mood. The Maharaja was one of the most easy-going men Tara had ever encountered. Even more so than her vast array of private tutors, whom her family paid a great deal to put up with her entitlement and that was saying something. However today, the princess noticed a deepened furrow in his brow and his lips were in a tight line that was hard to discern beneath his voluminous moustache. His eyes, a light brown, had further pigmented with worry. Tara squinted her eyes at the clock on the wall—it had been nearly an hour since they had settled down to eat. If the children were on schedule, they should be arriving shortly.

Tara knew exactly what to do during her last few hours of freedom. Rushing to her room, she picked up an easel, stretched canvas, paints, palettes, brushes, a small cup filled with water and her ancient, filthy painting rag and hustled to a window in one of the highest guest bedrooms in the palace that overlooked the forest. The room was supposed to be for lodging the head teacher of the children's camp; but, the latter would be arriving tomorrow, Aarti had informed her, which gave Tara an opportunity to paint at leisure. For now.

She splayed her materials, pulled up a rickety wooden chair beside her canvas and got down to painting. The princess wasn't very imaginative with her subjects—she usually needed references to bring her talent to life. Her muse for the day was the forest that stretched beyond the palace, bathed in a delicate, amber glow. Her palette was a careful infusion of soft grey-browns and golden yellows, the latter shade similar to that of an egg yolk. The trees had thick, textured barks and jagged branches protruding from their sides. Some of them had wispy leaves that reached the ground and crept across the lush grass beneath, sometimes further, while others were nearly barren.

Tara admired the contrast between these ethereal elements, quickly sketching out proportions and doing a quick wash of her canvas before getting to her favourite part—mixing colours. Each stroke was careful, deliberately placed. Tara knew she could never render a more skilled representation of nature than nature itself, but how it rewarded her to try! She didn't care to notice time as it slipped away; her precise strokes ensured her full attention remained on the artwork. She occasionally stepped away from the easel for a while to take a few rounds of the room, careful not to look at her artwork, just as her mother had taught her to do. 'Never look at it for too long. You will always be tempted to find fault in it somehow.'

Her mother had taught her to paint as a means of escape from her eventual responsibilities as the wife of a future king. Tani had usually been too restless and impatient to revel in the process, much like their father, but Tara and the Maharani had both been blessed with this gift, which served the princess well. By the time she had finished the artwork, final details and all, almost two and a half hours had passed. Tara had deliberately used a smaller canvas to manage her time as efficiently as possible. Though she hadn't been able to paint for quite a while now, she walked a few steps back and looked at the picture, marvelling at both her talent and her mother's teaching.

The painting was nearly as accurate as a mirror reflecting Tara's view from the window. The only exception was that she'd managed to capture the glow that the morning sun had enveloped the forest in before the harsher noon light, the forest now gleaming as if it held the embers of a raging fire. The trees stood seemingly unnerved by both the beauty they were a part of and the volatility of their primary sustainer, while Tara tried to imbue the grass with a more soulful essence, spotting some remnants of dew on them. Though Tara would not venture anywhere near wet grass (the squelching sound it made and the feel beneath her feet was an auditory and tactile nightmare for her), painting dew nestled unsuspectingly on solitary blades of grass that captured rays of raw morning light was a favourite of hers. The princess smiled, feeling free to admire her own work—this might have even been her best work so far. Absence did truly make her heart grow fonder of this passion of hers.

Lost in reflection, she nearly missed the sound of two lorries bumping and heaving their way through the palace gates, across the gravel path leading up to the palace's doors and the main entrance itself. A cold realization dawned on her. *They're here? Already?* She raced to the window, looking down as the chatter of children filled her ears. She backed away a bit, scared they would notice her and try to initiate contact. She watched the top of their heads—some blonde, others brunette, a few wearing hats—and counted 22 children.

Her back pressed against the wall, Tara contemplated whether she should lock herself in the room the entire day (the staff wouldn't be able to find her) before she heard a sharp rapping on the door. *Of course, Aarti had seen her come up here; the woman had seven sets of eyes.*

'Tara ji, bacche aa gaye hain! Aapke Papa aapko neeche bula raha hain unko milne ke liye. (Miss Tara, the children have arrived! Your father is calling you downstairs to meet them.)'

Tara made a last-ditch attempt to get out of it. 'Didi, meri tabiyat kaafi kharaab hai aaj. Main bacchon se nahin mil sakti hoon—agar vo bhi beemaar pad gaye to kya ho hoga? (Didi, I'm feeling quite unwell today. I can't meet the children—what if they fall sick too?)'

Aarti scolded her, not because she made an excuse to wriggle out of meeting the children, but for the lack of originality regarding the excuse. Tara giggled before allowing her to enter, the stout woman, clad in a new maroon sari, not even appreciating the beauty of the painting before criticizing the mess Tara had made.

'Mere paas ise saaf karne ka samay kaise hoga? (When will I get the time to clean this up?)'

Aarti told Tara that her father was very flustered and wanted her down at once, which she abided by instantly—she had only ever seen her father angry once and reasoned she shouldn't be the cause of it again.

Deftly picking up the cotton heap that tickled her ankles, the princess dashed precariously down multiple flights of stairs, knocking over a few (mercifully unlit) candelabras along the way. Her father and sister were already waiting at the main gates, which were open wider than Tara had ever seen them before. They were greeting the children, Tanisha even pulling them closer to embrace them. As Tara walked up to her father, the odour coming off the children struck her so violently that she felt as if she had run into a brick wall of the scent. Wrinkling her nose, she turned to her father, who widened his eyes as an immediate warning to not wear her emotions on her sleeve.

Tanisha was speaking to a few of the younger children, kneeling to be at their eye level as they replied excitedly. Tara overheard one of the girls, who couldn't have been older than seven, thanking Tani—the girl was so grateful to finally speak to someone who understood them. *I can understand you too.* Tara would have surely gone up and made conversation with the older children, if not for the god-awful odour that emanated from each of them. They looked considerably bedraggled as well. Tara skirted behind a few columns, sizing up the children and trying to avoid any who made attempts to approach her. She made herself look busy by talking (albeit painstakingly) to some of the nearby staff or asking her father inane questions regarding the children's routine and acting as a translator for him and the children. Tani, however, seemed to revel in their company, quite a few crowding around her and pressing her with all sorts of questions, from which Tara made out, 'Where will be staying?' 'What'll we be doing now?' 'What's for lunch?'

Even from a distance, Tara felt stifled by their pervasive stench. She was relieved when her father announced that they should make their way to the camp, reasoning that the open air would do the children some good. *And maybe a bath too, while they were at it.* As the children picked up their suitcases and followed Tanisha, the Maharaja held Tara back for a moment.

'Is there something bothering you, Tara?'

'Nothing at all, Papa, why do you ask?'

'It may just be the excitement of these children's arrival, but you seem more distant than usual.'

What was that supposed to mean?

'I would deeply appreciate it if you would cease this standoffish behaviour at the earliest. These children have so little and being snobbish is not the right approach. I'm doing this to honour your mother. Are you truly telling me this is what she would have expected from you?'

Tara took a small step back. How did her aversion to filth relate to dishonouring her mother? *Maybe the stench has driven Father out of his senses.* She tried to end the conversation civilly. 'I understand.' She was beyond relieved with the sharp nod she got as a response.

'Follow me, for now the onus is on us to show these children the hospitality they've been so thoughtlessly denied.'

Tara rolled her eyes as her father turned his back to tend to the steady procession of worms that oozed out of their palace. Knowing them for the better part of 10 minutes evidently put them far above her in regard to his priorities. The 10-minute walk to the cabins in peak afternoon did not sit well with the princess, only exacerbating her irritation with both her surroundings and the people that filled them. She observed Tanisha revelling in the epicentre of it all—overseeing the work of the managers they had hired to take care of the children as they were briefed about their accommodation, education and recreation. Tara stood with arms crossed, nose wrinkled and eyebrows furrowed, ready to scramble off in the opposite direction should any child choose to approach her.

After storing their baggage in their respective cabins, the children were gathered by the camp managers at a large wooden table in a clearing designated for meals. The children chattered incessantly, reminding Tara of the crickets that dotted her gardens. They looked, smelled and sounded just the same, so did it not stand to reason that they would act similarly? Her father sat at the head of the table, gesturing for the sisters to sit down on either side of him. Tara was assiduously engrossed in squashing any ant that came near, as opposed to her father's 'historic' welcoming of the children; the pre-rehearsed speech had been run past the sisters several times, well before the day the Maharaja had to deliver it to his intended audience.

'Children,' the Maharaja began, Tanisha duly translating for him. 'It is both my honour and privilege to welcome you to your home for the next few years. I do understand that the current circumstances are not the most favourable; however, I present you with the chance to take these misfortunes in your stride, and though the war may seem terrifyingly unending at this moment, from it will emerge a beam of hope spearheaded by you, the youth of Poland. I hope that we shall be able to instil the values of great leaders and exemplary citizens in you, so that if you choose to return to your country, may it be with a renewed appreciation of the values that are dear to your people and your nation. But, as of this moment, the citizens of Bramsadha shall ensure both your safety and well-being until this conflict comes to a close.'

As the children applauded and cheered, Tara tried to fend off the ants from beneath her skirt. Now seemed a good time to feign illness and return to the palace as soon as possible. She already felt delirious and dehydrated from the heat bearing down relentlessly on them. Tani, ever selfless, had found a seat in the shade, leaving Tara exposed to the sun that filtered through the canopy of the trees that encircled them.

Her father continued. 'As of today, you are all officially Bramsadhans. You are now our adopted brethren, our brothers and sisters, and you shall be integrated into our society with immediate effect. However, I urge you to not lose sight of your national identity, which has brought you here today. We will support you in preserving your cultural heritage as well as ensure you do not lag behind in your education. We want to instil a culture that reminds you both of home and makes you feel at home here with us.'

This final assertion was met with a mixture of contended murmurs and polite claps. The Maharaja smiled. 'Now that the formalities are out of the way, let us welcome you with a feast!'

It was at this point Tara excused herself from the meal and for the entire day. 'Papa, I truthfully feel I might faint in this heat. Let me return to the palace with Aarti and I shall brainstorm activity ideas for the children.'

Her father excused her, albeit hesitantly, from the proceedings on the condition that she be present for dinner. It was sure to be another situation rife with sentimental drivel, something she had no interest in witnessing, but Tara could tolerate it at best after resting for a few hours. She admired Tanisha's willingness to put up with the children. They seemed to exude a scent worse than the forest itself. The first thing she planned to do upon returning to her room was invest in her own hygiene. Tara barked for Aarti, and silently trudged back to the main palace, irked beyond belief.

Aarti was no stranger to the princess' silent seething sessions, being the person Tara usually went kvetching to after each disagreeable interaction with her father or Tanisha. Tara was especially livid today, stomping up the steps of the palace, her stout minder fighting valiantly to match her pace.

'I have been cursed with all the misfortune in the world, Aarti, I really have—these gremlins disguised as children in the dozens, a sister who seeks more attention than an exotic wounded animal and a father who succumbs to her charms like an insect to a Venus flytrap. My responsibility is to better our kingdom, not to entertain all variety of miscreants that my father desires.'

She swung open the door to her room, which was quite a feat considering it was a gilded chunk of metal. Aarti supposed that an infusion of anger and adrenaline had given Tara some sort of inhuman strength.

'And to think I am to tolerate their incessant demands. And this intolerable heat. It's as if my suffering knows no bounds.' Tara turned to Aarti. 'I plan on going for a very, very thorough bath. I'm afraid being in the vicinity of those children will give me lice or, worse, the plague. Please, launder these at the earliest—or better yet, burn them. Lay out a fresh set for me.'

Tara, true to her word, spent an hour in the bathroom. Aarti took apart the layers of her lehenga instead of setting it ablaze as the frenzied princess had requested her to do. She intended on resewing the pieces and donating them later to some beggars in the city. Tara, still agitated, grumbled to a disgruntled Aarti when the latter came to freshen up her hair. 'Aarti, how do you even suggest I deal with these rancid brats?'

The woman took a deep but carefully silent breath as she continued braiding Tara's hair. Whatever would the Maharani say to her beloved daughter now? Serving two generations of royals, each so vastly different, often tested her own sanity.

'Truthfully, if a genie appeared right before me at this very moment, the only thing I would ask for would wish for is to make these children disappear.'

Aarti parsed the princess' words. Her mistress wouldn't choose to wish away the war but the children who were victims of it.

'If only Papa would focus his attention on more important things; then, perhaps our time and money both wouldn't be wasted on such insignificances.'

Aarti felt overwhelmed. Perhaps it was her maternal instincts from watching the young girl she had partially raised evolve into this personification of selfishness and unkindness, or perhaps it was just her sense of humanity that couldn't allow the existence of hierarchies to further corrupt basic decency. Whatever the case, she dropped her hands from Tara's head and rested them on her shoulders. Tara looked at her housekeeper in the mirror, brow furrowed, her raven hair hanging in a half-done braid across her left shoulder. As Tara opened her mouth to protest, she was quickly hushed.

'Tara ji, I have known you ever since you struggled to pull yourself up from your crib. Before, even. I've held you when your mother got tired, I've calmed down every single teacher you have scorned and been at your every beck and call since you uttered your first word.'

Tara was aghast. This shared psychosis had infested Aarti's mind as well. She mentally braced herself for some lengthy lecture on 'the importance of giving'; however, Aarti's slight head shake and abrupt conclusion threw her off track completely.

'At the end of the day, it is up to you what values you choose to live by. But just imagine—what if you had been one of them?' Aarti braided the girl's hair, her touch gentler this time; more distant. 'One of the members of the security who helped transport the children from Bramsadha to Balganga informed me that most, if not all, of these children have lost somebody closest to them—their parents, their siblings, some even their entire families. Arriving here has been no easy feat for them. The last thing they would ever do is "steal" any of this family's wealth, believe me. They wish they were not here as much as you do. This is not their home but it is our job, nestled in this privilege, to make them feel like it is. What I'm trying to say is, Tara, that—'

'I should be more like Tani?'

'Not at all. In fact, I think you would be better than her at managing these *bacchas*. It just appears that right now she's putting in much more effort than you are.'

Aarti may not have been able to speak English, but foolish and close-minded were those who failed to notice what was underneath. Aarti, who had watched the sisters grow up, found that pitting one against the other in a friendly competition was the most effective way to rope them in. Not in a manner that rendered both the sisters bitter, but one that left one feeling (sorrowfully) superior and the other blissfully unaware. She further sowed the seeds of this rivalry. 'You both speak the language, but how is it that the children have immediately latched on to her and not you?' The fact was that the princess had actively avoided them but the woman skimmed over this convenient fact. 'You feel sympathy for these children and their struggles, yes?'

Tara nodded.

'Don't. That makes them feel inferior to you, detached from you. Your objective is to help them, but making them feel like they're but a charitable expense for you will serve to do nothing but further widen the gap. Don't feel sympathy for these children because you can relate to them. In some measure, you've experienced a loss that is comparable to some of theirs—your mother.'

The girl tensed as Aarti finished securing the loose ends of her hair.

'Empathize with them instead. Make them feel like they belong. I am well aware I sound like your father's parrot right now but do consider what I have told you.'

'I will. Wake me when it's time for dinner.'

Aarti smiled at her before seeing herself out.

Tara sat motionless, watching her housekeeper leave and slowly shut the door behind her. She felt anything but appreciative of the concern the elders in the household showed her. Despite feeling the need to act as mature as any of them, when push came to shove, she would still be treated as a child. Her sister, the one person who could empathize with her in this situation, was in fact their role model for how a princess should ideally behave. Somehow beating her sister at her own game would certainly be the sweetest revenge, even though it wasn't exactly what her dear Aarti had meant to convey. No matter, she would mull over it after a much-required couple of hours of rest. Mercifully, the camp was situated a substantial distance away from the palace, thus allowing her the sweet embrace of silence so long as she remained ensconced within the comfort of her quarters. As promised, Aarti returned after a few hours to rouse a very disgruntled princess, whose beautiful braid had now unravelled into stray locks loosely framing her face.

'Tani and your father returned about an hour ago. Your sister wanted to meet you as soon as they reached but I kept her from waking you. She told me it was about something important concerning the children. Now, please go talk to her and remember what I've discussed with you.'

Silana

Silana could feel her heart pounding in her ears as she rushed back to her house, Sunne following closely behind. Her ebony hair, tied in a bun, had come undone, occasionally getting stuck on stray branches that splayed out from the trees. This didn't seem to bother the girl who, upon reaching the front porch of her house, doubled over to take a much-needed breath before smoothing down her clothes and trying to fix her bun. Hesitantly, she knocked on the door.

Her mother swung the door open, her delicate features mirroring Silana's visible panic. Yvonne ushered her trembling daughter inside, helping her take off the multiple layers quickly and placing them on their designated spots on the coat rack. 'To the living room. Go, now.'

Something about her mother's voice shook Silana to the core. Her mother was the gentlest soul she had ever known, and her current stoic demeanour contrasted starkly with her usual bubbly and positive nature. This was the same Yvonne who had stood silently as Lukas beat their children, leaving Silana to wonder what was to become of her. Her entire form shook as she made her way to the living room, finding Sebastien, sitting tight-lipped across from their father. She quickly took a seat beside Seb, her eyes dropping as she noticed the blueprints for the week's poster spread across the expansive glass table. She kept her head down, gaze fixated on the plans and the other pages of her diary that she assumed her father had ripped out in a frenzy.

'My own dearest children. Rebel scum.'

Yvonne, who was standing a little distance away, stepped towards the table but stopped when Lukas sharply raised his hand.

'God knows how much I struggle for both you insolent children.'

'Father, it's utterly my fault. I pushed Silana into this.'

'That's a blatant lie, Sebastien. I was the one who proposed the idea! I pushed him into—'

'QUIET, THE BOTH OF YOU!'

The room went silent. Silana could hear nothing but the sound of her heart thumping in her ears so violently that she felt she might go deaf.

'The posters on Ulica słonecznikowa and Drugie skrzyżowanie—were they all you?'

Neither spoke.

'ANSWER ME!'

'They were.'

'And why would either of you commit such an act?'

Silence.

'Our family has held a particular position in this society for more years than you can possibly imagine. Your grandfather—my father—was one of the most respected men in this community. What would he think if he saw you two fools today, tarnishing the family name and everything our political affiliations stand for? And God forbid you had been caught. Everything I have worked so hard to achieve—our standing, our impeccable reputation, our prosperity—would have vanished in a moment. How dare you sit across me and eat my food, live in my house under my rules, and bite the hand that feeds you? Have you no respect or shame?'

Silana's eyes brimmed with tears and she let them fall as her father continued his verbal rampage.

'These disgusting, meaningless messages—"Don't let our youth grow up in a world filled with hate and plundered by greed"—do you hear yourselves? The Nazi party is a fair and just one, dedicated to eliminating all the undesirables from our world.'

Silana, through the corner of her eye, watched Yvonne flinch silently.

'Silana, is this truly what you've chosen to use the journal for? I gave it to you as a birthday gift, from a place of love, of understanding.'

Silana was frenzied. 'Father, it was a terrible mistake on my behalf. I didn't realize the impact this would have on our family, on our name. I cannot begin to express—'

Lukas Haydn stood up, his chair roughly grating against the beautiful tiled floor, and grabbed the diary from the table. Not that there was much left; the binder was practically destroyed, the pages falling out left, right and centre. Silana scrambled in his direction, nearly tripping over the legs of one of the chairs. Sebastien also stood up, concerned, while Yvonne rushed to restrain Silana.

The trio watched, stunned, as Lukas marched towards the fireplace and flung the diary into the scarlet embers of the smoky flame. Yvonne's hand went to her mouth in shock, and Sebastien too looked wide-eyed. They watched the pages burn, the fire growing into a blood-red beast, swallowing the delicate journal whole. The parchment melted into a black, tar-like substance, and the covers of the diary fell apart to reveal Silana's soul. She did not dare to make a sound as Lukas Haydn looked triumphantly at the time and effort of his eldest daughter over the past few months, all ablaze.

Silana turned, refusing to waste her tears any longer, and sat back down, eyes still fixed on the remaining blueprints. Neither was she going to beg nor was she going to cry. The indifference with which her father had discarded her most private possession stirred up an uncommon emotion in her this time—resolve. She was not going to give him the satisfaction of a reaction. She thought back to the last possession of hers he had destroyed in such a manner—nearly a month ago, in a fit of rage, he had destroyed her favourite lipstick because, according to him, Silana had been growing exceedingly vain and hadn't been adequately respecting her parents; she knew he meant himself.

Silana composed herself while her father walked back to the table, looking at her expectantly. She kept her eyes locked upon the blueprints, refusing to meet his. Her father doled out a list of punishments for both children, essentially stripping away any moment of respite. Additionally, he assigned them tasks, which included travelling to every neighbourhood they had targeted to remove the 'cursed, vile and untrue' posters. They were also required to attend Nazi party meetings with their father on the 'important days' and partake in spreading their 'righteous' ideology.

'It is a noble cause,' their father asserted, 'to eradicate

something that has been plaguing our people for centuries. The Jewish problem. Instead of assisting in ridding the earth of them, you are choosing to embolden them by rallying more people against our cause.'

Since when was this cause something we wanted? Silana wondered. Both her brother and she were completely perplexed by their father's behaviour—he seemed more erratic and urgent than ever before. This was completely unlike Lukas Haydn. Three years ago, during a financial turmoil that had beset his company, he had made a valiant (and successful) attempt to remain calm and composed throughout for his wife and three young children. He used to toil into the early hours of the morning and had eventually paid back every single penny he owed, getting the family enterprise back up on its feet. Yet here he was now, raving about the supposed infidelity of his children and the deviousness of a race of people he hardly associated with. His eyes were wild and glowing red as they reflected the dying fireplace.

As he spoke, he carefully picked up the plans for the posters, tearing them with deliberate motions. It was almost theatrical, the way he was moving, and he somehow perfectly timed the culmination of his monologue with the destruction of all the poster plans. At one point, Lukas Haydn even threatened to send his son to the Hitler Youth.

Silana was utterly bewildered by her father's behaviour, and so were her mother and younger sister, who were observing from the shadows, clutching each other tightly. Lukas Haydn concluded, 'What I do and say to you all comes from a place of concern.' *Always concern, never love.* 'I want any tangible evidence of your involvement in this rebel-affiliated scheme handed to me immediately. And both of you are grounded. Indefinitely.'

Sebastien clenched his jaw as Silana looked at him, her concern palpable as she contemplated the repercussions.

'I don't want to hear another word from either of you until tomorrow.'

Their father pushed back his chair, stood up slowly and glared at his. This time, Sebastien averted his gaze, turning to look at his mother; Silana stared straight back. Lukas looked away and trudged up the staircase, gradually disappearing. Silana released a breath she didn't even know she had been holding. *He didn't hit us.* All her mental preparation had been futile, leaving her wondering what had been different this time. This was certainly one of the gravest offences she and her brother had ever committed, not to mention they had done it together.

Silana and Sunne, who emerged from the shadows with her mother, began cleaning the tattered papers while Sebastien pulled Yvonne into the kitchen for a heated but hushed discussion. Silana would have normally criticized the absence of her brother's help, but they seemed to be discussing something important. She held off on the critical remarks and asked her younger sister about her day. Sunne chattered on happily about the abundance of sweets that had been distributed throughout the school that morning, owing to a few birthdays.

Sunne described in lurid detail her escapades after school—these involved her sneaking off to get ice cream with some friends, going to a movie unsupervised and not being able to finish her homework as an unfortunate consequence.

Silana smiled, laughing along as Sunne recalled her friends spilling drinks all over each other during a particular scene of the movie. *If only I were allowed this extent of liberty.* Silana sighed. But if one of them were to have a comparatively less closeted lifestyle, she would choose Sunne for it in a heartbeat.

Just as they finished disposing of the last of the blueprints and scrubbing down the table once more—their father didn't like it when people cried in the vicinity of the table, something about the salt content of tears damaging the furniture—a collected Sebastien and panicking Yvonne re-entered the room.

'Ma chérie, we don't have to do this,' Yvonne pleaded.

'Mother, I've kept it from them long enough. They deserve to know. We deserve to know together, as a unit, because that is what us four are and it's all we ever will be.'

'Powerful words, mi amour. Powerful. But will they match your actions?'

'Haven't they already?' Sebastien was firm in his resolve.

Yvonne sighed. 'I do hate to admit it but you are correct, though all of you do have a long way to go in coming to terms with this. It is not easy, I assure you. But we cannot continue to live in the bliss of ignorance for much longer.'

She ushered her children into the living room and waited quietly for the door of the master bedroom to shut with a final, disdainful thud. She flicked on a lamp that filled the room with a soft glow, permitting Silana to see her mother's fallen visage.

'Mother and I had quite an important conversation before things escalated to this point. Admittedly, it came out in a fit of parental rage but the bottom line is that it did.'

Sebastien glanced at Yvonne, who gave him a hesitant smile and motioned for him to continue. With his mother's approval, he carried on. 'Mother married Father 19 years ago; it'll be 20 years the day after tomorrow. You both know that she spent most of her life in France with her parents and met Father when he went to Paris for a convention—one of his first, actually.'

Silana wasn't exactly in the most well-suited headspace to hear the story she'd been told a hundred times before.

'What you may not know was that Mama's family wasn't very well-off then. Though happy, they struggled financially. Grandpa was determined to go to any lengths to secure Mama's future. The handsome and wealthy Polish gentleman who was courting her seemed like the best possible option, considering Grandpa himself was Polish and Mama could speak it fluently.'

'What are you getting at, Seb?'

'Patience, my girl,' Yvonne's soft smile morphed into a stoic reassurance. Silana drew her lips into a tight line as Yvonne motioned for Sebastien to continue.

'Papa hailed from one of Poland's most devout Christian families and Mama seemed like the perfect match—a young, beautiful Christian girl with a good education. However, there was a slight discrepancy in the narrative Mama told her fiancée.'

Sunne looked up at Sebastien while picking at a few loose strands of her dress and Silana furrowed her brows.

'Our grandparents were desperate to leave their hovel in Paris and give their daughter a better life, even if it meant going against their religious beliefs…because they were Jewish.'

Silana's stomach tightened.

'And by extension, Mama.'

'So, what you mean to say is Mama lied about her faith to marry Papa and move to Poland with her parents.'

'That's exactly what I was trying to imply, Sunne. But thank you for your valuable summation.'

Sunne was too shocked to retort. Their eyes eventually turned to Yvonne who was studying the flickering lamp in an uncanny silence that pervaded the living room.

'I did what I had to do to escape from there. Your grandmother used to beat me every day and tell me I was the reason we had no food—that I was the reason we lived in a filthy roach-infested house.'

Silana's heart ached a little for her mother as she realized why she was so particular about cleanliness all the time.

'You must understand that you three are also half Jewish.'

'Did Father not verify what you told him was true? I don't understa—'

'We were young, Silana, and in love. Such a deathly combination, no? Religion was the only thing that would have torn us apart and I was willing to do anything to prevent that from happening. I didn't just want happiness—I wanted it with the right person and I thought I had found that person in your father. Not just in him, but within him. In a way, we both deceived each other.'

What a healthy foundation, Silana thought.

'I just had to warn you children. I truly have no idea

where life will take us from here, but I can only hope it will be kind to us.'

'What are we supposed to do now, with this information? We're going to a Nazi party conference next week!' Silana whisper-shouted.

'I'm telling you this not to frighten you but because you have the right to know. The only people who know apart from you three are your grandparents and my dearest friend Ilse. When I left behind my life in Paris, I brought only one part of it with me to remind me of where I came from—a part of one of the candles we used during our last Sabbath. I painted it myself.'

Just then, a sudden movement from the far corner of the room caught Silana's attention. She dismissed it as her mind playing tricks—her father was asleep and so was the live-in help.

Her mother concluded, 'All I wanted to put forth is this—these people are a part of you because you are a part of me. I am truly proud of you for doing what you did, even while knowing the consequences. But please try to be more cautious in your endeavours. Now go off to bed! It's well past your bedtime. Don't forget you have school tomorrow!'

Lukas Haydn had left for work early that morning, not bothering to leave a note before leaving. Silana was incensed by his compulsion for her to write a note not being reciprocated. He was evidently still upset and Silana reasoned that he would eventually calm down after she and Sebastien abided by his suffocating punishment.

Yvonne woke up a while after her children had left,

finding three comforting notes on the table beside the main door as opposed to her husband's rather austere one. She freshened up and delegated regular household duties to her maids, Esther and Katarzyna. Walking over to her husband's desk to pick up the money he had left for a few groceries and her sewing materials, she noticed his desk, which had stood stoically in the same place for 19 years, the epitome of unwavering order and precision. Every item in his workroom had a purpose, but a single element was astray—small yet significant enough that Yvonne did a double-take.

Lukas' 'secret' drawer, the second one from the right, was unlocked. For as long as Yvonne had been married to him, she had never had the opportunity to observe what was inside. She quickly pulled it open, dust coating her fingers as she picked up a beige envelope. She turned it over and was met with glaring blood-red letters bearing the message—'NOTICE FOR THE ARREST OF YVONNE HAYDN AND HER CHILDREN'.

Tara

Tara despised it when Aarti took on a parental role with her. She would usually run off to her sister's room and this occasion wasn't much different. Tara was cooped up in Tanisha's quarters, avoiding the stout witch and bantering with her sister.

'There's something I've been meaning to discuss with you. It's about the children.'

Of course it was. No wonder Tanisha had provided her refuge in the first place; this conversation was certainly the reason for it.

'One of the stories I heard particularly struck a deep chord with me. I spoke with Wincenty at lunch. He and his sister led a normal and ordinary life. His father owned a successful bakery that had been in the family for two generations and they had expanded it quite remarkably, even during these hard times. That was until some Nazis sifting through old records uncovered their deceased grandmother's maiden name to be Goldstein—she had been Jewish. It started with their privileges being rescinded one by one before everything else was taken away as well. Their business was allowed to remain operational, one of the last ones under Nazi reign, to supply bread to the local Jewish people at predetermined quantities to ensure they didn't starve and also to the demanding Nazi officials.

'Wincenty's parents worked tirelessly, risking their lives to supply bread and help the near-starving Jewish population of their locale. He and his sister often helped their parents. They were able to sustain this covert operation of theirs successfully for months until the bakery was raided under the suspicion of selling bread "illegally", essentially, exceeding Nazi-regulated bread quotas.

'Wincenty tells me the only way they could have discovered their operation was if someone who knew about these happenings told the Nazis in exchange for a cash reward. His parents, when confronted, foolishly resisted and refused to admit to anything.'

Tara braced herself. Tanisha was a passionate storyteller who never spared any details, no matter how macabre and unsettling. Listening to her was not for the faint-hearted.

'Was it bad?'

'Terrible,' Tanisha replied, her chartreuse eyes flashing with intensity. 'When the Nazis raided the bakery, Wincenty's father answered the door and was shot at point-blank range. His mother and sister also met a similar fate. Wincenty, at just 10 years of age, had the foresight to escape from the back entrance of the shop before the Nazis burned it to the ground. What's worse, the raid occurred on a Saturday, with the streets full of onlookers, many of whom knew the family. The Nazis attacked them to prove a point, forever shrouding their memory and their initiative to help people.

'None of the passers-by even attempted to ask the boy running barefoot down the cobbled streets, clothes and face ashen, if he needed help. They were the same people whom his parents had died to feed, the same people who greeted his family each morning, for whom the family opened shop an hour early and worked late into the night to sustain.'

Tara had subconsciously shifted positions—first lying down, then resting her elbows on the mattress and now sitting upright, wide-eyed and uncharacteristically attentive.

'Wincenty was found shivering on the streets after a few days by one of the people Father coordinated with to bring these children here.'

'That's...quite depressing, don't you think? Not an apt bedtime story in the slightest. I do pity your children.'

Tanisha looked at Tara, confused. 'You're missing the entire point of this *bhaashan* (lecture). Don't try to find any humour in this; it's meant to resonate with you!'

'If you'd brighten this life of mine, marred by hues of grey, with even a speck of whimsy, any semblance of jocularity, I would be more inclined to interact with these children. That, and the assurance they won't give me the plague.'

'The plague? The bubonic plague?'

'I have no idea what viruses they may have carried with them. I've broken out in hives just from the smell.' As Tara wrinkled her nose at the advent of the unpleasant memory, her sister looked more disappointed than humoured.

'You want to help these children, yes?'

Tara nodded.

'A good start would be not accusing them of bearing the Black Death and not referring to them as either rodents or insects.'

'Worms aren't technically insects.'

'All right. With you, everything is off the table. I suggest you call them either by their names or just "child" will do.'

It both astonished and irked Tara how increasingly her sister looked and acted like their mother with each passing day.

'And try not to look so overtly disgusted by them. You do know you can speak more fluent Polish than I can; you will be able to communicate with them better.'

Being cooped up in a library with teachers who smelled like aged onions while Tanisha roamed their kingdom 'studying' did thankfully prove to be helpful in such situations.

'Today's dinner will serve as an opportune time to mingle and associate with some of them. You know that I work with a lot of children as extensions of Papa's many charities.'

The Maharaja had offered Tara this role but she had politely declined, choosing to hand the reins of the social aspects of royal charity to her sister instead.

'What I suggest is starting with some of the older children, gradually earning their trust and making communication with the younger ones more effective. Also—'

'Why are you helping me, Tani?'

Tanisha paused for a few moments to consider her answer. 'You're my sister. We are bound to squabble over petty things and get on each other's nerves—we may even rip them out at times. However, we must not let our childish rivalry interfere with our commitment to helping people, especially children, through difficult circumstances.'

'I hate to say it, but I think you may be right in this case.'

'Could I have you sign a claim to that effect? "Tanisha is always right". What do you think?'

'Don't push it, Tani.'

'Get ready for dinner! I've made sure its outside for your utter comfort,' Tanisha commented with a smirk.

The ceasefire was not going to last for long anyway.

On the way back to her room, Tara bumped into Aarti who was running about the palace in preparation for dinner.

'Dinner will be served in an hour on the terrace in the east wing.'

'Tani told me.'

'Did you talk to her nicely?'

Nicely? They weren't children. They were monarchs, having complex political discussions that affected their people. Tara rarely found herself at odds with her ageing housekeeper, thus said nothing. She went into her room and slammed the door shut behind her. As Tara sifted through her closet, her goal was to find an outfit that was elegant but not extravagant, considering the children's situation. She ended up deciding on a navy blue sari with gold streaks lining the hem. The embroidery was intricate and the overall attire reflected a quiet class. Best of all, the material was thick enough to shield her from the night's chill. *Perfect.* She decided to pair it with faded gold heels and a miniature tiara that took a while to braid into her hair, considering she wasn't quite used to wearing ones that size.

Tara had a brief internal conflict regarding make-up—her sister wasn't planning on wearing any. Not that she needed it; Tanisha bore a striking resemblance to their mother, who had been one of the most beautiful women Tara had ever known. She also needed to retain 'awareness' regarding those hapless children. Conversely, Tara needed to feel human one last time before this shadow overtook her entire life. Her quiet rebellion shone through in the guise of indigo eyeshadow and bold, scarlet lipstick.

The hour had passed faster than she had anticipated, much to her disappointment, and she made a dash for the terrace wearing only three gold bracelets and her cheapest polki earrings. She hustled to the east wing of the palace as quickly as she could—one of her father's pet peeves was a lack of punctuality. For this reason, he asked that both his children be by his side 15 minutes before any event began. Tara reached the terrace in the nick of time but Tanisha was already by their father's side—*of course she was*. The sun had nearly set upon their palace, prompting a flood of servants to light all variety of candles on and around the long table.

'Girls, joining us for dinner are not just the people who these children here but also a few members of the armed forces who have been crucial in facilitating the last few legs of their journey. They should all arrive in 10 minutes.'

The family resorted to nervous banter until the sounds of shrill chatter filled a relatively quiet night; the three stood up, greeting the children as they were shepherded in by members of the armed forces, who were still in their uniforms.

The palace staff had done a rather decent job decorating the table, laying out scintillating silver cutlery in preparation for a three-course meal. Tara wondered if the children had ever eaten so much in one sitting. A young rosy-faced boy no older than eight sat beside the princess. She greeted him. 'How are you?'

'You can speak Polish?'

Tara smiled. 'A little.' That was a lie; she had been fluent since 15.

'Is that your sister?' He pointed a timid finger at Tanisha, who was surrounded by four eager children talking excitedly about their new accommodation.

'Yes, she is my baby sister. Do you have any siblings?' Tara kept up the conversation the only way she knew how, smiling down at the sandy-haired boy.

'I also had a baby sister.'

Had? Oh dear. She swerved from the topic. 'My name is Tara. What's yours?'

'That's a nice name. What does it mean?'

'Star, because my mother told me I lit up her life.'

'I am Rafal. "God heals" is what my name means.'

Ironic. Tara wasn't quite sure what to ask him next, so she pretended to be very invested in the announcement of the first course, which was some variety of soup. As servers placed the bowls in front of the children, most started to wolf it down as soon as they hit the table. The silverware had been laid in such a manner that one would have to work their way inwards, as was the norm. Tara had anticipated having to teach the children how to use the cutlery properly and was taken aback when most did so themselves. Even little rosy-faced Rafal, whose skin looked yellow in the soft, pervasive candlelight, displayed proper dining etiquette.

'You know what cutlery to use?'

He looked up at her while ladling the soup into his mouth.

'My parents and sister were killed by the Nazis. We used to be rich like you before.'

Tara wished she had had the sense not to ask such an inane question. She would now have to do damage control. 'I'm...truly very sorry.'

Rafal didn't reply and resumed silently mulling over the contents of his soup rather than eating it. From beside him, a slightly older-looking brunette girl (maybe 11- or 12-years-old, Tara guessed) joined the conversation. Her eyes were wide with curiosity.

'Do you also speak Polish?'

Why all the children felt the need to ask her that was beyond her. 'I do. My name is Tara, what's yours?' She already felt exhausted. When the princess walked into a room, the people there generally flocked around her like moths to a flame. But here, sitting at this table so ridiculously overdressed, nobody seemed to care at all who she was.

'Don't mind Rafal, he's a little serious,' the girl said

Tara couldn't imagine why.

'I'm Valery from Kraków. Your dress is very pretty. I've never seen something like it before!'

Finally! A tolerable worm. 'Thank you, Valery. I for one quite like your...hair.' Unfortunately, there wasn't much to compliment the girl on. Her hair had been braided neatly into two sections, tied with off-white ribbons that matched her grey blouse, which was held together by three loud vermilion buttons. Her earrings, the only jewellery she had on, were nothing more than microscopic silver studs in her ears.

'I'm here with my brother, Jerzy. JERZY!'

A younger boy with an uneven buzz cut looked over from the other side of the table, gave Tara a crooked grin with what teeth he had left (much to her horror) and turned back to talk to a few equally dishevelled-looking boys.

'We lived with our mother before the war. There were not enough supplies for her to also come; she sent us to Balganga after promising that she would meet us again, at our favourite bookstore in Kraków.' This time Valery picked uncomfortably at her soup. 'I like it here but I miss my mother and what our life used to be.'

Tara nodded empathetically, sneaking a sideways glance at her sister. Tanisha was giggling with a few of the older children. She was tempted to demand switching seats—somehow her sister had all kinds of luck when it came to these charity cases, and here she was—stuck listening to their sob stories. She tried to maintain a poker face.

While Tara shifted from nodding mindlessly at the children's conversations to glaring daggers at her sister, Valery coaxed rosy Rafal into switching places with her—plates, cutlery and all. She tapped the princess lightly on the shoulder. 'I heard your name means "star".'

'It does.' *Oh no.*

'Is this palace your home? I've never seen any house so big before! Jerzy and I, before the war, lived with our parents and another family in one apartment. My father was a janitor and my mother was a housekeeper. This is so bright and shiny in the day! How old must it be?'

'A few generations.'

If Valery was so smitten by this summer home of theirs, Tara wondered what the girl's reaction would be upon seeing their main palace in Bramsadha. She tried to change the topic but it was quite difficult to get a word in between Valery's constant jabber.

'...and these gardens! Can we play in them? We're in some part of the forest behind this side of the palace but there really isn't much to do there, apart from one small play area.'

This was a start. 'What would you like to do there, given a choice?'

The girl flopped back in her chair to think for a moment. 'Well, none of us would mind a few more swings. And benches. Maybe umbrellas too, because of the heat.

'Could we swim? I saw a stream nearby,' a quiet Rafal interjected.

This was the first Tara had heard of it. 'I have never noticed this stream before; I really am quite ashamed.' She wasn't; self-deprecation seemed the best way to appear approachable to these children. A few of them seemed as timid as helpless animals—each time someone would try reaching out to them, they backed up into a small corner. Tara was learning to approach them with caution.

'It's not too far, around 10 minutes away.'

The princess, while in the summer palace, generally never stayed awake to notice petty things that didn't require her full attention. The nauseatingly winding drive uphill was enough for her. Not that she was enthusiastic enough to swim in any case. Her sister compared Tara to a cat in her aversion to water.

'I could arrange something for you.'

This was the first time Rafal was fully attentive to and acknowledged the princess, his eyes staring directly into hers. She wasn't anywhere near her sister's level of sociability with the children but was inching towards it. By the time Rafal began whispering some new questions to her, the second course had already arrived. Biryani—*finally something to relieve her of the conversation.*

Tara began wolfing it down as soon as they placed the steaming, ornate plate in front of her, not even waiting a moment for the servants to lay everybody's portions on the table. This behaviour, of course, was in complete violation of royal table decorum—but then again, there wasn't anyone present to appreciate a well-mannered princess any more. The night had become chilly and the princess shivered while shoving more biryani down her throat, the mild spices and utter deliciousness of it proving to be a welcome distraction. She looked around the table in search of similar expressions of appreciation but, to her astonishment, could only discern disgust.

Valery tapped her shoulder, panting and gasping. 'It's very…' She took a sharp breath before finishing her sentence, 'spicy.'

Oh dear. The chefs they had hired seemed unable to cook for their key demographic. All across the table were children wiping tears from their eyes, snivelling and rubbing their noses until they turned scarlet. Tara looked over at her father, who seemed equally concerned. Tanisha lay a soft hand on the shoulder of a nearby girl who was coughing violently. Dinner was turning into a nightmare quicker than any of the royals could fathom. A few children were able to take the piquant flavour in their stride, alternating between water and the food; however, that was not the case for the majority of the group. Towards one end of the table were seated the few army personnel who helped the children there, taking the reins from Tanisha, who was rushing back and forth, calling for more beverages.

'Papa, you instructed the kitchen to use less spice, didn't you?'

'I did, Tani!'

'If that's the case, we now have another issue to resolve.'

Tara was desperate to one-up her sister and find a solution. Suddenly it hit her. 'Papa, what if we lend them our palace chefs instead? They can definitely prepare less strongly flavoured meals for the children.'

Her father smiled. 'I knew my brilliant daughter would shine through sooner or later.'

Tara smirked, even choosing to ignore the 'sooner or later' part of his praise. Through the chaos, the Maharaja directed for dessert to be served instead. Servants wearing white-and-black outfits waddled around like very rushed emperor penguins, picking up the biryani deftly and bringing in the dessert the chefs had prepared—rasgulla.

Tara, upon observing her sister rushing around the table checking on the children, decided to follow suit. Though her indigo sari and ever so slightly smeared lipstick made her feel like a wandering banshee, it was in her best interests to outdo the charitable Tanisha. Making her way along the length of the table, stopping intermittently to ask the children how they were faring, she eventually reached the last few seats where a few high-ranking army personnel were seated. A few were laughing heartily with the children, humouring their excessive reactions, what with the spice being so routine for them.

Doing a final scan of the table, Tara went around it once

more before hurrying back. At that moment, her tiara fell through her loosened braids, clattering on to the floor. Tara stopped in her tracks, squeezing her eyes shut, dreading to bend and pick up her tiara. As she opened her eyes, Tara encountered a uniformed gentleman, perhaps in his late 20s or early 30s kneeling on the floor, holding the glimmering headpiece in his hand. He looked up at her, muttering to the princess in his sonorous voice some incomprehensibly respectful greeting that was lost in the crescendo of the children's chatter. But Tara only noticed his sienna-coloured skin that glowed in the light of the candles and deep, expressive chocolate eyes she tried ever so hard to pull her gaze away from. His chevron moustache accentuated his youthfulness but it was betrayed by the lines beside his eyes that deepened as he smiled.

'It is an honour to meet you, Your Highness. My name is Colonel Vijay Singh.'

Silana

Silana's rush to get to her room made her oblivious to the lack of activity in the house. Though she could discern whispers from the study, she assumed it to be either Sunne or Sebastien engaging in some manner of tomfoolery. She was hardly bothered by that—she had more pressing issues on her mind. Her primary concern was that she had forgotten to prepare a speech to address the party members for an event she and Sebastien would be accompanying their father to.

The day before, in a fit of ambitious stupidity, when her father had asked the siblings which of the two was prepared to make a fitting speech for the crowd, Silana volunteered, citing her elevated literary proficiency, hoping to alleviate his bad mood. Never mind that she had less than an hour to complete the two-page speech. Silana had sped home from school with the sole intention of finishing it.

She burst into her room, nearly toppling over due to the weight of her backpack. She had kept a few blank papers on her desk in preparation and had mercifully planned out the speech before falling asleep the previous night. Silana dipped her trusty quill in ink, careful not to spill any of the liquid in her haste. Her introduction had to be captivating, pristine.

As a young student and proud citizen of our nation, I have experienced first-hand the decline of both our situation as a country and the waning passion of our youth. Our nation has been consumed by an unwavering threat that will not cease until people like us step forth and take action. We must never let our fellow countrymen fall victim to the detestable manners of

Yvonne rushed in at that moment, her face red, eyes welling with tears, eyeliner streaming down her face and melding with the foundation. Her hair looked half-done and Silana noticed that all her jewellery was missing—including her wedding ring.

'IT'S YOUR GRANDFATHER! HE'S HAD A HEART ATTACK!'

Silana was shell-shocked. She rushed to her mother in a vain attempt to comfort her, but Yvonne was manic. Her mother's intonation reminded Silana of butterflies flapping their wings—barely noticeable but painfully beautiful. Yvonne usually didn't speak much; the most she'd ever speak was while comforting her children. Even that was generally done through silent pats and well-cooked meals that catered to their preferences.

Sebastien had rushed in behind their mother, reiterating the narrative and adding, 'Pack the essentials, Sil, we'll only be gone a few days. We're visiting Grandma—she's all alone. Hurry!'

He led their mother out of Silana's room, giving her time to process the news and pack. Yvonne had calmed down a bit but her voice was still raised as she directed Sunne to pack. Silana flung open her cupboard and stacked enough clothes on her bed for four days. Though anxious, her packing skills remained commendably sensible. She called out for Katarzyna, assuming Esther, the nicer of the two, would be busy assisting Sunne and their mother.

Esther popped her head in. 'Katarzyna isn't here today, miss; her aunt was sick and she asked for the day off.'

'Thank you, Esther.' Silana was frustrated. Katarzyna had either kept her suitcase in storage or tucked it away in the abyss of her cupboard; she had neither the time nor the energy to retrieve it. Thus, she stuffed all of her most precious belongings into an aged travel bag, clearing out the small treasures she had kept inside—including her precious sewing basket and a pure silver thimble. As she slung the carry-on pack over her shoulder, the nearly complete journal she had replaced with the one she was given for her birthday caught her eye. There were a good 10 pages remaining, even though the completed parts dated back a few months. Silana grabbed it off her desk, bounding towards her parents' room as she clutched it tightly. Her only source of comfort would now be the old leatherbound journal.

Her family hardly opened up to one another—the children confided in neither parent for fear of being dismissed. The only thing they had in common with each other was their pain, and none of them wanted to share it. Their happiness hardly came from within the household—each of the children's passions had led them down their own paths of early maturity.

Silana entered her parents' room, where Sebastien was reading from an important-looking piece of paper as Yvonne looked at him expectantly. Upon seeing Silana, Yvonne snatched the piece of paper from her son's hands, folding it deftly.

'What's that?'

'Just a letter from your father's office.'

Silana had seen many of those before when her father was on his business trips. The seal and margin of those letters looked nothing like the one her brother had just been holding.

'Then I'd like to wait for Father to return before I finish packing,' Silana lied.

Her mother looked up at her, furious. 'My instructions are not worth less than those of your father.'

'But my trust evidently is!' Silana yelled back. She'd never raised her voice at her mother before. However, there was something about the tension in the air that overpowered any reason she possessed, the same contagion that possessed her mother. She expected her mother to yell back, if not worse, and mentally braced for it. What Silana didn't expect was for her mother to sink to the ground in defeat, put her head down between her knees and sob.

Sebastien took the letter from Yvonne and led Silana out of the room. 'Sil, I must pack, and I'll make sure Sunne does too. I suggest you read this later and comfort Mama for now—the letter is important, but less so than the immediate situation. Do as she says. Trust only her.'

The siblings dashed in opposite directions. Silana returned to her parents' room, parting the curtains to let a soft cascade of sunlight infiltrate the space.

Her mother looked up at her. 'What's the time, my dear?'

'2.26 p.m.'

Silana's father was meant to return by 3 p.m., and the family had to be assembled in the living room in anticipation of the same.

'Have you read the letter?'

'Sebastien said to read it later.'

Her mother got up from the bed, walked towards her daughter and embraced her tightly, then squeezed her hands. 'We're going to Ilse's house for a bit. The lie about your grandfather was to give you a sense of urgency. Read the letter when we're out of this wretched house.'

'Wretched? It's your home!'

'It is now none of our homes, ma chérie. Today is a dark day, though deceivingly sunny. As soon as they are done packing, we must take the tram to Ilse's house. Help me with my bag, will you?'

Silana slung her mother's pack, considerably heavier than her own, on to her shoulder and waddled down the stairs in a very unladylike fashion, which would have been heavily criticized had her father been present. Yvonne soon entered the living room with Sebastien and Sunne in tow. She was in quite a rush, urging her children to hasten.

The nearest tram station was hardly a block away and as they half-jogged and half-walked in that direction, an eerie silence enveloped them like a thick fog. Silana no longer felt welcome in the neighbourhood and a small part of her was considerably relieved. She felt like she had avoided something evil—the same evil that pervaded the house down the block from where the couple had been taken. They quickened their pace and reached just in time to catch the tram. Sebastien took the luggage from his mother and sisters and quickly hauled it up into the tram. The family scrambled in, grabbing what seats remained, Sebastien ensuring to get the one closest to Yvonne. Silana never understood why they'd always been so close—perhaps a firstborn tendency. She had tried to have the same relationship with her father but he was never particularly keen to reciprocate. He did try, but only when Silana showed him how well she'd done in a test or anything academia-related. Sebastien's connection to their mother seemed effortless, unconditional.

Silana looked out of the window and watched familiar places turn into unfamiliar ones. The tram journey to Ilse's house was relatively short—about 20 minutes. Silana was seated next to a lady whose feather hat kept brushing up against her—a very well-dressed frail woman with beaded jewellery and a large, tacky basket. She had a distinguished air around her but not a wardrobe to match. Sitting in her presence almost hypnotized Silana into silence before the woman finally noticed the girl staring at her and said, 'Awful lot of people today!'

'Uh, yes.'

'Well, it's such a bright, sunny day—no wonder people may wander out to enjoy the weather!'

The woman introduced herself as Sylvia. She was recently widowed and would soon move to France. She was just visiting old friends before doing so. She had no children, but made up for them with a vast array of pet fish.

'Fish?'

'Fish are the most perfect species in existence.'

'What makes you say that?'

'When I was a young girl, not younger than yourself, I had a quaint house by a very noisy brook. I used to visit it in an attempt to silence it and there I found the most beautiful fish, delicate as snowflakes, swimming through raging currents and unforgiving riptides—resolute to travel further. I thought us as humans to be quite like those fish—beautiful and in pain; hopeless, yet brimming with hope. They were separated from each other, lost in tides 10 times larger than they could imagine, but they fought against it. They fought even when they sometimes lost sight of what they were fighting for or who they were fighting with. In perilous times such as these, I look at them and thank them for reminding me to keep fighting.'

'My father never allowed me to have pets,' was the only response Silana could muster, grateful it elicited a laugh from the kind woman.

'My fish remind me because no one else will. A bright girl such as you must have had someone to raise you this well!'

Silana was touched. Beaming, she looked over to her mother and Sebastien. The girl's smile waned a bit, prompting the older woman to turn to see what she was looking at.

'Ah, siblings. Can't live with them,' commented Sylvia.

'...Can't live without them?'

'If you insist, my girl.' The old woman, pleased to have distracted Silana from whatever was plaguing her, continued the conversation until the tram conductor announced the next stoppage. Silana noticed her mother frantically beckoning to her, and she gave a tight but careful hug to Sylvia, who smiled and mumbled, 'You will do exceptional things, my dear, but you mustn't ever lose sight of those who help you to accomplish them.'

The family rushed towards Ilse's house, their suitcases rattling along the uneven path. Silana made sure to keep Sunne ahead of her and in check as their mother guided them to her friend's house. Upon reaching, Yvonne buzzed the doorbell anxiously, her trembling fingers only resulting in Silana's unease growing. Ilse opened the door, blissfully unaware, the large smile plastered on her face melting into worry as her friend and her children seemingly barged through the door and subsequently begged Ilse to bolt it.

'The staff told him.'

Ilse held a hand to her chest—she was a dramatic woman but Silana had a feeling that this time there was no scope for exaggeration.

'Sunne, third room to the right. Wait there for a bit, darling. Lucyfer has been so eager to meet you!'

Clearly, the prospect of meeting Ilse's cat proved to be immeasurably more important than the letter their mother had found for Sunne, as evident by her yelp of excitement and immediate disappearance. Ilse looked around as if there were spies hidden in the very picture frames that crowded the living room and, once satisfied, led the remaining family members to a makeshift library. 'I would normally extend you an invitation for tea but that tremor in your hands will not bode well for my new carpet,' Ilse joked—a valiant attempt to lighten the mood.

'I found this letter in his desk today,' Yvonne began,

smoothing her skirt and clenching her hands together. 'I would read it to you, but I—'

Sebastien, ever the devoted son, cut his mother off. 'Allow me, please, Mother. You've done enough for us today already.'

Now Ilse was teetering between anxiety and downright fear. She had known Yvonne for nearly 30 years and considered her to be family. The latter was almost frustratingly level-headed and rational, rarely showing any emotion.

Sebastien, who had inherited this quality of Yvonne's, cleared his throat, hesitating only for a brief moment before reading.

To
Inspector Borys,
Commander-in-Chief of the Policja,

From
Lukas Haydn,
32, Ulica slonecznikowa

Dear—

'I don't understand the formalities...Aren't your husband and the inspector childhood friends?'

'It will all make sense soon, Aunty Ils.'

Ilse was practically a sister to their mother, so the children considered her their aunt (though Ilse was utterly flabbergasted by how they had managed to shorten her name any further). Sebastien cleared his throat as Silana, seated across from him, waited with bated breath.

Dear Inspector,

As a valued and active member of the National Socialist German Workers' Party, I come to you with an issue so severe it may have a lasting impact on our community. My family has been both devoutly Christian and beyond charitable in regard to generosity towards the development of our town. Our stature has, in some cases, left us vulnerable to exploitation by third parties who seek to inflict harm on us and our loved ones.

Yvonne Werber is one such facilitator of this truly horrific pattern of behaviour.

Yvonne cringed at the mention of her maiden name.

Late last night, I happened upon a barrage of incriminating evidence that, in my humble opinion, is proof beyond reasonable doubt that she is a Jew. My suspicions were confirmed after I found said piece of evidence through a questioning of one of my staff members, who heard her last night confirm the same to her children. This, by extension, makes them half-Jewish too. Yvonne Werber, upon our marriage 20 years ago, had constructed a false narrative that was employed by both her parents and her to secure the marital union with my family.

Silana felt icicles forming within her throat and her entire face felt hot, almost detached from the rest of her.

My acquaintance with the party has led me to sever any ties with those even remotely associated with

> *the Jewish race, and thus, though this revelation has shocked me to my very core, I shall take the necessary steps to punish those responsible. I am unfortunately unable to discuss this matter with you tomorrow owing to an urgent international business meeting; however, my associate shall provide you with any further details required, and I have made due arrangements to sever all legal ties with Yvonne Werber and her children.*

Silana felt as though she was being pulled down to the floor by invisible hands, and if she were standing, her knees would surely have buckled. *Her children?*

> *Therefore, not only do I request their arrest effective immediately, but a trial suitable for their actions against both me and the state.*

Silana's heart burned through her chest—she did not want to hear any more but knew she had to. A part of her remained in firm and unwavering denial—this was her father—her rock, her teacher, her biggest supporter. Had it taken just a year in politics to snatch him away and turn him against his own family? Did his wife and three children mean so little to him?

> *I shall expect them to be home by 1600 hours and I would request you to make arrangements in accordance with the same. Your cooperation is truly invaluable and I am indebted to both you and the state.*
>
> *Regards,*
> *Lukas Haydn*

Ilse was completely bewildered, perhaps for the first and only time in her life. 'Lukas? He would never. He could never. How could he? I've seen him care for the children; he values them more than his own life—'

'The same children he beats as a lesson, Ilse. The same children whose wounds I've had to care for, wounds he causes. Lukas never valued anything more than his own life and considering his life is now the Nazi party, he will move mountains to redeem what he perceives to be the gravest of ills that has befallen him. We have nowhere else to go; every wretched person in this city is loyal to his money. Is it poss—'

'How is that even a question, Yvonne? You are my sister, my family. You, Sebastien, Silana and Sunne are welcome to stay as long as you like. There's no question about jeopardizing or compromising my safety—I'm a widow with an indifferent cat. Hardly a viable suspect, now, am I?'

'Ilse, it does not matter to Lukas how innocent you are. There are just two homes left in this city where the inhabitants don't report either directly to Lukas or his political allies—your house and my parents'. They will search my parents' house first but mercifully it's on the other side of town. I don't know what will become of any of us if they find my family here.'

As if the betrayal of her father wasn't enough to throw a wrench in Silana's now shattered heart, she found herself caught between resolve and despair. Had it been those posters? Or maybe the biology test? If Sigrid were here, she'd have told Silana to stop overthinking so much. *Oh, Sigrid*—Silana had left her friend without even a goodbye, let alone any explanation. The group sat in sombre silence for a few agonizing minutes, with Yvonne periodically looking at Silana, expecting her to break down at any moment. However, Silana's emotionless exterior seemed to unnerve not only her but every other person in the room.

Silana's thoughts returned to that haunting memory of the night her father had destroyed her diary. She could almost smell the pages burning in Ilse's fireplace, emitting an acrid odour that matched the bitterness now churning within her. That same feeling of helplessness and violation resurfaced, now mixed with a cocktail of betrayal, disbelief, rage and unfathomable sorrow.

'What does this mean for us?' Sebastien voiced her most pervasive thought.

Yvonne, who looked as heartbroken as Silana felt, shook her head. 'I don't know, my love. Ilse, I refuse to endanger you any longer than I already have. I can neither apologize nor thank you enough for all you've done—not just today, but throughout our sisterhood. It won't be long before Lukas finds us here, that's certain. There's no telling what he'll do to me or the children and I do not intend to find out. I know that you would hide us as long as we need, but I cannot in good conscience allow you to do that. If there's any means of escape, please do tell us now.'

Ilse looked thoughtful and Silana could discern an internal debate raging inside her. Silana had a talent for reading people; one could be the most proficient liar but their eyes would always tell the truth. She could read almost everyone except her father—she was too blinded by emotion to notice his thoughts. Ilse, though grimly, finally spoke up.

'I have an acquaintance who feels very strongly about this cause. I shall write to him now and I expect a response by tomorrow. Even if they check your parents' house, they won't be here by then. For now, I suggest we all settle in and rest. Come, Silana, I'll show you and Sunne your room.'

Tara

Tara had never felt so flushed before.

The uniformed gentleman, who seemed as taken by her as she was by him, had scurried to his seat after handing back the princess her tiara. As the children figured out how to eat their rasgulla and rejoiced in its sugary flavour, Tara stole glances at the tall man seated at the opposite end of the table. He was alternating between talking to his colleagues and gesticulating with the children. Occasionally, he would turn for a split second to meet her gaze, but Tara would break eye contact just as quickly.

Meanwhile, her sister and father were deep in discussion about the children.

'I've spoken to a few of them, and they seem quite happy with their lodging. But more playing areas would definitely benefit them.'

Their father nodded in agreement. 'Their teachers should arrive by tomorrow and classes will commence in two days' time. Can you inform them of that?'

Tanisha turned to the children, conveying the news. Their confusion was apparent even to the Maharaja; they had evidently not expected this trip to involve any academia. The few murmurs of discontent soon gave way to exhaustion, brought on by both the journey and the socializing. The servants, after clearing the last round of dishes from the table, finally herded the children from the terrace through the palace—which took a while as some members of the group would break off at times to admire the features of the palace corridors—and back to their cabins.

As Tara bid them goodbye, promising Rafal and Valery that she would see them the next day, the only image swirling through her mind was Colonel Vijay Singh's soft smile. She wanted to feel that unfamiliar emotion forever—their eyes locked in a moment where time stood still. But that would be foolish. A voice in the back of her mind was screaming all sorts of warnings to her. He was an armed guard, after all. Low ranking by definition. Colonel Vijay Singh was just that, a colonel. He was not a prince who might some day be a king.

Still dazed, Tara was watching the children leave when Tani tapped her on the shoulder.

'I hope you're not too tired. We have a meeting now with the armed forces.'

Her luck had been absolutely impeccable these past few weeks, hadn't it? Tara hung her head; declining was out of the question as it would not only insult the army but also their father. Tara knew she didn't exactly have a real choice.

The Maharaja had begun greeting the officers, shaking hands with them and patting them on the back as they stood in a somewhat haphazard line. Tara counted four men, with her colonel standing at the very end of the line. The anxious princess and her sister walked towards the group, watching their father thank the officers. He finally reached the colonel who, after the routine acknowledgement, was oddly pulled into a tight embrace, a gesture the Maharaja hadn't bestowed on the other officers. The men were talking too softly for Tara to hear what they were discussing.

Spotting the princesses, their father beamed at them.

'Tara, Tani, these are the brave officers who brought the children to Balganga from Bombay, overseeing their transport and necessities. These three are Aman Sahay, Munna Singh and Aakash Verma.'

The princesses smiled politely at them as each of the officers bowed their heads in respect.

'And this is Colonel Vijay Singh. Tara, I hear you two have already met?' her father quipped, prompting a polite chuckle from Tara. 'Regardless, I feel like a formal introduction is in order. You see, the colonel's father was one of my oldest friends. He has, most unfortunately, passed recently owing to health complications.'

Tara and Tanisha muttered their condolences.

'I've known Vijay since he was a child. His spirit then was the same as it is now—bold, forthright and resolute.'

Vijay put his hand over his chest, bowing his head in gratitude.

'The colonel is not just a family friend but a family member. Not only does he supports our initiative wholeheartedly, but has also recruited higher-ups for our cause and has been instrumental in ensuring the safety and comfort of these children throughout their journey.'

Not just a family friend but a family member. Tara wanted nothing more than to vanish into the night. Her chest tightened uncomfortably, and she hoped it was serious.

'I can only do so with your continued support and guidance, Maharaj.'

'Come, let us move indoors. We do have a few pertinent things to discuss.'

Tara kept pace with her father and sister, trying her best not to turn around to look at the colonel. Being so closely affiliated with her father and now the children meant she would inevitably be seeing a lot more of him. A small part of her rejoiced, revelling in the mystery and excitement of the soulful glances, but another, more critical, part reprimanded her for straying from her responsibilities and royal decorum.

The group made their way to a grand salon within the palace, adorned with dangling tapestries and ornate yet comfortable furniture. Tara recalled the few vacations she had spent here; she would often sit beside her parents as they entertained guests and try to latch on to each and every word they said. She used to wait in patient anticipation for the day she'd be able to talk to guests as they did. But now, sitting between her sister and father at this ungodly hour and in a sari that was slowly cooking her to death, Tara found it less than ideal.

Three trusted cabinet ministers joined them to discuss the pressing matter of dealing with the British. As the days passed, the British authorities were becoming increasingly nosy. The Maharaja explained to the seven men the need to strengthen the existing precautions in place in case of any official visits or searches and to buy more time to create an additional layer of security for the children.

'That is where I will need your help, officers.'

Major Aman Sahay said, 'I've already managed to snuff out any rumours about their arrival. We were extremely careful while bringing them to Balganga. In order to protect both your family and these children, we've stationed guards near the forest and in front of the palace who are loyal to us and now to you. We will also be monitoring communications to prevent any leaks about the happenings here from reaching the ears of the colonial directorate.'

The Maharaja thanked him before adding, 'We have a plethora of issues to concern them with instead, one being the very real issue of a suitor for Tara.'

The princess tensed when she felt several eyes turning to her. Remaining unmarried due to the passing of her mother, at her age, was far from a desirable quality in a princess. Though her father loved her to death, at the end of the day, his only wish was for her to marry into a wealthy and influential family to bring 'honour' to her own. Tara couldn't see the honour in being someone's trophy wife.

'There are a few princes of neighbouring kingdoms ready to propose marriage when the time is right—we just need to inform them of the princess' desire for marriage; that will effectively shift their focus away from the children.'

Tara felt her anger rising. She hadn't even been informed of this plan to use her as a pawn in a bigger scheme without even considering her willingness to go along with it. She would have gotten up and left in one of her patent huffs were it not for the fact that, firstly, she was wearing too many layers to either walk or move normally and, secondly, Tanisha was sitting on at least half of her pallu, which would prevent her from making a dramatic exit.

The men seated across murmured in agreement, complementing his majesty for his ever-apt reasoning. Finally dismissed after some concluding banter, the sisters discussed their takes on the meeting as they walked to their rooms. They were rarely allowed to voice their opinions formally, so they usually resorted to informal chats after such gatherings. Tara felt some comfort in knowing she wasn't alone in feeling like a pawn in her father's gambit to win respect.

'Considering it is your life on the line, I do agree that not asking or even informing you about this was not wise on his part. However—'

Tara turned to look at Tanisha, furrowing her eyebrows. 'However what?'

'Don't be too harsh on him. Papa's only trying to do what's best for both us and the children. God forbid the British discover our plans, they can threaten him to abdicate, or worse.'

Tara certainly had a lot to think about. She hugged her sister and closed the heavy door to her room, and latched it. Changing into her night clothes and crawling into bed, she decided to give her father and sister the cold shoulder for a few days. Her methods of forgiveness were indeed strange but they seemed to work, so no one really complained too much.

Morning arrived before Tara's will to wake up, heralded by Aarti's aggressive pounding on her door, alerting her that her father expected her at breakfast. The princess considered ignoring her persistent maidservant but didn't want to risk her father's intervention. Breakfast was filled with chatter revolving around Tanisha's interactions at the previous night's dinner.

'Tara, I noticed you talking to some of the children yesterday too. What did they tell you?'

'Hm?' Tara looked up with a mouthful of toast, swallowing quickly before replying. 'Oh, they were just telling me their stories and how they reached Balganga. Which reminds me,' she straightened up, trying to evoke an air of authority, 'the boy I spoke to, Rafal, made a few suggestions regarding what we could do to improve their camp.' She decided to make Rafal the poster boy for this campaign. 'There's apparently a stream nearby where they would like to swim on hot days, and they've requested benches and shade in the compound to shield them from the heat.' Tara added that last part to make the request seem more feasible.

An emboldened Tara faltered slightly, noticing her father's expression.

'Is there an issue?'

'Well, Tara, Tanisha already informed me of this. The benches and tarpaulins are being installed as we speak. We are vetting the safety of the stream as well, to discern whether it is fit for swimming.'

'Oh!' Well, that would certainly be the last she would offer any ideas. The princess redirected her attention to her toast.

The Maharaja glanced at one of the ornate clocks above the door frame. 'The children's teachers will be arriving this afternoon. I'd like you both to join me in welcoming them, showing them their accommodations and introducing them to the children. I will be leaving to attend to some matters outside the palace and shall return by 1.30 p.m. for lunch. Visit the children, see if they are settling in well; make the most of the four hours.'

The need to be a good host had been eating Tara.

She was excited to show the teachers around, relieved she would not be one of the only two people who would act as a translator for the 20-odd children and the rest of the palace any more. The sisters walked to the cabins together, sharing a comfortable silence. Upon their arrival, Tanisha was immediately swarmed by the children while Tara watched from a distance. She spotted Rafal and Valery bounding towards her.

'I've informed them about the stream; they are doing a recce of it.'

'Thank you for the benches and these blue things!'

Tara looked up at the dodgy blue tarps streaming above her head. One of the children ran up to her, tugging at her sleeve. 'Miss, would you like to play football? Your sister is joining us.'

Tanisha beamed at her sister's horror.

'Perhaps I could...watch?'

The child shrugged and ran back to his companions.

'They've already recruited the army people; now they want the princesses too!' Valery joked.

'The army people? They're here? Right now?'

'Yes.'

Tara's eyes scanned the area until they landed on three men at the centre of some commotion. She hadn't noticed them before; they had been squatting to talk to some of the children.

'TARA!' Tanisha hollered at her from a distance. 'There's a football in the storage area near the palace. If you're not playing, please get it!'

Her sister was acting as juvenile, if not more, as these

gnats hovering about them. The game between the two teams kicked off the moment the football arrived, fiercely violent—well, at least by Tara's standards. She'd never seen Tanisha more in her element, watching her tumble to the ground multiple times, her bare feet caked with dirt. Any pride Tara felt came second to the fear she felt for her own safety, running awkwardly in the opposite direction each time the ball came within five feet of her. Throughout the painfully humid and lengthy ordeal, she exchanged several glances with Colonel Vijay Singh—his hair now scruffy and white shirt brown due to the mud.

Tara glanced towards the palace, desperately hoping for the first time in her life that a flushed Aarti would rush in and reprimand both princesses for their tardiness. Alas, the game concluded but Aarti was still nowhere to be seen. As both teams finally settled around the table in a truce, Tara's eyes remained fixed on her sister, who was drenched in sweat, her hair undone, now successfully initiated into the community of gnats. Tanisha finally locked her gaze with Tara's, the latter still rooted to her spot on the bench, yet somehow perspiring more than her sister.

'Tani, we have lunch in half an hour!' Tara hollered across the playing field. She stopped for a second—princesses should never ever raise their voices. She was quite impressed with how loud she could be. *I can see why people like doing this.*

Her sister bounded over, yammering excitedly about the game.

'Yes, Tani, I watched you play the entire thing. You look like a vagabond.'

'Gosh, stop complaining for once, will you?'

'All right, go to lunch looking this way. Papa will be perfectly fine with that.'

'Maybe I will.'

'Don't blame me if he mistakes you for an insect and gets someone to whack you with a flyswatter.'

Tanisha rolled her eyes.

'I'll help you get ready. Just get me out of the sun.'

'Fine. You're really the epitome of a princess.'

'Fine by me, as long as you see me out of here at the earliest.'

Perhaps if Tara hadn't hinged much of the day's expectations on lunch, it would have panned out better for her. Tara adhered to a strict diet set by the palace doctor, which she never failed to follow, except for social obligations. Imagine her horror when the absolute opposite of what she had asked for was laid out in front of her. The meal, in addition to being plated abysmally, had been doused in copious amounts of ghee. Tara was so aghast that she was momentarily speechless.

'Girls, I have decided the palace chefs will prepare our food while our personal chefs from Bramsadha will make food for the children. That does mean they will not be able to stick to your diet any more, Tara, because they have a slightly restricted skill set.'

Tara opened her mouth to respond but no words came out. When her vocal cords did finally decide to cooperate, it resulted in an unabashed telling-off. 'I MEANT LEND THEM THE CHEFS, PAPA. LEND. FOR A DAY. MAYBE TWO.'

'Tara, princesses do not raise their voice,' the Maharaja tried to pacify her, but to no avail.

Tara refused to eat and summoned the head chef, lecturing him for 20 minutes about both his incompetence and his use of ghee. All the while, her father and sister carried on with their meal, watching Tara's hands flail in every possible direction.

Tanisha whispered, 'This is more entertaining than our usual mealtime conversations. Do remind me to get her angry more often.'

By the time Tara had finished her frenzied caterwauling at every single moving object, the other two royals had finished their lunch and were preparing to meet the teachers. Tara hadn't even had lunch yet. *Her family was so unapologetically inconsiderate.*

Dismissing the chef, the Maharaja said, 'The teachers have arrived. Would you like to try a few bites of your food before we greet them?'

Tara made a face at the heap of food on the gold-rimmed plate. 'I'd rather not.'

Greeting the teachers was a quick affair. Tara didn't suspect anything was amiss until after they had shown the teachers to their rooms. Their father confided to them when they were alone. 'We're running short of a history and a mathematics teacher. The only ones we could find who spoke Polish were averse to helping us, fearing repercussions from the British.'

An unusual pang of guilt had been building up inside Tara up until this point due to her behaviour during lunch. As their father rarely admonished them, the girls often felt compelled to take responsibility and initiative on their own for flaunting their freedom.

'I can step in, for whatever it's worth. I'm proficient in maths and can read up what I can on Polish history. I could even create a syllabus.'

'Are you sure, Tara?'

'If duty calls, that is where I will be. You seem to have handled matters just fine so far. There's not much for me to do in my spare time—honestly, how many more impulsive paintings of mine can you frame?' (The answer so far was an entire room.)

It took some convincing but Tara eventually persuaded her father to allow her to draft a syllabus. The next few weeks were bound to be a challenge, so she enlisted the help of two children from each age group for maths—7 to 9, 10 to 13, 14 to 17—with the rest being given the choice to self-study and come back with any doubts they had regarding the topic. Similar age groups were organized for history. With the teachers' help, Tara also crafted a feasible timetable, adjusting it so she could teach around two classes a day. They cleared out a few rooms in the palace, and the Maharaja was able to secure an abundance of notebooks, textbooks and stationery for the children.

Initially, Tara struggled to relate to the children and gain their trust. That was until she snuck into her conversations the ace up her sleeve—her mother's passing. As she let her guard down, so did the children and one by one they began opening up to her. The group, Tanisha included, participated in various activities such as nature walks, picnics and even bonfires on cooler evenings. Tara found herself sitting closer to them, no longer wary of contracting the plague from them. She could feel her initial animosity evaporate with each passing day. The children even somehow managed to convince her to kick a football. Fuelled by their constant pleading, Tara was in the process of organizing a trip to the nearby stream for them.

Colonel Singh had decided to remain posted with the family for reasons no one quite understood. They had struck up a conversation after one of Tara's history classes, bonding over a shared love of art. Tara wasn't sure how her father would react to their newfound friendship so the pair opted instead for clandestine walks around the garden, which were now blossoming into full-fledged dinners together. Tara usually lied to the Maharaja about these dinners, claiming she was dining with the children.

It had been a few weeks. Tara had just returned from teaching the older children and was in a better mood than usual. The younger ones still created a ruckus sometimes, even with royalty teaching them, which Tara found most amusing. She settled into a chair in front of a vanity mirror, telling Aarti about the children as her confidante braided her freshly washed damp hair.

'They are not as bad as they seemed, Aarti. I should take your advice more often,' Tara joked.

Aarti held her breath—the last thing she wanted was to jinx it.

The princess thanked Aarti, bidding her farewell after instructing her to wake her up in a few hours for dinner. As Aarti exited the room, closing the door behind her, she sighed in relief and a broad smile spread across her face. This was the first conversation wherein Tara had referred to the children as something other than rodents or insects. It was progress, a tangible one at that. Aarti was truly just as proud of Tara as her mother would have been.

Silana

The first night at Ilse's house passed uneventfully, yet tension hung heavy in the air, casting an unyielding shadow over the family's spirits. At some point in the night, they received a frantic phone call from Yvonne's parents. Silana's grandmother was beside herself, sobs and incoherent babbling echoing through the receiver, while her grandfather spoke to Yvonne in a shaky voice.

'It was a mockery of us, a pretend Kristallnacht. They had come to arrest us—we heard shouting and yelling. I can only thank God that Ilse had telephoned us in advance. They somehow missed the attic—the detachable ladders were a stupendous idea, my dear girl. Hush, my dear, we're all right. Now do tell me, how have my wonderful grandchildren been?'

Yvonne was openly sobbing at this point but in a room away from her sleeping children. She knew the Gestapo would be heading to Ilse's house next. Ilse remained seated beside Yvonne throughout the duration of the call.

Her father continued, 'It's so lovely to hear your voice and know you're all right, my dear. I hope you will remain so. Your mother and I have made arrangements to hide in an old church where your wedding officiator, Pastor Yuri, works. He has agreed to shelter us until this passes, which I'm sure it will very shortly. You and the children must come here too—the pastor advises it. This church, which we have been patrons of for so long and attended so many masses at, is sure to ward off any evil.'

'And you believe churches protect Jews?' Yvonne half laughed, her voice dripping with sarcasm.

'And who exactly gave you the idea that they don't? Don't you dare mention Lukas' name.'

Yvonne laughed out loud this time.

'The only people who use religion as a weapon to exercise repression are godless ones. All of us have a purpose in this world and we must serve it as God intended. Not a single religion condones any form of hatred, repression or acts of violence. The times we are living in are confusing—one that none of us can comprehend—but we have to somehow equip our children for them. My love for any other religion as a Jew comes from the fact that we share a common goal of uniting our multifaceted beliefs into a beautiful tapestry of progressive humanity. Yvonne, at the end of the day, our religion should be of the least concern in any regard. What should be most important under any circumstance is our character. If one is a good person, then that is a religion in itself. It seems that nowadays this is as rare as common sense.'

Yvonne had not spoken to her father for this long or had such a purposeful conversation with either of her parents since her marriage to Lukas. Lukas disapproved of her maintaining a close relationship with her parents, believing she should devote all her time to caring for and tending to his needs and those of their children. Yvonne rarely engaged in such conversations with her parents, and they also never attempted, hardly visiting and keeping contact to a minimum.

Though Yvonne's parents had wanted her to get married to someone with as revered a social standing as Lukas, they always secretly disapproved of the way that he treated their daughter and the children. However, they could not openly oppose him for fear of being exposed as Jews; additionally, stirring conflict with a family as reputed and 'charitable' as Lukas' would not bode well for them, considering they were perceived as outsiders and their credibility was through their link to him. The dissolution of Yvonne's marriage was a relief for both her parents, especially her father, despite the tragic circumstances.

As her father pleaded with her to join him at the church, Yvonne agreed to consider it, given their perilous commuting situation. The call ended around 3 a.m., with Ilse trying to comfort her friend with the most idiotic jokes conceivable.

'It's the witches' hour, Yvonne. Let's rest now or else Lukas may summon them to chase after us.'

'Summon them?'

'What with him being the devil and all!'

Silana felt lethargic and her restless sleep the previous night did not help her mood either. She and Sebastien, who had also risen early, made a pact never to tell Sunne what had happened until she was at least 15. They deemed it to be only fair, and besides, Sunne's reaction would cause a major upheaval. Their mother was already burdened by a myriad of challenges; the very least Sebastien and Silana could do was guarantee Sunne's civility—they both already had quite a lot of practice in this regard.

The siblings discussed the events of last night in subdued

voices. 'I was too worn out last night to comprehend the gravity of what was written in that letter. I feel I still haven't completely understood it and I probably never will.' Silana had not shed a single tear.

'It's as if my tears have dried up. I have none left,' Sebastien concurred. 'Hardly a day before, he wanted us to attend the Nazi meeting to feed us this sick ideology. It repels me that he would sacrifice us to retain the Haydn repute and political connections. Sil, frankly, there's no room for sadness here. I've filtered out all of the irrelevant emotions and I'm left with anger. I feel anger not for our father but for our situation. How could we have been so unfortunate as to be stuck in such a dreadful time, in the midst of this godforsaken, never-ending war, with a father who will run for cover with his tail between his legs to save himself, essentially using his family as human shields? We live in an era of power-hungry cowards with no one to cling to but each other, and a responsibility to protect one another, which is the case with Sunne.'

Silana nodded in silent agreement, gently buttering her toast. Sebastien's eyes had clouded too much for her to see through them but she didn't need to. His intentions were clear.

'I didn't mean to overwhelm you, Sil.'

She laughed. 'Don't give yourself too much credit, Seb. Most of it goes to Father.'

'Ah well, then, I better pull my up socks and be eviler!'

He snatched the piece of toast away from his sister and stuffed the entire thing into his mouth, grinning as Silana lashed out at him.

Sunne strode in an hour later to find a very grumpy Silana lying on the couch and a contrastingly satisfied Sebastien sitting on the other end.

'I fell asleep last night, Sil! What did you discuss with Aunty Ilse? She told me to go to my room like I'm a child.'

'That you are!'

'And you are not?'

Silana clicked her tongue in irritation, beckoning her ever-persistent sister to take a seat. Sunne strode through the salon, traipsing across the vermilion carpet, brushing her fingers against the fine-grained texture of the wooden island table before sitting down near her sister. As the rays of the golden morning sun streamed in through the open window, it seemed like the sun was eavesdropping on the trio,

Silana and Sebastien exchanged a brief look before the former spoke. 'Father is away on quite a long business trip. He's safe and all is well with him. But a few bad folk are trying to hurt us.'

Silana felt the need to stress that her father would never have taken such a drastic step in his sane mind; it was almost as if she was still trying to rationalize what he had done.

'Hurt us? Why? What have we done to them?' Sunne asked in a tone that echoed the musings of a child still innocent to the true evils of the world. This was in sharp contrast to Sebastien, who had used the same question last night as a confirmation of his suspicions.

Silana silently marvelled at the gap in experience and their differing levels of trust in people. Both Sebastien and she had changed considerably these past few months, especially since starting their poster initiative, Sebastien losing Jakub and Silana losing Anna. Silana knew that the circumstances they were in were beyond her control and the only way she felt she could exert some control over the situation was by keeping Sunne shielded from it.

'Sunne, what they do should be of little concern to us so long as we have each other. Aunty Ilse and Mama will keep us safe from everything and everyone who may try to harm us. All you, Seb and I need to do is ride this out. But, my dear, at least we're not doing it alone.'

Sunne seemed relatively satisfied with this; she took her sister's hand and led her to the kitchen, whispering to Silana, 'I heard he ate your bread! Come, share mine.'

Yvonne and Ilse joined them not long after. Breakfast seemed to pass uneventfully. Ilse delegated the children the task of clearing the table as she went outside to check the mail. Yvonne helped the children, commenting, 'The future is tumultuous and inexplicably uncertain. What I want you to keep in mind is how fiercely proud I am of you. You must never compromise on your safety. I pray you don't have to learn this in any sort of detrimental way.'

Silana was surprised by how much more her mother was speaking. It was as if leaving the Haydn household had drawn her out of her shell for the very first time. She fervently wished she could travel back in time and plead with her mother not to marry their father. As her mother pulled the three of them into a tight embrace, Silana was overwhelmed by a surge of emotions—a mix of fear and self-pity. She allowed herself to wallow in the latter until the guilt set in, forcing her to confront the reality of who was truly responsible for their situation.

Just as Yvonne released them, Ilse rushed in, waving an envelope. 'Remember that friend I told you about? I just received a response from him! See, I told you he hardly takes a day to answer, the prompt fellow!'

Sebastien nearly fell off his chair in anticipation as Ilse quickly tore the envelope and scanned the letter while the Haydn family collectively held their breaths in anxious silence. Ilse looked up from the letter, her friendly grin spreading from ear to ear. 'I have a way for you to escape from here!'

Yvonne rested a hand on her son's shoulder, seemingly to calm him down, before turning to her friend. 'Ilse, my dear, what does this escape entail? I don't believe you have told me about this, but you do know I'd much prefer an alternative wherein I do not have to seek sanctuary in a church with my children alongside my parents. We'd be sitting ducks.'

'You do recall Jeremiah Karas, don't you, Yvonne? The freckled Jewish youth with a passion for humanitarianism? Lucjusz's nephew?'

'Ah yes! Such a bright young child. He and Sebastien used to be quite wonderful friends until he moved to this side of town and switched schools.'

'Yes, him. I was fast friends with his mother, who was busy most of the time, so Jeremiah spent a rather substantial portion of his childhood with me. He has escaped to India due to threats but we remain in frequent touch through letters. He has moved to Bramsadha, a princely state in India, after acquainting himself with the ruler. This Maharaja is providing shelter to Polish children in his summer home until the war passes and they can return to their home country safely. I can arrange safe, albeit slightly uncomfortable, passage to India for you all.'

'Travel to India? Under these circumstances? How can that be possible?'

'But it is, my dear.' Ilse walked around the table to where Yvonne was sitting, kneeling in front of her until she was at eye level with her friend. She took Yvonne's small hands in hers, clutching them tightly. 'I know that this could not be any more difficult than it already is, Yvonne, I do. I understand that as a Christian I am in no position to agree that I relate to what is happening to you at any level.'

Ilse's dearest friend looked at her, tears welling in her already scarlet, puffy eyes.

'But I will offer all help I can to you and your children as I have reiterated multiple times. My love for you should never be in doubt in your mind,' Ilse's voice quivered as she spoke. 'It is possible for the four of you to leave as soon as we finish an early afternoon lunch. You will covertly travel through the country on a supply train that carries different types of amenities and medicines. The train will take you to Moscow, from where you will board another one to reach Baku; there, you will take a ferry to Iran and finally get on cargo steamer from a local port and make your way to India. Upon your arrival in Bombay, the Maharaja will arrange for your passage to the camp.'

'And you are absolutely certain that you can validate this Maharaja?'

'Yvonne, during an epidemic last year, he allowed his

ballroom and a few other rooms as well to be used as treatment centres when he got to know there was a dearth of them. Additionally, he is famous throughout India for his humanitarian work, which has put him on the wrong side of the British. But the Maharaja not only takes all this in his stride but also encourages others to do the same. He is one of the most selfless people you may ever encounter.'

'Ilse, really, you're making it seem too good to be true,' said Yvonne, a smile spreading on her face. 'I will be eternally grateful if you make this happen for my children and me.'

'I shall write back to Mr Roshan. He's the connection to the Maharaja I had spoken to you about. I first met him during a stint I had in India when my husband had travelled there for work.'

Ilse never referred to her husband as 'late'. She preferred to allude to him as though he were alive in an attempt to immortalize him through her words.

'Roshan was a doctor who worked with him for a while; the two of them became fast friends and kept in touch through letters. He studied here, too, and has a house that he visits each month. When my husband passed away, Roshan wrote to me a few times to tell me that I wasn't alone in my grief. In any case, he will be the one to facilitate your transportation and I'm certain he will be quite ready to help you four. Though he cannot possibly afford to help people commute more than once every fortnight in light of security concerns, I have also been told that he has ready accommodation between the commuting gaps. If you're especially lucky the trains might even leave tomorrow.'

Silana chewed the inside of her cheek—*a fortnight?* She

wouldn't bet on her luck regarding whether the trains would be available tomorrow or not. Still, a lot could happen in a fortnight. All Silana wanted to do was wake up from whatever nightmare this was and write in her journal about what an adventure this had been and toss it aside, running into the waiting arms of her father before she took off to school and met with Anna and Sigrid. Silana felt displaced and rootless, like those nomadic gypsies her father used to speak about: 'They are wild, uncouth and uncivil because they have no means to ground them.'

She wondered if her father now thought the same thing about her.

Silana

That same evening, Yvonne Haydn was taken by the Gestapo.

The afternoon had been anything but eventful and a lazy atmosphere pervaded throughout Ilse's house. The air was stuffy with dusty books, parchment and the earthy aroma of aged wood that seemed to envelop all the furniture. Silana and Sunne had retreated to the bedroom after a hearty lunch, the latter still expressing concerns regarding their father's whereabouts. Every time Sunne did this, though unintentionally, Silana's heart sank further. Still, she refused to react—it could have been the shock or the utter depletion of any energy she possessed.

The bedroom Silana and Sunne were sharing had seemingly been unoccupied for a while, judging by its cobweb-ridden curtains. They sat cross-legged on the muted pink bedsheets and discussed anything and everything besides their current situation. Sunne rambled on and on about how she missed her school, her friends and even Nadia, a bully who taunted Sunne for her untameable curly hair. Sunne didn't fail to bring up the fact that Silana also had the same type of hair, leading her elder sister to laugh and fluff out Sunne's strawberry blonde curls—something Silana used to often do to Sunne when they were children.

Sunne squealed and tried to flatten her now poofy hair

while Silana commented, 'Nadia's not here now, is she? There's no one to stop you from looking as pretty as you do. And since when has she become a beauty expert? Did you see the eyesore of a red dress she wore to the Christmas party last year?'

Sunne giggled and covered her mouth almost instinctively—Father never liked it when they made fun of other people based on appearance, no matter how cruel they were to the sisters. 'And what will I tell Lech?'

Lech was Sunne's 'boyfriend'—the two would do scandalous things such as go for moonlit walks on weekends, hold hands in the library and cycle home together.

'Lech gave me flowers before we left, you know,' her sister rambled on. 'He told me to keep them in my room and take a whiff whenever I missed him and wanted to remember him.'

'Sunne, darling, wouldn't those flowers have died in a few days?'

'That's precisely the point, Sil. The idea was that he would replace the flowers as soon as they withered to remind me that though our love may wane due to distance, it will rekindle like fresh flowers when he sees me.'

'Love?' Silana laughed. 'What do you children know of love?'

'Definitely more than you.'

Silana gasped, taken aback, and playfully swatted her sister. The girls bantered back and forth for a bit before being joined by an anxious Sebastien.

'Mother is calling you both downstairs right this moment. God knows what you've been up to.'

They thudded down the staircase, amazed by how the surrounding walls were animated with pictures and colourful wallpaper—a contrast to the silent, soulless staircases back at the Haydn residence. The three siblings filed into the salon to find Yvonne and Ilse sipping tea. 'Chamomile. Would you three like some?' Ilse held up the kettle. The trio shook their heads and thanked her as Yvonne nodded her approval.

'All right.' Ilse set down her cup next to a stack of newspapers. 'I've written to Mr Roshan, who's thankfully in town for work, and I expect a reply very soon.'

'I'm surprised no one has been to search your house yet,' Sebastien remarked.

'We have a plan of action for that too. I've written the letter in a code that my husband taught me during the war. Another important thing I've called you down for—I do expect the Gestapo to come knocking soon. When they do, remember that there is a small crawlspace behind the drawer to the right of the bed.'

Silana didn't like the fact that Ilse had used 'when' instead of 'if'.

'It is most certainly big enough to accommodate the four of you and you can adjust the drawer before closing the crawlspace's door; once they leave, I shall come and retrieve you. If they happen to take me instead, wait until all is silent. I will lie for you four until the very end.'

The conversation had left Silana feeling hopeful. Hope—what a cruel thing to believe in during such times.

Hardly an hour later, around 4.15 p.m., the siblings were playing cards in the bedroom when they heard the sound of motor cars fast approaching on the road leading towards Ilse's house. Sebastien and Silana shared a look; Sebastien dimmed the lights and rushed to inform their mother while Silana hastened to unlock the crawlspace, grabbing Sunne and dragging her towards it. The girls crawled into the small opening, which led to a relatively dusty but significantly larger space. There was a singular lamp that they didn't dare turn on. They waited with bated breath for their brother and mother to join them.

Silana was relieved when the door quietly opened and her brother slinked in. Her heart was pounding and her mouth felt dry as Sebastien climbed into the small space, pulling the drawer in front of the crawlspace door to shut it quietly. Silana began to panic. 'Where's Mother? Where is she?'

'Take a breath, Sil. She's downstairs, hiding in the broom cupboard to listen for any updates regarding Father.'

Silana was not to be pacified—in fact, she was on the verge of tears. 'How could you have left her?' she whisper-shouted.

Before Sebastien could reply, the trio was silenced by the distant chaos of dogs barking and raised voices, exacerbated by the noisy motor engines going silent. *They're here*, Silana thought, a frost enveloping her insides. The siblings sat in painful silence, Silana squeezing her eyes shut and burying her head between her knees as the sounds grew louder.

The trepidation in the air built to a crescendo, the stuffiness of the crawlspace triggering Silana's claustrophobia. The hairs on her arms stood when she heard the familiar sound of a woman's elevated pleas, recognizing the voice to be her mother's. Sebastien too had the same realization. Silana felt trapped, on the verge of screaming and she knew Sunne was as frightened as her because she could feel her sister trembling.

The voices outside had now turned into full-blown screams, the noise creeping into the crawlspace and echoing eerily off the walls. Silana felt Sebastien tense up next to her but the only thing flashing across her mind was what would become of their mother. She crouched further and covered her ears; it reminded her of how she used to cope with her parents' fights when she was little. *Go to her room, cover her ears, read her book and pretend everything was all right. Everything would be normal by tomorrow.*

But tomorrow was bloodied by the realization that she and her siblings had been orphaned by their circumstances, with no place to call home if this war ever ended. All Silana could do was pray for a miracle, but they were hard to come by these days.

Another 10 minutes passed before the myriad of noises quietened. The silence unsettled Silana more than the noise had; she dug her fingernails into her palms, nearly drawing blood. Her father wasn't around now to scold her for this bad habit, which resurfaced whenever Silana was stressed. She kept her fingernails there even though her hands stung.

Their eyes had now adjusted to the darkness of the crawlspace, allowing Sebastien to notice her and subsequently unravel her hands and hold them in his much sweatier ones. The two stretched their arms across Sunne, shielding her and edging her as far from the door as possible. Silana felt the vibrations of quick steps coming up the stairs translate into audible and frantic footsteps that seemed to stop outside the door of the room. *Too light to be anyone armed*, Silana reasoned. *Too heavy to be her mother.* She foolishly hoped that her mother was coming to tell them that Father had come to his senses and was inviting them back home.

The door creaked open as the footsteps made their way towards the crawlspace. The three could hear the painful screeching of the metal desk along the wooden floor, with the obvious intent of revealing the entrance. There was banging—no, knocking, at the door.

'Children?'

Sebastien wasted no time crawling towards the entrance and flinging the door open, nearly taking the rusted piece of metal off the hinges. Silana noticed the outline of Ilse crouching at the entrance of the crawlspace. But something about her voice sounded different. *Is she choked up? Why on earth would she be crying if she wasn't injured? Unless...No.*

Ilse stood up after Sebastien had crawled out in an obvious attempt to hide her face from the girls. Silana managed to squeeze through the door before Sunne, shivering at the cold emptiness of the room—something she hadn't felt there before. Her gaze settled on Ilse, whose eyes were red as the scarlet throw pillows on the bed. She'd never seen Aunty Ils like this.

Ilse had certainly cried when she lost her husband but her journey to heal involved helping others more than herself. Emotions and Ilse were hardly ever two words used in the same context.

'Aunty Ils, where's Mama?' Silana's question came out

sounding much less urgent than she intended. Ilse's mouth opened but no sound came out, prompting her to close it once again.

'Aunty Ils, please,' Sebastien begged, stepping forward and taking his mother's best friend by the shoulders.

'What happened to her?' Sunne asked as Ilse broke down into tears.

'They took your mother. They took Yvonne.'

The two older siblings' immediate thought was to pacify Sunne. Silana led her extremely bewildered and shell-shocked sister out of the room as Sebastien took the responsibility to calm Ilse down—not a particularly easy task. As Silana took Sunne to the master bedroom, which was just a few doors down, clutching her sister's hand tightly, she caught a glimpse of the downstairs living room.

Most of Ilse's beautiful floral curtains had been ripped from their hangers. Her grand dining table had been smashed, with one of its legs broken, and most of the downstairs drawers had been opened and crudely searched, resulting in items being strewn all across the floor. One of the large mirrors near the main door had been shattered, glass scattered across the floor and the carpet, silently reflecting the dying glimmer of one of the last lamps left intact.

The broom closet that Mother was supposed to have hidden in was wide open, beckoning Silana into its darkness where her only companions would be a scraggly-looking mop, an overused duster and a large bucket. The chandelier Silana had admired so much was the only thing left relatively intact and it too looked at the massacre splayed out in front of it. The girl prayed her mother would step out from the darkness of the broom closet any minute now, hands outstretched, assuring in her gentle French accent, 'It's all right, ma chérie. All things have passed.'

'All things have passed' was the phrase her mother used to say to her when she scraped her knee after falling off a bike or she ran home crying after being made fun of for her weight or her round, moon-like glasses. But nothing had passed. Quite the contrary—Silana's nightmare had only just begun. She quickened her pace, distracting Sunne by asking her to look at one of the frames on the wall. 'What a funny-looking cat!'

Once in Yvonne's room, Sunne said fervently, 'You may think me a child but I am far from that. I deserve to know what happened to Mama as much as you and Seb.' Her eyes welled with tears as she tried to be assertive.

Silana knew that, to a certain extent, her younger sister wasn't wrong. In fact, she had grown quite apprehensive about Sunne's newfound independence. The latter was used to having everything more or less handed to her on a silver platter—Sunne's crocodile tears generally paved the way to their father's iron heart. Her cloudy eyes meant something more profound this time—for the first time, Silana saw her loss reflected in someone else's eyes. She struggled to formulate words, which was quite unlike her. How was she to tell her sister any of this? How was she supposed to break her heart for the nth time? She wanted to lie; she really did. Every bone in her body was telling her to keep their mother's fate from Sunne. But reasonably, that plan wouldn't take very long to fall apart. Sunne was still looking at her accusingly, wide-eyed and trying to look as offended as possible.

Silana watched as her sister grew more impatient, a part of her willing Sunne to forget all of it. Sebastien would not appreciate her telling Sunne any of what was transpiring. She gestured for Sunne to sit on the bed, carefully shutting the door as the girl complied. She didn't even bother flicking a lamp on as the dusky remnant of the evening cast sweeping shadows across the wooden floor. Silana settled next to her sister, hardly knowing where to begin. She decided to start where her thoughts began—their father. But she tried to condense his role to whatever extent she could. Her telling Sunne about their father's role made it seem that she was actively defaming the memories of both their parents. And her mother—she still hadn't fully processed what had just happened. How was she to tell someone that they had lost both parents in the span of just a couple of days or that they were now orphaned?

'...and the political party that sought to exterminate all Jews? Father is affiliated with them. Mama is a Jew and we, her children, are thus Jewish. Father believes that he had been tricked by Mama and his anger has manifested as revenge.'

Sunne's tears had evaporated in the remnants of the evening sun. 'But I'm not Jewish! I go to church every Sunday!'

Silana sighed, overlooking her sister's lack of comprehension. 'We're her children. Her blood flows through us as much as Father's does; thus we are only half Catholic.'

Sunne was silent for a moment and then shook her head. 'Since when does religion have anything to do with blood?'

Silana didn't have an answer.

'So what happened to Mama?'

Now it was time for the difficult part. Silana steadied herself—not to stop her tears from flowing but to try to describe what had happened in the simplest way possible. 'We left home because Papa wanted to punish Mama for lying to him by hurting her and us.' *Simple indeed. Seb would be proud.*

'Hurt us? In what way would he want to hurt us?' Sunne persisted.

She would just have to be candid with her sister. Deception would not do either of them any good at this stage. 'By killing us, Sunne. We are a plague—cockroaches meant to be exterminated for world peace that will begin with bloodshed.'

'And they're going to kill Mama?' was Sunne's only concern, but Silana was exasperated by this point.

'I don't have all the answers, Sunne! I pray they don't but how can you expect me to be sure?' Her sister recoiled, prompting Silana to lower her volume. 'We're a unit, Sunne. Nothing can ever take that away from us.'

Silana's next move was to divert Sunne's attention before she could grasp the severity of the situation. It was like the games of chess she had played with her father as a child—Silana was constantly bewildered by how he would create a problem in the centre of the board and distract her while developing pieces elsewhere, tactically exploiting her weaknesses. 'Chess is so similar to real life; how you play it reflects who you are as a person,' he would say.

Silana, using this strategy, added, 'We're a unit except for when Sebastien steals my food and you steal my vanity kit. Then you two are on your own.' Silana was surprised at her own lack of sorrow but she was satisfied that Sunne had managed a smile.

Silana

Sunne and Silana spoke about anything and everything to distract themselves from the ordeals of the day—from Sunne's boyfriend and her sporting escapades to Silana's cursed biology test and teacher. Silana found herself adding anecdotes in order to elicit a laugh from Sunne. She realized how little the two spoke even though they lived together, admitting that she quite enjoyed their conversation—it reminded her of the ones she used to have with Anna and Sigrid. A small part of her suddenly didn't feel so alone in this journey any longer and she hoped Sunne would be this responsive and open to her and Seb should something bad (or worse) happen.

Darkness finally shrouded the room, and the two siblings got off the bed and tiptoed back to Ilse and Sebastien. The house looked even more terrifying at this time, increasing Silana's unease. The water spilt across the salon downstairs captured the moonlight, making it seem as though the house was bleeding. Silana deduced that Ilse had stopped crying only shortly before the girls' return; Sebastien's eyes had grown small, the lines in his forehead more prominent than she had ever seen before. Thankfully, Ilse seemed to have regained her ability to form coherent sentences.

'Children, we must move quickly. I can arrange transport for you in the late hours of tonight.'

Silana cut in, 'Tonight? But Mother—'

'I am well aware of your mother's situation, my child.' Ilse's voice sounded grim. 'They will keep your mother alive for now.'

'How do you know that?' This time Sunne was the one panicking.

Sebastien shot Silana a glance as if to say 'I thought it was your job to keep her in the dark', but she conveniently ignored it.

'They didn't even have to open the broom closet for your mother to step out. She had realized something I hadn't— they would have ransacked my entire house in any case, and if they had found Yvonne hiding, I too would have been arrested. As they barged into my house, Yvonne pretended to walk in from the kitchen. She bribed them with her diamond necklace, earrings and her engagement ring to not take me away too; the reward for her arrest was far too great. Then they asked where you three were.'

Silana's stomach tightened.

'Your mother cleverly told them you three had gone to stay at another acquaintance's house. She offered to take them to the location.' It took all of Ilse's willpower for her not to break down again. 'She gave them a name— Bronowski. She claimed that they are distant cousins who recently moved into town to raise their children closer to you three and Yvonne. Are they familiar to any of you?'

The siblings shook their heads, looking at one another.

'Then I believe that she's certainly led them to some distant corner of town in order to give you three time to escape.'

Silana was a mixture of hurt and confusion. *They were a family, a unit. Weren't they supposed to stick together?* Then, again, that would have probably led to all of them being discovered and rounded up like animals, taken to a fate most certainly worse than death.

For a minute, no one spoke, allowing Silana to hear the soft echo of her heartbeat—fast-paced at first, but quieting down as the girl allowed the silence of the room to envelop her.

'Your friend…Mr Roshan. What did he reply?' Silana noticed her brother's attempt to take initiative. He might have assumed it to be his responsibility, considering he was the eldest in their family now.

'That was just what your mother and I had been discussing. Roshan has written back, informing that the last commute for this fortnight would be leaving at 0100 hours. I don't mean to be dramatic but your last hope is the Maharaja. The Gestapo will return, this time exceedingly agitated after the wild goose chase your mother has led them on.'

'In that case, we need to leave as soon as possible, Aunty Ils.'

Ilse seemed to gather herself as the siblings looked on expectantly. 'Silana, Sunne, go pack your bags quickly. Meet me and Sebastien here in no longer than 10 minutes.' Ilse glanced at the teal clock above the bed. 'I want you both back here by 7.40 p.m. Hasten but be as quiet as possible. Go, quick!'

Silana and Sunne had each packed light for the journey, their travel bags as old as the girls themselves. Unfortunately, they had unpacked their bags, thinking they would be spending quite some time at Ilse's house. Their clothes, though neatly placed in the cupboard, were now hastily shoved into their respective bags.

They returned downstairs, avoiding stepping on the scattered glass shards. Navigating through the dim glimmer of the moonlight was difficult, but they managed. Ilse stood in a corner of the room, her shoulders more hunched than usual—the storm raging within her reflected in her tempestuous eyes. Silana wondered if Aunty Ilse was, perhaps subconsciously, in silent penance for what had befallen Yvonne.

'I so wish I could keep you children and hide you away until this terrible storm passes us. But it seems to have only just begun. My hope for a speedy end to the conflict that started with the idiotic calls for anti-Semitism has ended with your mother's capture.'

That last sentence was spoken with difficulty, the wound still quite fresh for them all. Silana and her siblings, however, were still numb from shock.

'I hope the street lamps dim quickly. We need to leave as soon as possible. Roshan will be waiting for you. I'm anxious to introduce you three to him. Don't fret, he's a lovely person.'

The children seemed to feel exactly the opposite, looking decidedly apprehensive.

'The journey you undertake may be long, perhaps even perilous at certain stages, but like your mother has repeatedly told you three—rely on each other. You three are each other's most precious asset, more than any materials you may possess.'

The siblings nodded in agreement as the light of the street lamps finally ebbed away and melted into the night.

'Children, we must leave now. Load your luggage in quickly—it's quite a long drive. Watch your step!'

As their eyes adjusted relatively quickly to the darkness, the children came out of the house and piled into the back of her aged motor car. Starting the car, Ilse instructed them to remain quiet if they were stopped and if interrogated, to tell the authorities Ilse was their mother and that they were going to visit their sick grandmother in the emergency unit at the hospital. As Ilse sped down the road, Silana couldn't help but ask where she had learnt to drive; as per her knowledge, women weren't supposed to. It just wasn't proper for a lady, according to her father.

'My husband taught me a year before he passed away.' Ilse smiled faintly. 'We used to drive past these very roads, wondering if some day we'd have enough money to buy one of these big houses.'

'I think your cottage is beautiful, Aunty Ils. So quaint!'

Silana glowered at her sister. *Quaint? How could she be so insensitive to Ilse?* As she was about to scold Sunne for being ungrateful, Ilse chimed in, 'That's what my husband used to say, too. Our dream to have a larger home was... well...my dream to have a larger home. It had always been a singular ideation. I had sole creative liberty over the interior but my husband was most enthusiastic about the so-called "character and charm" I was able to infuse into our home.'

The darker corners of Silana's mind replayed the state of Ilse's house she had last seen it in—shattered glass, smashed furniture and spillage—all taking away from the tranquillity of the house she had aspired for. She wondered how badly it must have affected Ilse, considering the house was a testament to the memory of her husband.

'That's beautiful, Aunty Ils.' Sunne, stuck in between her two older siblings, forced a smile, which Ilse returned.

'We shall be there in no more than half an hour. I suggest you children sleep for the duration. You may not have much opportunity after this drive.'

Silana found it wise to heed Ilse's words, resting her cheek against the car's rattling windows as Sunne elbowed her in an attempt to make some more space for herself. Much to Silana's relief, Sebastien allowed Sunne to rest her head on his shoulder, freeing up room for her to lean closer to the window. Her favourite part of car journeys was surveying people as they blissfully went about their lives. Not that there were many out at this time—except for the odd homeless person and the occasional officer who never failed to make her blood run cold.

This one will stop us, I just know. I can feel it. They mercifully never did, not even as Ilse's car, louder than an entire orchestra, navigated the rugged roads, going further into the city suburbs. Each jolt was accentuated by the slow percussion of the gravel, building into a crescendo. The motor car's dim headlights cast beams that danced lightly on the road while the sidewalks glinted faintly in the car's backlight. Just as Silana was about to drift into a brief sleep, Ilse's voice pulled her out of her near-catatonic state. 'We've reached, my dears.'

Sunne clambered over Silana to exit the car while Sebastien was already standing outside, unloading their luggage from the boot. As Silana got out, she was greeted by an inconspicuous neighbourhood of apartment buildings that stretched across an entire block. Silana recognized the area to be one of the less fortunate locales in town—she had once visited an orphanage nearby, helping her family distribute Christmas presents to children. She noticed a glaring green sign that read 'Train Station—500 metres'. Silana was too tired to make anything of it as she gingerly took her bag from Sebastien and followed Ilse, eyes still half shut, towards the front door of the closest building.

Ilse knocked thrice, paused for three seconds and knocked two more times. The door creaked open to reveal a tall Indian man dressed in a pinstriped navy blue suit and tie. He beamed upon seeing Ilse. 'My dear! It's been far too long.'

His accented Polish immediately caught Silana's attention.

'Roshan! It's so lovely to see you again.' The two shared a hug.

'Ilse, if only we met under less grievous circumstances. Please, come in.'

Ilse motioned the children to follow Roshan, and they scuttled in, placing their bags on the chairs in the living room before going up to Roshan and shaking his hand. His grip was firm and warm.

'It's so nice to finally meet you children. Please, take a seat.'

They settled quietly into the narrow-framed wooden chairs as the man turned to look at Ilse. 'And where might their mother be? I was expecting…'

Silana tensed up. Ilse pulled Roshan aside, leading him

into what seemed to be the parlour, leaving the children alone with their thoughts. They knew exactly what she would be telling him. A clock perched high above a console table filled the silence that pervaded the room.

Tick, tick, tick.

Silana scanned the room, studying everything from the peeling wallpaper to the island glass table. Silana watched as the clock, its surface embellished with ornate patterns, continued to deliberately click away in a smooth cadence.

Tick, tick, tick.

Ilse and Roshan returned, the man looking more sombre this time, his voice tight as he addressed the siblings. 'Children, I had no idea what befell your mother. I am so sorry. You have my deepest sympathies.'

'It's all right,' Silana was as shocked by the authority with which she answered as her siblings were. 'You couldn't have known. In fact, we should be thanking you for what you are doing for our family.'

Roshan smiled. 'Ilse told me about how brave and mature you all are. I believe her with even more conviction now.'

Father would have been proud of her newfound 'conviction'. Or maybe he wouldn't have been—more questions for him to answer, a more evident streak of rebellion.

'I assume Ilse has briefed you about where you are going; it's my duty to tell you how. I hope that you three understand the kind of risks that may be present during this journey.'

Silana nodded her head as Sebastien stared intently into his lap, not meeting Roshan's gaze.

'This train is one of the last that we are able to organize out of Poland. Our informants have recced the political climate and ascertained that the Gestapo have been closing in on our operations. We have assisted hundreds of children escape to India—mostly orphans. So far, we've not had any difficulties during the journeys; however, we must always be careful.' He took a breath. 'Would you children like any refreshments? Water, perhaps?'

They all shook their head, even though Silana's throat was parched with anxiety.

'Are you sure? All right, then. Do tell me if you change your minds.'

'Talk of the train, Rosh.' Ilse was leaning against the doorframe, hands crossed over her stomach.

'Yes, yes. I've been informed that there are around 20 children in total this time. They will be your travel companions. About the journey itself, you children will be accompanied by me and Mrs Nidhi Dulari, my wife. Don't fret about the visas; we have officials who will arrange it for you as soon as we reach the Russian border.'

'Once we reach Bombay, what shall become of us?' Sebastien posed his first question in a rather interrogatory manner, even if it hadn't been meant as such.

'From there, the Maharaja will organize transport for you and all the other children to reach Bramsadha. The train departs in half an hour, but I would like to get you children acquainted with your fellow passengers before we leave. If you'd like to use the washroom, now's your chance; we will be leaving in 10 minutes.'

None of the children moved a muscle. Silana looked at Sunne, who looked to be nearly on the brink of tears.

'Sunne!' Silana hurried over to her sister and knelt down

beside her chair. 'We're a family, Sunne. A unit. I promise that Seb and I will not leave your side for a second. Matter of fact, you'll be begging us to, because you'll be squashed in between.'

Sunne gave her sister a smile, but there was a clear sadness behind it. Silana spent the remainder of the 10 minutes braiding and un-braiding Sunne's beautiful, voluminous hair, while Sebastien switched between fiddling with his bag and admiring some vases on a nearby table.

Roshan, who had gone to retrieve his own bag, finally called the children. 'It's time to leave!' The children exchanged glances, grappling with their respective suitcases as they followed Roshan. He led them out of the door to his motor car and helped the three load their suitcases in the boot.

'The train station is not far from here. I would have definitely walked there with you but I'd rather not risk any guards on night patrol stopping us.'

Sunne tightly embraced Ilse first, with Silana and Sebastien following suit. Sebastien thanked Ilse on behalf of their family. Silana recognized that the unspoken order reflected the direct involvement she had had in their lives. She wanted nothing more than to pull out a piece of paper and write something to Aunty Ilse because she couldn't form the words—even if she tried, she was afraid she wouldn't be able to get through more than a sentence before her emotions manifested in a rainstorm of tears. Silana remained steadfast though. She promised herself that the next time she would see Aunty Ils was going to be soon, and she would write her a plethora of poems to express how eternally grateful she was.

Ilse huddled them together, her voice quivering, 'My dear children, as much as I would like to accompany you to India, my duties here are still unfinished. The circumstances have torn us apart but I do hope that, in due time, they will reunite us. I am leaving you in the more than capable hands of Roshan, but you three must take care of each other also.'

She got into her car and started it, peering teary-eyed at the children from her driver's seat before pulling on to the road and speeding away into the thin fog that had settled on the neighbourhood. 'Come, we must be quick. Even the slightest delay could prove to be disastrous.'

Silana

The train station was far less glamorous than what Silana had imagined. The Haydn siblings had been promised a certain level of comfort back home as long as they did what they were told. Silana had to constantly remind herself of the bleakness of their situation.

The entrance was weather-beaten and dimly lit, with several letters missing from the sign overhead. The space, intended for accommodating hundreds of travellers each day, certainly didn't look wide enough and bathed in the intermittent glow of the overhead station lights, seemed all the more foreboding.

Roshan instructed the children to take their bags and follow him as he presented a few papers to the security guard on duty. The guard scrutinized them intently for a tense few seconds before nodding his approval and allowing the four to pass. Silana was relieved that her fear-stricken face hadn't affected the guard's assessment.

The station was eerily empty. The lack of passengers and the surrounding silence seemed to amplify the sounds, which echoed off the tiled floors and abandoned ticket booths. Flickering signs displayed various destinations, their chaotic neon lettering quite a jarring detail. The walls and floors, once possibly white, were now a muted brown.

Roshan finally led them to an open platform that extended

into cobbled train tracks. That is where they encountered their companions—some 20 children, all between the ages of seven and seventeen. Guiding them was a kindly-looking woman in her mid-30s, whom Silana assumed to be Roshan's wife. Her sprightly demeanour and bright clothes stood out in the sombre situation. Looking up, she gave the group a quick smile and quipped, 'You four are just in time! A minute later and we may have even left without you.'

Some of the children were quietly waiting for the train, while others were bursting with excitement, their energy spilling over into the station's passive midnight serenity. The children's voices dipped slightly as Roshan cleared his throat. 'Children, many of you have already met me. For those who haven't, my name is Roshan Dulari and this is my wife, Nidhi Dulari. We shall be accompanying you to India. The train will arrive in just a few minutes time and I trust none of you will cause ruckus till then.'

His words elicited a few chuckles, the loudest from his wife, who waded her way over and quickly embraced him. The two conversed effortlessly in a beautiful dialect Silana didn't recognize. Nidhi then turned her attention to the Haydn children, her smile never leaving her face.

'Hello! I'm Nidhi. It's lovely to meet you three.' Her Polish accent was even richer than her husband's. The siblings all smiled in response, exchanging glances, hoping one of them would say something in reply. 'You must be tired; it is getting quite late. Don't worry; you will be able to sleep on the train.'

Nidhi came closer to the Haydn children, lowering her voice so as not to be overheard, which wasn't difficult considering the anxious chatter of the children. 'Many of your companions have lost their entire families and have gotten here by some miracle. Those fortunate enough to have surviving siblings have had to leave their parents behind because our resources do not permit us to accommodate adults.'

Silana stole a glance behind Nidhi at the rambunctious group and wondered how the station had seemed so deceptively quiet when they first arrived. Nidhi drew her attention back. 'These are some of the children who will be your camp-mates during your stay in India. Keep an open heart—their pain is but a fragment of who they are.' Her next sentence was drowned out by the sound of the incoming train's whistle. 'Stay right here. We'll be boarding soon!' Nidhi rushed over to Roshan, helping him push the children back from the tracks.

It struck Silana how different the children looked in that very moment. Some, like the Haydn siblings, wore relatively comfortable-looking, well-stitched coats. She noticed a few girls, herself included, wearing flowery hats and patterned scarves. Some boys, the ones standing in the vicinity of these girls, donned pearly white shorts and sweaters. Silana deduced that these children had probably found themselves in situations similar to the siblings'. They tended to keep to themselves towards the back of the platform; a few looked quite unsettled at the prospect of having to board a train with the rest. But this was just a small portion of the group.

The majority of the children in Silana's line of sight reflected a vast disparity between those who came from comfortable backgrounds and those who did not. The chattier bunch was mostly dressed in tattered, worn coats, brown or grey in colour, the colours faded and the clothes quite likely second-hand. Some of their scarves had loose threads dangling idly, at the risk of being snagged. Silana noticed hardly any hats in this particular sea of heads; the few that she did spot reflected many years of wear. Both her siblings had fallen quiet, any will to make small talk effectively overpowered by the bustling swarm of their fellow passengers.

Soon, the platform was flooded by the obtrusive glare of the train's headlights. The siblings remained rooted in their places as the train finally came to a stop, creaking out a symphony of groans. Silana had mentally braced herself for the train's appearance, but nothing she had imagined compared to the weathered hunk of metal just over 10 feet away from her. Sebastien's shock was almost laughable; Silana turned to look at her brother, whose mouth hung hopelessly agape. She lifted a hand to his chin and clamped it shut quickly.

'This? Are we expected to undertake such a long journey, under these terrible circumstances, in whatever that may be?'

In any other situation, Silana would have laughed and reprimanded her brother for acting entitled, but he did have a valid argument; she tried fervently not to doubt their safety. They'd come this far already, and Aunty Ilse had, after all, assured them that many people had made this journey before. *There was no need to worry.* However, this train seemed to have shorter carriages, almost half of the usual ones.

'Twenty children! Do they truly expect all of us to fit inside one carriage?' Sebastien whisper-yelled at his sister.

'I'd assume so, unless they expect us to ride on top of it.'

'At this rate, I wouldn't put it past them.'

Silana shot her brother a look of contempt suitable for his behaviour.

'All right everyone, gather here. Be silent about it, please.'

The excitement of the train's arrival quickly turned into an eerie and deafening silence as the children realized why it was there in the first place.

'I trust everyone has their relevant documentation; we will check that before you board. A few instructions: when we stop at any security checkpoints, please remain quiet and stay in your respective seats. The documentation we have provided is your most important possession now and the only thing that you should hold close to you throughout the journey. I cannot emphasize this enough—please keep it with you at all costs.'

What documentation? Silana looked over at Sebastien, who looked as though he had completely dissociated. *He's not going to do anything about it.* Her concern for her brother's odd behaviour would have to be put off temporarily, she reckoned, as she raised her hand. 'Um—'

'Don't worry. I have your papers with me.' Roshan continued, 'I hope that you will acquaint yourselves with each other. Look around—these people shall be your family until this war is over, perhaps even after that.'

Nidhi smiled all the while as her husband spoke. 'All right, children, make two single-file lines—one at the front entrance and one near the back. Hurry!'

Silana and her siblings had been standing closest to the front entrance and shouldered their way through scrambling children towards Roshan, who handed them each a grey envelope with their names written in black ink.

'Put your bags in the overhead racks, dear, and find three seats adjacent to each other.'

Silana boarded the train first, followed by Sunne and then Sebastien. Somehow, the carriage seemed even smaller on the inside, with tiny over the seats meant to accommodate their luggage. Silana's foremost priority was finding seats, preferably near each other, which she urgently conveyed to Sebastien.

The carriage had three seats on either side and two in the middle. They were uncomfortably close and the colour of dirty sunflowers with bright blue foam cushions, a painful contrast to the muted grey train interior. The haphazard usage of colour made Silana shudder with disgust.

'Sunne, Silana, give me your bags,' Sebastien said, desperately trying to avoid the flurry of people. He hoisted his own luggage onto the overhead racks and then his sisters'.

'Sebastien, sit there next to Sunne. I don't want her to be alone. I'll sit here.'

Sunne and Sebastien sat in the left-hand row of the train, and Silana took the middle seat in the row right next to where her siblings were seated. Sebastien was busy reassuring Sunne, who looked terrified at the prospect of undertaking the journey on a train that was in such a dilapidated condition. Internally, Silana was panicking even more, considering a stranger would soon be seated next to her.

The siblings had taken their seats close to the middle of the carriage and were thus witness to the evident divide.

At the back, children with haughty expressions grouped together, wrinkling their peevishly long noses at anyone who dared sit near them. *These types of people exist? Even in this situation?* Seated at the front were the children who appeared less privileged than the Haydn family.

Silana, who had been watching her brother calm down a distressed Sunne, turned her attention to the seat next to her after it was rocked by a resounding thud. A nervous-looking boy settled next to her, his short, untamed hair a mess, a dirty white shirt accompanied by equally drab beige pants and speckled hazel eyes that stared directly into Silana's. She realized she had spent a little too long studying him when he spoke, holding out his hand. 'I'm Levi. It's nice to meet you.'

'Silana. It's nice to meet you too, despite the circumstances.' She shook his hand, noting how rough his palms were. He mustn't be from an affluent background, she reckoned. 'No coat? Aren't you feeling cold?' she blurted out. Levi replied slowly that he was not able to afford one. She tried to change the subject as quickly as humanly possible. 'I've heard India is quite warm though. You should be all right.' *What are you trying to do, stupid girl?*

To her relief, the boy chuckled. 'I certainly hope so.'

She opened her mouth to say something but closed it when she heard a few loud claps from the front of the carriage—Nidhi, standing next to Roshan, was the source of the sound. 'Settle down, please. I hope everyone has found a seat. Roshan and I will be taking a headcount. When we call out your names, please raise your hands and acknowledge so we can tick your name off. We would greatly appreciate it if the rest of you maintain silence—after all, we do want to leave as soon as possible, don't we?'

'Marina Godlewski? Valeria…Lukaszewski?'

Her pronunciation amused Silana thoroughly but she refrained from laughing at Nidhi's expense, appreciating her valiant attempt to say each name even though she knew she couldn't possibly get them correct.

'Jan Tomaszek? Levi Floreck?'

Levi Floreck. Silana marvelled at how musical the name sounded. Nidhi called out a few more names before proclaiming, 'All right, it seems everyone is here, thankfully. We shall be leaving in another few minutes. Do check once again if you have your papers handy. I'd advise you to keep them in any pockets your clothes may have.'

A few children rose to take their respective papers out of their bags, and once they had settled, Nidhi continued, 'You will need them for crossing borders and upon arrival in Bombay. Keep them as close to you as possible.'

Silana clutched her little envelope tightly, nearly on the verge of crumpling the paper.

'For now, the journey does promise to be smooth and you can use this opportunity to rest. I suggest you all sleep for as long as possible.'

The couple took their seats at the very front of the carriage just as it heaved loudly, startling its passengers and setting off slowly with a puff of smoke. Though Silana noticed children around her settling into some semblance of sleep, she was in no mood to do so. Her eagerness to converse with her reticent travel companion, combined with her anxiety to leave her city behind as quickly as possible, left no room for sleep. Looking at her siblings, it was evident they didn't share her worries. Sunne's head rested on Sebastien's shoulder, with Sebastien somehow trying to sleep with his arms crossed. Silana, grateful that she didn't have to engage in any difficult conversation with them, directed her attention back to Levi who (much to her relief) asked her a question, 'Are those your siblings?'

'Yes,' she replied. 'Are you here with yours?'

'I'm an only child.' He smiled.

Silana tried to further the conversation. 'You aren't sleeping?'

'How can anybody in such situation?'

Silana smiled in agreement. 'You're quite right. I'd love nothing more than to leave this city and everyone in it behind as soon as possible.'

'If you don't mind me asking, Silana, why are you going to India?'

'The same reason you are. Sanctuary.'

'From what? I don't see the Star of David sewn into any of your coats.'

The only thing each child aboard the train, except for the siblings, had in common was the bright yellow Star of David stitched into all forms of their clothing, branding them and ostracizing them from the rest of society.

'It's not quite as interesting as you might hope. My siblings and I happen to be half Jewish, which we discovered around three days ago.'

'Now this I must hear.'

Silana chuckled at his enthusiasm. 'Well, to put it briefly—'

'Briefly? Why so? By the looks of it, we've got plenty of time.'

'Very well, then.' Silana described as much as she could about her journey. She began from her days at school, detailing about her controlling father, their rebel initiative, their father's betrayal, Ilse's assistance, their mother's arrest and the sibling's subsequent attempt to escape.

'So, we left Aunty Ilse and arrived at the station with Roshan. And here we are.' She hadn't realized how much she had been dying to tell an uninvolved third party what had happened to her these past few days until she finally did. Though nothing had changed, sharing her reality with Levi made Silana feel slightly better.

Levi raised his eyebrows. 'I thought you said your journey wasn't interesting?'

Silana smiled. 'Well, some parts are truly stranger than any fiction I've read. I'm terribly sorry! I realize I've been talking too much. Do tell me about yourself, Levi.'

He became quiet for a moment, and Silana was terrified she had unknowingly said something that may have offended him.

'It's all right. You don't have to—'

'I'm fine, Silana. Don't worry. It's only fair that I share my story with you, too.' He shifted a bit in his seat, evidently uncomfortable at the prospect of opening up to the extent that Silana had. Silana looked at him, silently admiring how well-structured his nose was from the side, creating a sharp linear bridge that gave him a deceptively stoic demeanour. He turned back to look at the girl, and in the dim light of the train, shared his story.

His upbringing had been entirely different from Silana's and much less lavish. At first, there had been no conceivable divide between the Christians and the Jews at his school but as the Nazis began tightening the noose around the necks of Polish Jews, Levi steadily lost most of his closest friends. The public pool, library, movie theatres and eventually even his school shut down. His father also lost his job, spiralling into alcoholism and domestic violence. Levi would sneak out to visit his friends while his father lay drunk and barely conscious in his room after his nightly drinking sprees. His family were forced to sew the Star of David on his clothes by this point.

Levi tried to find employment. However, being a young Jewish boy didn't bode too well for him. Sometimes, when he stood in line for the mandatory rations since all Jewish grocery stores had been closed, he was made to do menial labour. Soon enough, his friend's mother, aware of Levi's domestic situation, informed him of a Maharaja in India sheltering Polish children. He asked whether his mother would be able to undertake the journey, but the reply was negative. Levi's mother encouraged him to undertake the journey while she took refuge in Levi's grandparents' house, away from her abusive husband.

'After incessant begging and pleading, she eventually convinced me that there was nothing left for me any more in our town. "Forge your own future and never let anybody cite your religion as a reason that you cannot," she said.' Levi slowed down a bit after reaching the climax of his story.

'A week ago, I left my mother at her parents' place and, with two of my friends, made my way to Mr Roshan's house.

He directed us to a large shelter, near the train station, where we had to stay till we boarded the train to India tonight.'

'You mentioned you're accompanied by two friends?'

'Yes, they're seated in the seventh row.'

Silana peeked around the corner to see two sleeping boys.

'The one in the navy coat is Fryderyk, and the one sitting to his right is Rysio.'

Levi and Silana chatted for a few minutes before drifting off to sleep, the weight of their circumstances finally taking over them.

As the train came to a grinding halt, the screeching of the metal against the train tracks progressively increased till the duo had to resort to covering their ears. The entire group was jolted awake as the train pulled into a shabby-looking station, not entirely dissimilar from the one they had boarded from. This time, however, the platform was bustling with anxious travellers and equally agitated porters and conductors. Silana could hardly see out of the window since she was in the middle row, but she did witness her brother and sister nearly falling out of their seats in shock at the train's sudden halt. She giggled and tried to speak to her siblings over the ensuing cacophony.

'WELL RESTED?'

'WHAT?' her sister shouted back.

'I ASKED, WELL RESTED?'

The two shouted back and forth, much to Sebastien's embarrassment. Levi was similarly trying to signal his friends, but his attempts were futile. After a few minutes, the train's caterwauling eventually subsided, allowing Nidhi and Roshan to stand up and announce their next set of instructions.

'Once again, please check that you have all your documents in order. This is one of the places where they are mandatory.'

Silana patted herself down, rummaging through her pockets and pulling out the now slightly crumpled but still sealed envelope, glancing over at her siblings, who held similar ones in their hands.

'I will take the silence as an affirmative. All right, we are now going to be splitting into two groups.'

Roshan walked up to a few rows beyond Silana, indicating the division.

'Everyone seated in front of where Roshan is standing, please stand up and exit from this door, please!' said Nidhi.

They obliged, slowly emptying out of the train carriage and lining up on the platform.

Silana nearly dropped her bag in anxiety while retrieving it from the rust-devoured overhead racks. Making her way to the platform, Silana caught a glimpse of an overhead sign that read 'Liliya', recognizing it to be the station Nidhi had told them would be from where they would be travelling to Baku. She made sure to hold on to the sleeve of her brother's coat to avoid losing him in the sea of people. Sebastien also held on to Sunne's sleeve as the siblings navigated the ever-shifting crowd.

Silana whispered to check whether Sebastien had his travel documents in order; he replied in the affirmative after checking Sunne's as well. At that moment, Roshan attempted to gain the children's attention while his wife made the rounds to take their count.

The station was a chaotic maze of people and luggage as the children navigated their way to the other platform, the air filled with the mingled scents of coal smoke and the stench of the passengers. Silana's eyes widened as they approached a dark train that gleamed under the dim station lights.

'This is it,' whispered Sebastien, his voice tinged with trepidation.

Roshan and Nidhi led the way, their authoritative presence reassuring the children. As they boarded the new train, the interior was markedly more comfortable, with plush seats and polished wood panelling. Silana found a window seat this time, her heart racing with anticipation for the journey ahead.

Sebastien and Sunne settled next to her, their eyes reflecting the same mixture of anxiety and hope. As the train's whistle blew, its long, mournful sound seemed to echo the sentiments of the travellers.

'We're really going to India,' Sunne murmured, half to herself, as the train began to move.

The train's whistle blew as it pulled into the station, the sound mixing with the distant cries of seagulls and the salty scent of the Caspian Sea. As they disembarked, Nidhi and Roshan gathered the children together, their voices barely audible over the clamour of the passengers.

'All right, children. Remain in your groups and follow either Nidhi or me. We will be taking you through two different exits to board the bus. It is hardly a 10-minute journey to the port. Keep your travel documents ready. The security at the exits will be checking those.'

The journey had been long and tiring, but the children's spirits were lifted by the sight of a bustling port city teeming with life. They had arrived in Baku, from where they would take a ferry to reach Iran.

Silana and her siblings, standing at the back of the line, teetered between anxiety and pure terror as the guard, an older man with dark, furrowed brows and tired eyes, mechanically stamped glaring red notices of arrival on their documents.

As the children filed out of the station, the train also chugged away with a final ululation. The group must have walked for no longer than five minutes before hitching a virtually vacant bus bound for the nearest port. They settled in quite comfortably, and Silana found herself again in the company of Levi, the two effortlessly picking up the conversation from where they had left off. They took this opportunity to introduce themselves to their travel companions.

Levi's friends shared with Silana their journeys, which differed from Levi's. Fryderyk was from a wealthy Jewish family in town that Silana recognized from her mother's gossip sessions with her friends. Rysio too seemed quite pleasant. She met his sister, too—a beautiful blue-eyed girl named Sanja. They bonded over their shared love for the ice cream parlour in the city centre that they had frequented with friends. Silana tried to not let the memories of Sigrid and Anna cause her too much pain.

Silana noticed Sebastien and Sunne conversing with a few of the children and was glad that so far they had been able to maintain composure even under such severe circumstances. A very pale-looking Nidhi, who was seated beside the bus driver, was urging him to accelerate every few minutes, much to his annoyance. After a few minutes, Silana felt the bus shudder as they arrived at the port.

Nidhi lightly tapped each child's shoulder, as they disembarked, to take a headcount. Silana was able to get to her siblings and grasped her brother's hand, allowing him to pull her through. She thanked Nidhi, who smiled kindly and instructed them to go to the second gate.

'Stay close, everyone,' Nidhi instructed, her eyes scanning the group to ensure no one was missing. 'We're heading to the ferry terminal now. Keep your documents handy.'

The siblings wasted no time pulling their documents out from their bags and taking off down a boardwalk. Nidhi followed close behind them, having finished with her tally, while Roshan already stood near the ferry.

The ferry was an imposing sight, its hull painted a deep blue and its decks bustling with activity. Workers were loading cargo, and passengers were lining up to board. The ferry's horn blared, a deep, resonant sound that echoed across the port. The engines roared to life, and the ferry began to pull away from the dock, the water churning as it moved. Silana stood at the railing, watching as the city of Baku slowly receded into the distance.

When the ferry finally docked in Iran, the harbour was a hive of activity, with ships of all sizes docked along the piers, their masts reaching towards the sky. Nidhi and Roshan guided the group towards the waiting ship for their final leg of the journey. The anticipation was palpable among the children.

Silana looked up at the ship with a sense of recognition. The vessel had a sturdy, robust build, reminiscent of those her father used to transport essential cargo for his business. *So, that's how they're going to get us to Bombay.* She felt a pang of nostalgia but quickly pushed it aside. The sight of the ship confirmed their next step—they were truly on their way to India.

Silana knew the journey would be tedious and braced herself for it. But some part of her felt slightly more uneasy—a cocktail of nostalgia and another emotion she didn't wish to unpack. Looking back at the city's lights sparkling through the gloom like holes punctured in black paper, she had a feeling that this goodbye was more permanent than she was willing to admit.

Silana

Five days at sea felt endless for Silana, the time passing slowly as the gentle ocean breeze tousled her hair. The ship was scheduled to arrive in Bombay on the sixth day, and the children were buzzing with rumours and theories about what awaited them.

'I've heard we're going to be taken there on elephants!' said one of the girls, much to Nidhi's amusement. She allowed the discussion to continue for a while, enjoying the wild speculations.

'The Maharaja will be organizing your transport to the camps. Armed guards will escort you there.'

Silana wasn't quite sure how she felt about that. This initiative seemed oddly politicized and she dearly hoped that the Maharaja was not using them for some hidden agenda. Their journey had been harrowing enough, with constant rejections from countries unwilling to allow a boatful of Jewish refugees to dock at their ports, arguing that it would not bode well for their political ties. Silana had hoped they would be safe once in international waters but skimming across the vast, unfamiliar ocean had only heightened her fear. The journey, though arduous, had been made bearable by the people she undertook it with. Sanja...Levi and his friends...Silana had been pushed out of her comfort zone, leaving behind memories of her old life with Anna and

Sigrid, which now felt like a lifetime ago.

The afternoon sun was so hot it blurred the colours of the surrounding boats with the sparkling sea and the strip of land Silana had spotted.

Silana clung tightly to her siblings while they stood a little farther from the deck where the rest of the children had gathered. She was yet to process that this was to be their home until the war ended and their father came back to his senses. As much as she tried to convince herself otherwise, the emptiness caused by the disappearance of Yvonne extinguished any hope of reuniting with their father or returning to their old life in Poland.

The captain announced that they would be docking in a lesser-known port to avoid scrutiny by the British. Bombay was a hotspot of British interference; however, the Maharaja's contacts at the docks would be able to divert any such unwanted attention. The children would once again be split into two groups and then taken to their final destination.

'It has been an honour and a pleasure to assist you on this journey. I wish you all lasting health, safety and peace,' the captain said.

It was peak afternoon when the boat finally bumped against the dock, startling a half-asleep Silana. The children weren't given a chance to greet the armed men who quickly ushered them into lorries, which had large black words painted on either side of them in a language Silana didn't recognize. Ten children were loaded into each lorry and informed that they would be taking bathroom breaks every 90 minutes. They would spend the night in an army camp en route to Balganga and leave at first light in order to arrive at the camp around noon the next day.

Nidhi, once more in Silana's group, translated the driver's instructions. The guards sat in the front of the vehicle as the lorry jerked its way across Bombay's roads.

While Sunne slept with her head on her sister's shoulder, Silana mulled over how little time she had spent alone since leaving Aunty Ilse. Despite being surrounded by wonderful people and witnessing the breakdown of social barriers among children from different classes, she felt increasingly drained with each passing day. Initially, she chalked up these bouts of fatigue to nothing more than homesickness, but after sharing her thoughts with Sanja, they concluded it was the constant stimulation—physical, visual and emotional.

'How long will it take us to reach Balganga?'

'The driver said we will travel for approximately five hours today before resting for the night, and then for another five hours tomorrow, maybe more.'

Silana took that as a cue to try and squeeze in as much rest as possible, convincing herself it would make the journey quicker. After persuading Sebastien to do the same, Silana positioned her travel bag as a makeshift pillow and slept for the first half of their journey, waking only when they arrived at their overnight stop.

At the army base, Nidhi and Roshan rested in the commander's quarters while the children were made to share bunks. Silana, too drowsy to seek out or converse with her friends, fell asleep quickly and only fully woke early the next morning when a blaring bugle jolted her awake. After a quick breakfast, Nidhi introduced the group to some of the army officials—Colonel Vijay Singh and decorated officers Aman Sahay, Munna Singh and Aakash Verma. As they boarded the lorry again, the conversation between the children and the officers continued for the entirety of their journey—Nidhi acting as the translator. The officers, who were seated beside the driver, spoke through an open slit that could be latched from the driver's area, discussing a variety of topics—sports, the local cuisine and the Maharaja himself.

'He has two beautiful young daughters, one of whom is set to reign, and the other pursuing some field of education,' one of the officers shared, prompting a buzz of chatter.

'She is apparently quite the princess.'

The conversation veered towards camp activities.

'We know that the children there play football. We also join them sometimes.'

'Aman, football ko chodo (forget about football). We should teach them kabaddi instead!'

'What's that?' one of the smaller boys piped up.

Suddenly, Silana realized how filthy they all were. She had washed her clothes in questionable conditions on the ship. The water they had bathed with at the base yesterday had felt like icicles piercing her steadily browning skin. This prompted one of the more pertinent questions, 'Can we freshen up once we reach?'

'Yes. Once you've cleaned up, the Maharaja would like to dine with you all.'

Silana suggested they give Nidhi a break from the unrelenting translation. She had been speaking for a few hours already, which no one really seemed to notice. As the conversations piped down, Nidhi flashed Silana a grateful smile. With her siblings fast asleep, Silana resorted to re-reading one of the three books she had carried for the journey. She had read each of them countless times, and took her time to decide which to read by skimming her fingers across their crinkly spines and pulling out the one that felt right. She flicked open the page, the words of the first chapter practically ingrained in her memory. She was nearing the end of the book, just two chapters shy, when the lorry began slowing down in front of expansive, pearly gates. The children were shaken awake and scrambled to collect their hats, coats and bags. They had disposed of their travel documents upon arriving in Bombay—Silana was certain she would have misplaced them by now.

The lorry rumbled further into the compound before stopping in front of the palace's entrance, and the children clambered out, talking amongst themselves excitedly. Silana saw two important-looking individuals standing at the base of the stairs leading inside the palace, surrounded by staff—a beautiful, elegantly dressed woman adorned in sparkling jewellery and an older-looking man with an unexpected air of authority and goodness.

The man, probably the Maharaja, wore a headpiece unlike anything Silana had ever seen before and clothes that gleamed with various colours in the afternoon sun. Upon moving closer, Silana couldn't help but notice the wide, sparkling, kohl-lined eyes of the elegantly dressed woman—they were an identical hue of green to Sunne's. She introduced herself as Tanisha and spoke decent Polish with a rich accent. Tanisha explained that she was the younger daughter of the Maharaja and that the entire kingdom had been eager to welcome the children. She explained that she and her sister knew a substantial amount of Polish and would act as translators between them and the palace officials.

Although the children weren't able to understand Hindi, they were silenced by the Maharaja's rich baritone. He expressed the same sentiment as his daughter, adding, 'I know you have come from Poland, and will always be Polish natives. But as long as you are here, you all are Bramsadhans. We shall make our full effort to protect you and facilitate your return, if you so choose, to Poland once this violence has ended, giving way to peace.'

Tara

The final batch of children had arrived by the time Tara finished teaching her classes for the day. She would have liked to meet them, but duty called in the guise of another suitor. She was beyond frustrated by the fact that she had to get married in order to attain the throne, finding it a colossal waste of her time. However, her father had not been in the best of spirits lately. Although hesitant to show it, he was considerably burdened by the prospect of his activities being discovered by the British.

A representative of a neighbouring kingdom was coming to meet after lunch to discuss the potential union of the two kingdoms through matrimony. The princess was apprehensive about meeting a representative instead of the prince himself. Her suitor was apparently caught up in some pressing affair and was thus sending an emissary to meet with the council instead. *What a lovely precedent it set indeed.*

But Tara was well past the optimal age of marriage and her father was growing steadily impatient. Her purpose in life was to ensure her father's happiness, even if it was at the expense of her own. She had confided this to the ever-attentive Colonel Vijay Singh. Over the months, the frequency of their interactions had skyrocketed, and their friendship had blossomed. However, being a princess, her commitments were pre-ordained. She couldn't let her father find out about their late-night walks or the lunches.

Tanisha had passed comments about her sister's recent lack of apathy towards the idea of marriage. 'Are you finally coming around to the idea of a suitor? Have you already found one?' she teased.

Tara hadn't denied it—her sister wasn't entirely wrong.

Her lunch was a 10-minute rush job of clearing a plate of daal chawal before hurrying to the great hall where her father, his council and an ancient-looking emissary were already in discussion. Tara quickly bowed, greeting the man, and sat down beside her father. The courtier didn't even bother to explain the situation to Tara, continuing, '...and he commands a mighty army and wealth beyond measure. We are also on very good terms with the British. You see, we are possibly the most attractive option you have now, considering the restraints on your time.'

'Restraints on our time? What kind?'

The courtier looked quite offended that the princess had spoken to him so directly. 'From what our King has been made aware of, the British have threatened your father with annexation, should a matrimonial alliance not come to fruition.'

Tara was aghast. 'Annexation? That couldn't possibly be true. We have been informed of no such threat.'

'You'll be quite surprised to find that you have, Princess,' he spat out her title. 'Might I remind you of the festering protests? The British are cracking down on...ahem...disloyal ruling sectors. They've offered us a tremendous amount of compensation to respond to these protests as we deem fit.'

Tara couldn't believe this ancient fossil was trying to threaten her into an accord. She looked to her father, eyes widening in confusion, wondering how he could tolerate such an insult—that too on his turf. Her father put a hand on hers. 'I am well aware of our situation, Minister. I would be pleased to introduce my daughter to Prince Mahadev Jethi, so long he decides to grace us with his presence.'

Though the dynamic between the two men was clearly established, her father had a knack for politely snubbing officials.

'Very well. I shall make arrangements for the prince to come and see Her Highness at the earliest.'

They argued over some logistics of the 'exchange' before the minister gave a shallow bow and saw himself out. Tara followed shortly behind, despite her father's exhortations to stay. There was nothing to discuss.

Teaching the children had been her sweetest escape. She'd even somehow grown to tolerate their smell. Sure, Tara could never have imagined that her teaching endeavours would involve copious investments in earplugs and clothing better suited for peasants, but she loved every second of it, even growing to feel affection for a few of the rats. And Vijay—what would she tell the warm-hearted colonel? She was not a diplomatic tool to be exchanged.

Her sister tried to sympathize with her. 'You have the perk of ruling two kingdoms...You've always known that it would come at a cost. You can't blame Papa for trying his best to prepare you.'

God, how she hated it when her sister spoke sense. 'There's tension brewing here and in the neighbouring kingdoms. Aarti told me the citizens are campaigning for the British to leave India.'

'More protests? These have never come to any sort of fruition. They won't last very long.'

'Aarti seems to hold out quite some hope this time.'

'Too much hope is never a good thing. Disappointment almost always follows.'

'On the contrary, it wards off bad tides.'

'I've hoped that some force of nature would make these protests disappear, but no luck so far. Just unending, entirely expected disappointment.'

'I'm sure not all of these potential suitors are the antichrists you make them out to be. Rumours have been circling about you and some fetching colonel strolling in the garden at ungodly hours.'

Tara stiffened. 'Any conversations I have with him are strictly professional...about the children. He's been telling me how they want more time outdoors, and I've just been trying to manage that.'

'All right, no need to get defensive. I reckon you've come up with some fabulous ideas with all the time you've spent together. Care to tell me about a few of them?'

Silence.

'Really, Didi, no need to lie.'

'Tani, it's really not your place to question me; I'm still your older sister.'

'You're right. It isn't my place. All I want is for you to be careful. I know it may feel like Papa's doing nothing but pressuring you when it comes to this suitor business, but I can assure you there are more forces at play here. Don't rush…the decision is important, and I agree with your philosophy of finding someone respectable. But do try to do it before we all die of old age.'

'I'm trying. I really am. The suitor today didn't even come to meet me himself; he sent some elderly minister of his instead.'

'And was he any good?'

'The fact that you would ask that is entirely blasphemous. He looked as old as this palace.'

'Well, at least he has life experience!'

'You're evil.'

'Quite admittedly. Should I call for some chai?'

Their conversation covered a wide range of topics—the children, their latest activities, the weather, Tanisha's degree, their father and back to the children.

'I've been trying to organize that excursion to the stream, but some diplomat or the other always seems to want to visit us.'

'Don't worry too much about that. Something will come up and we'll be able to sneak them to the stream for at least an hour.'

'At least their morale is high. I wouldn't be able to see anything good in life if I'd lost everything.'

'They may have lost everything but they are grateful to be alive. That is where their happiness lies.'

'I really wonder why it's going to be me ruling this kingdom instead of you,' Tara joked.

'Well, for starters, you do have plentiful life experience.'

'You're more of a child than Rafal is.'

'I'll take that as a compliment. The boy is wiser than the both of us.'

The princesses' back and forth lasted as long as the afternoon sun. Tara's classes had exhausted her entirely, and it was only Wednesday. She had to draft lesson plans for the rest of the week and the next because they were returning to Bramsadha over the weekend to attend to some duties. Though Tara had started tolerating the children, she was relieved to be going back home. She missed not having to scream to alert Aarti about spiders nestled beneath her sheets in the middle of the night and her spacious room at the main palace. Not to mention she'd been away so long, the court ladies would have to keep her at the central palace for another aeon to update her on all the latest clandestine affairs. They'd also press her endlessly about her absence from court.

Tara wasn't one to keep secrets. But she was quite inclined towards breaking that rule this time—the fate of the throne depended upon it. Those frivolous ladies of the court were not beneath spreading any and all snippets of gossip told to them by the future queen, even if it compromised their own titles. It was all about the attention. She expressed these concerns to Vijay that evening during their walk. 'They are all below me, in rank and in intellect, and what they think of either me or my absence should not matter. Yet, for some inexplicable reason, I feel the need to be relatable and please their insatiable thirst for entertainment at the expense of another's privacy.'

He nodded. The colonel would never interject when Tara vented to him, until she began searching his expression for some form of a reaction.

'Humouring them isn't understandable to me. From what I can tell, you seem to you seem to be considerably headstrong. Look at how you handle those children; why not channel that around these women?'

'That's a lot easier said than done.'

'I don't think so.'

Tara hated being surrounded by such stubborn people. 'In any case, Tani and I may have figured out a few more events for the children. I'm yet to meet the newcomers, which I shall before I leave for Bramsadha. I have to organize their schedule, seating…we need a bigger classroom—sometimes dealing with all this is utter madness. We may even have to build an entirely new dorm to accommodate them. Tani informed me their accommodation is approximately two to a bunk bed right now.'

'Have you conveyed all of this to your father?'

'We're not exactly on the best of terms right now. It's…complicated. The entire suitor business has made him extremely anxious and detached from me. I'm certain he sees me as the root of all the problems and wants to marry me off at the earliest.'

'I doubt that is true. Your father is nothing but concerned for you. You're his daughter.'

'The only true daughter of his is our kingdom.'

The colonel went silent.

'With all these protests against the British, I'm not sure that either this kingdom or the one I marry into will last very long.'

Silana

On their first day at the camp, Silana found herself in an entirely new world. Each child she spoke to had fled from similar circumstances, but each one had a different story to tell. While Silana and her sister had no problem making friends, Sebastien had been oddly quiet ever since they had left Poland. She attributed it to homesickness, though her brother wasn't the type to be reclusive around strangers, especially those his age.

Lunch with the Maharaja had been an overwhelming affair. The Maharaja and Tanisha sat at the head of the table, smiling and conversing in that unfamiliar and melodious language, which Silana could discern on rare occasions, owing to the noise pollution surrounding her. The new batch was introducing themselves to the old ones over the din of the usual affairs of a meal. 'Give the jug to the boy on the left...No, not your left, my left.'

The meal itself was richer than Silana expected, with a mild infusion of spices and an assortment of chapattis and rice that treated her taste buds to a delightful dance of flavours. She asked a very loud girl sitting next to her, who introduced herself as Aneta, what the days here looked like.

'Well, we usually have classes for around five hours. They've divided us into different age groups. The elder princess teaches maths and Polish history. Oh, and both the princesses speak Polish as well!'

'They mustn't have much to do then, do they?'

Aneta laughed, humouring Silana's off-handed comment. 'Perhaps not. Come, I'll take you to the cabins; you can share my bunk. From what I've heard, there's not enough space now, so the Maharaja will be building another cabin!'

The cabins were much less extravagant than Silana had expected, even though Nidhi had mentally prepared them for what to expect when Silana had asked how many girls to a room there would be. Luckily, Silana had already begun establishing a good rapport with most of her camp-mates.

'Your bag is quite small. It might be a tight fit with the two of us, but I'm sure we'll manage. The bathroom is at the other end of the cabins,' Aneta told Silana.

Sunne was similarly receiving orientation from a girl around her age. Silana looked on proudly as Sunne organized her belongings in the little space she was allotted. The cabin was soon swarming with girls, prompting Aneta and a few other girls to take Silana and Sunne to a more peaceful and secluded sitting area beneath a tree. The girls briefed the sisters about what a typical day at their camp looked like—from the classes and activities to the group dynamics of the camp.

The tree they were seated under invoked a distant memory in Silana, of her and Sigrid and Anna sitting under a similar one during lunch, having similar conversations about their peers. Its branches hung low and whispered in her ears the same song she had heard long ago in her homeland. She didn't let either her homesickness or her worry about Sebastien's behaviour dull her interactions with the girls.

The infinite blue sky slowly darkened as the sisters became engrossed in their own sphere of conversation.

'You are supposed to meet the elder princess this evening. We think she was a bit apprehensive of us all at the start, but she's come around. Tanisha is beautiful but I wouldn't be able to tell she was a princess from a distance. With this one, you can tell.'

'She teaches maths and history?'

'Not us, the older ones. She's far too busy to devote all her time to teaching all of us. We're expected to study from the few textbooks they've given us.'

'You all share the books?'

'Yes, for now. The Maharaja is trying to get more supplies.'

One of Aneta's friends interjected, 'But he's being discreet about it. Too many stationary supplies like pencils, paper or books may raise suspicion. According to a guard I spoke to, the British aren't supposed to know about us.'

Just as Silana was about to ask a follow-up question, the group was interrupted by a frantic girl running towards them, red-faced and proclaiming she had important news. 'The princess just arrived at the cabin; she wants to meet all the new girls. Nidhi sent me to fetch all of you.'

They scurried back to where the princess was greeting the girls, seated in the sitting area outside the cabin, which had makeshift wooden chairs, tables and miscellaneous furniture. Silana had never been as mesmerized by a woman before—the fact that this woman in plain traditional clothing, conversing in soft Polish with all the girls, was a princess was evident. Her collected demeanour and tangible grace gave her away. Edging closer to her, clutching Sunne's hand, Silana could discern some snippets of the conversation the princess was having. It was mainly about the food that day, if any changes could be made to the accommodation, the activities and such. Silana noticed that her voice was slightly raised, an oddity that the untrained ear would have dismissed. She had probably trained it all her life to be soft and appealing, but that training of hers was in direct contradiction to her new reality. In the chaos, Silana had been pushed up to the front and somehow found herself standing in front of the princess.

'I'm Tara. What's your name?'

'Your Highness—'

'There's no need for any of that. I am a citizen of Bramsadha just as you are.'

'I'm Silana.'

'That's a lovely name, Silana.'

The princess turned to greet Sunne as Silana replayed their conversation in her head. Tara, after shaking hands with a few more girls, announced she would be joining them for dinner.

'We understand the concerns of an influx of new members at the camp and are working to build a new cabin at the earliest. In the meanwhile, dinner is in an hour and I suggest you collate new activities you would like us to introduce. We will try and facilitate as many of those as possible.'

The Princess and her guards left the children to freshen up for dinner. The hour passed sooner than Silana expected, as they got ready and gossiped about the royals—Tara in particular.

'She seemed fairly put together, more so than her sister.'
'She's so beautiful...is she still unmarried at this age? She looks well into her 20s. I've been told royals here marry very young.'

The low-hanging branches of trees were adorned with beautiful decorations. As the twilight's scattered glow faded, the lanterns became the only source of light as a moonless night blanketed the camp. Tara's creative initiative with the decorations drew audible gasps and looks of awed wonder from the children. Meanwhile, Silana hunted for her brother in the group of boys streaming out of the boys' cabin, eventually finding him involved in whispered conversations with one of the older boys.

The princess was quieter this time around, focussing mostly on her food until she finished it. She then signalled for the children to tell her what they had come up with. All sorts of suggestions popped up—more sports, more lessons, more accommodation. Tara could only definitively promise the last one.

'Do you perhaps have musical instruments?' Silana blurted out over the chaos.

Tara scanned the girl's face, her brows furrowed. 'What do you play?'

'Piano,' Silana answered right away. *Father had been right; his piano lessons did come in handy.* 'What with all the sports and the lessons, I think it would be nice to have some creative outlets. Maybe we can try learning Indian traditional instruments if those are more readily available.'

'I could look into it. We could manage it but there

would have to be certain days and hours when you wouldn't be able to play. Additionally, we'd need to figure out where to store all of them…I'll talk to the Maharaja. In any case, you must come play the grand piano we have in the palace. It's languishing as a decorative piece, collecting dust. I hope you'll breathe a little magic back into its perpetual greyscale.' Tara raised her glass slightly in a mock toast.

Silana returned her soft smile, wondering if the princess truly meant any of what she said. If Silana had been in her position, she wouldn't exactly be open to a pungent, dishevelled child performing on the grand piano in her palace.

'Do you have any Indian instruments?'

'Yes, I play the sitar. My mother taught me how to when she was alive. We have an old one sitting unused in some storage room. I could show you how it is played, though I haven't played it in a while either.'

'What say we convince the Maharaja to have a musical day? You could play the sitar and I could play the piano for him.'

Their conversation seemed to have the impact of two flames merging together and burning twice as bright. Silana edged closer to Tara, speaking in excited Polish about her favourite classical composers for the rest of the dinner. No one had held a conversation with the princess for that long before.

'Are there many Indian composers?'

'A vast array, as precious to me as uncut diamonds. I don't suppose you know any of them. I suggest you play for my father and me tomorrow. Perhaps after lunch? We can schedule half an hour for you to practice.' Tara quickly wrapped up their conversation as dinner came to a close, the staff swooping in front of them to place large bowls filled with rasgullas on the table.

Silana, quite accidentally, had stuffed her face with the small desserts, resulting in the sugary syrup dribbling down her chin. She flailed about, trying both to clean it and reach for more at the same time.

'The key is to hold them above your mouth!' Tara giggled, watching her struggle.

As that night passed and Silana was squeezed in a bunk with Aneta, she had neither her mother nor her siblings on her mind but the conversation she had had with the princess and her promise.

Tara

'She's a bit funny-looking but seems quite respectful. She's of a higher social standing than most of the other children—I can tell from the accent,' Tara said to her sister. 'The children were very pleasant but so terribly loud. This girl sounded as frustrated as I did.'

'Do you remember her name?'

'No, but I remember her face. It shouldn't be that difficult to find out her name. I'll ask Aarti.'

'You've been raving about her yet failed to catch her name? That's such classic Tara behaviour.'

'At least I was invested enough in the conversation to remember it happened! That was one of the most constructive discussions I've had in a while.'

'I know this is an attack on me to learn classical music but I'm putting my foot down—I have absolutely no time for that.'

'But you have time to play in the mud with these... children?' Tara braced herself, glad she had caught the 'rats' comment in the nick of time.

'They enjoy that a lot more than classical compositions, Tara.'

'And you're supposed to be the intellectual, Tani.'

Nobody in the family would ever let Tanisha forget about her degree, referencing it whenever she acted out.

'She's to play the grand piano tomorrow.'

'And how exactly are you going to organize that?'

'That is my concern. With a few tweaks to my schedule, I could make it seem as though I'm the one practising the piano. We don't have any visitors I'm aware of tomorrow, though I'll check again with Papa.'

Tanisha nodded. 'I've never seen you take such a shine to any of the children before, apart from Rafal. But be very careful, Tara—don't jeopardize the safety of the rest of them for this.'

As morning came, so did a few British diplomats. The Maharaja murmured to his daughters how sick he was of hearing threats from this band of 'criminals'. He was hardly incorrect in this fervent sentiment of his as prissy, sour-looking officials began flooding the palace. Their conversations were the same repetitive ones that bored the princesses out of their minds—protests against the British, civil unrest, the war... the list was endless. They were only around for the sake of their duty to the throne, no matter how mind-numbing these discussions could be. As the minutes stretched into hours, Tara became antsy. She didn't want to miss her first class.

'The protests in your kingdom, of course, have been few and far in between. The neighbouring kingdom of Ganaka, though in good favour with the Crown, hasn't exactly had the same luck. The crackdowns on these protests haven't worked either.'

The Maharaja agreed. 'We cannot say we are very surprised, having spoken to their administration ourselves. Anshugava has proposed a union between my eldest daughter and their prince, but he was apparently caught in pressing royal affairs and couldn't undertake the short journey to meet his prospective queen.'

The diplomats looked at each other, but the Maharaja was far from done. 'They did inform us about how close their relationship was with the Crown and how the union would help further our territory and our wealth. Has the administration of Anshugava informed you of this proposed alliance?'

Tara couldn't help but smile—she loved this side of her father.

'We were not informed of this administrative decision. It's a good thing you put off the union; Anshugava is not nearly as prosperous as it makes itself out to be. We are connected to it as intimately as you, so their alleged "close connection" to the Crown consists of nothing but base-level diplomacy.'

Tara was so greatly relieved at what a large bullet—nay, missile—she had dodged.

Another diplomat backed the first one. 'Forging this matrimonial union would also mean taking on the responsibility for dealing with protests and their repercussions—not to mention the inevitable spill of rebellion into your territory. We'd advise you not to muddle up your politics and are glad you waited to consult the Crown first.'

The Maharaja nodded.

Finally, this conversation had something worth paying attention to. He was almost always blaming Tara for the failure of marriage alliances; even these prissy British people were taking her side. The absence of chivalrous princes was hardly her responsibility. Perhaps these diplomats could, for a change, consider the possibility of her managing the kingdom until she found a suitor.

'Though this proposal for a union has not been successful, it is imperative that the Princess finds another prince willing to marry her. She is already well past marriageable age. We can acquaint you with a few kingdoms that are reasonably wealthy and connected. Bramsadha is one of the largest kingdoms in the state and we cannot leave it under incapable management for long. At this stage, annexation should be your greatest concern.'

Incapable? Annexation? Tara flared with both anger and shame, and she felt herself turning scarlet. Luckily, a diplomat decided to further the conversation before she could say something rash.

'We would like to maintain our relationship with Bramsadha. The protests will certainly reach your kingdom at some point. Containing those hooligans is extremely difficult, as we have experienced and you have been made aware. The Crown would like to therefore extend its full support to Bramsadha, in return for a few minute favours. Our administration has devised a very comprehensive strategy.'

Tara almost fell to the floor. *More diplomacy?* These diplomats, with their noses in the air, chattered in their ever-so-posh accent for the next two hours. It would have been more feasible to turn this encounter into a mealtime affair.

By the time the officials bid them goodbye, Tara had already missed her first two classes. She quickly changed from her regal attire into her teaching clothes, slung a bag of books on to her shoulder and hurried to the classroom. But she didn't run. Princesses never ran. What if she tripped and fell? That would be considered most disgraceful.

Tara was out of breath by the time she reached the classroom, having missed three of her classes. She had a 10-minute gap before her next one, which she used to catch her breath and explain where she had been to the children. She was glad that she had to teach only one class that day—she couldn't cope with the stress of finding a suitor, the inability to confide in anyone and the children's lack of comprehension of the maths she was desperately trying to explain. *Perhaps she truly was 'incapable' if she couldn't even handle teaching a class of mere children.*

Finally, Tara's sweet release from the day's scorching sun and the endless questions of children who had somehow misunderstood basic algebraic addition arrived in the guise of a servant calling the children for lunch. Tara wiped her frenzied attempt at introducing brackets to the children off a large blackboard, the entire dusting process taking as long as it took for the children to gather their things and leave. Usually around this time the colonel would stop by the makeshift classroom to greet the princess, and a familiar cycle of her either griping about the children or the heat and his words of comfort, serving as reminders of why she was helping them in the first place, would begin. They would then agree to continue their discussion further at some later hour. But for the past week, Colonel Singh had been required to return to the main base in Bramsadha to be briefed about the recent protests and their potential ramifications.

Servants coming in to clean the room offered to help the

princess with her half-hearted attempt to shove the lesson books in her bag but she waved them away. Just as Tara left the classroom, bidding goodbye to the scattered groups of children and began trudging her way back to the solace of her room, a tap on the shoulder caught her attention. A familiar-looking girl flashed a hesitant smile at her.

'I'm Silana. We spoke during dinner...about the piano?'

'Yes, I was just coming to talk to you about that!' Tara lied. 'Unfortunately, there have been a few administrative issues and we're going to be expecting some British diplomats over this weekend. Also, I'm going to the main palace tomorrow.'

'Main palace?' the girl asked, seemingly in awe of the prospect that this was merely their secondary home.

'There's a lot to explain; I'll organize the piano for you once I return.'

Silana nodded and thanked her profusely. The princess spoke with some staff members before leaving to check on the children's activities and food. She also consulted a few teachers to ensure the children's academics were up to par. Her father had put her in charge of a tight schedule and she was determined not to fall behind in the one aspect of all this chaos she was supposedly good at—ensuring order.

Packing for Bramsadha was initially quite a private affair for Tara for a change. Aarti, who had tried to help the Princess fold clothes, was dismissed after teaching the girl the basics of packing. Tara managed to fill the suitcase halfway before giving up and begging Aarti to finish sorting out the mess she had made. Usually, seeing Aarti pack her stuff awakened a sense of return to civilization in Tara, filling her with enthusiasm. This time, however, she experienced no such excitement. Leaving Aarti to curse at the pile of outfits, Tara picked up a book from the palace library and sat on a rooftop swing that overlooked the garden, wondering if it was just fatigue or something else that contributed to her lack of enthusiasm. As she flipped through the yellowed pages of her novel, she found herself unable to focus, the words steadily blurring together. Going back to her 'real' home didn't truly feel as real as it used to any more.

Silana

The days at the camp passed slowly, each one dragging more than the last. Silana found herself caught in a routine of sorts—drawing daisies in the margins of her books during class, eating lunch and dinner with her friends or circling the camps and sitting under Aneta's tree as the afternoon turned into a dusky evening. Silana was no stranger to routine and she settled in quite easily. She, Sunne and Sanja had formed a coalition of sorts; though they had branched out and acquainted themselves with the rest of their peers, they always had each other to fall back on.

Silana had at first found it relatively simple to introduce herself to the other residents of the camp. As she made more friends, she felt little need to put in any more effort to socialize, perfectly content to have a good rapport with 10–15 girls and a few boys. However, Silana began to feel increasingly drained each morning and she couldn't understand why. She tried to put on a brave face for Sunne but often woke up in a cold sweat at odd hours of the night, haunted by terrors of a past she tried desperately to forget and, perhaps, change. Her nightmare usually involved her siblings and their mother running from a demon—their Father. After this red-eyed reaper swallowed Yvonne Haydn, he would drag her children back to Poland, banishing them to Tartarus for sharing her blood. Silana yearned for nothing more than this creature's redemption.

Sunne often talked about their mother—during meals or when the girls sat together knitting under woolly clouds. They would talk about reuniting with her, even though Silana saw these conversations as futile, preferring to distract herself and her sister by joining some of their peers to spot varieties of parrots and flightless fledgling pigeons the boys had found. Despite the servants' warnings about handling fledglings, the children continued to play with them, finding joy in their innocence.

Another aspect of the camp was very successful in distracting the girls from their situation. The Maharaja could only give a few textbooks to each batch of children as the risk of getting caught by some British patrol with a truckload of them was too high. The Maharaja had these books specially imported from Poland, disguised in shipments of copper wire and then delivered to the camp.

Silana, at 15, was among the older children at the camp. She and others her age would work late into the night to handwrite copies of these textbooks, the Maharaja applauding this initiative by providing the best-quality pens to support their endeavour.

Outside of their routine, Silana would go on quests to find her brother, who would be either invested in some inane football game with his peers or off somewhere in the surrounding forest, away from the familiarity of the camp but always in its proximity. She grew more and more frustrated with Sebastien. Every time she would manage to catch him, he would make some feeble excuse and scurry away. This left Silana to deal with Sunne's fantasies of reuniting with their parents after the war. Silana hated it when her own dreams were spoken out loud—somehow that made them seem even more impossible. She had never wanted to oust her mother from her mind but only distance her memory till she was equipped to deal with the grief that came from losing her. But her sister wouldn't even allow her that solace. She felt a growing void inside her that steadily began to expand into a cold realization. She and her siblings had nothing waiting for them back 'home' in Poland. Silana wasn't pleased to be saddled with the responsibility of Sunne while Seb indulged in whatever whims struck his fancy.

Tara had long returned from her weekend excursion to Bramsadha and joined the children for meals. With no conceivable prospect of being able to play the piano, it had quite slipped Silana's mind until Tara sought her out after class one day.

'Silana, yes?'

'Yes, Your Highness.'

'Please, like I've said, there is no need for that. Tara, if you please.'

Silana nodded.

'We, fortunately, don't have any visitors today. I'd like to offer you an opportunity to play something on the piano.'

Silana found herself in seventh heaven and practically skipped to the palace, the anxiety of playing for royalty only enveloping her once she encountered the grandeur of the claviature and the hall. The last time Silana had practised seemed like generations ago—the day before they had left their father and his house in Poland for good. She had finished learning a piece a few weeks prior to that day, intending it to be a gift for her mother. Silana began to play Chopin's 'Nocturne' in E flat major. The gentle notes of the piece filled the hall, quieting Tara and the Maharaja. Silana poured not just her passion into it, but her mother's too, as she played the piece with a steady memory of its notes, evoking the essence of Poland through the sound. In no time, she had reached the bridge of the music, her hands fusing with the piano's ivories as she let them guide her towards the end of the piece. Though the piece was around five minutes long, Silana felt as though she had been sitting there only for a moment before she finished with a flourish, lifting her hands as she pressed the pedal, pausing only to acknowledge the polite applause she received after her final note resonated in the room. Silana was surprised at her muscle memory, considering it was such a fresh piece and she hadn't had a chance to practice it in ages.

'My dear, why didn't you tell us you were this talented?'

Silana was beyond flustered—the Maharaja was speaking directly to her. She hadn't smiled as wide as this in weeks.

The Maharaja continued, 'My family and I have been ardent patrons of the arts. Though you may not have the opportunity to play here every day, my girl, I will personally ensure you can take advantage of every free moment at your disposal. Such raw talent cannot be allowed to waste away. Tell me, for how long have you been playing?'

'Around seven years.'

'If you provide me with the names of the books you'd like to learn from, I will arrange for them at the earliest.'

Silana profusely expressed her gratitude as the Maharaja

left her with the princess, citing some urgent work.

'That was "Nocturne", wasn't it?'

'Yes, yes it was. Did you enjoy it?'

'Thoroughly. My mother used to play it and tried teaching it to me. I always cited I was too young and weaponized that excuse to force her to continue playing it for me.'

'My mother has always loved classical music too.'

'Seven years…That's quite a long time to be playing. Do you know "Claire de Lune"?'

'Very well. It was actually one of the first advanced pieces I learnt and it was…a terrible struggle. It took me a while to perfect but was worth every hour I spent practising.'

The princess chuckled. 'When I was young, my mother used to play it for me. Apparently, that was one of the only times I wasn't yanking out her hair or doing something similarly destructive. She passed away a few years ago… Silana, it would mean the world to me if you could play it in her memory.'

Tara

'...and then I bothered her to play a few more pieces she knew, because her "Clair de Lune" almost had me in tears. Tani, I may not listen to classical music daily, but she is one of the best—a most passionate player. At such a young age, too! You should have seen how effortless it was for her. Frankly, even I was motivated to try, though it was complete and utter gibberish. I have no idea how she did it.'

Tara and Tanisha strolled through the garden, stopping intermittently to admire the flowers scattered among the lush green leaves as they conversed.

'I wonder why you've suddenly taken an interest in these children. You seemed least bothered by them before, if not finding them downright hateful.'

'Hate is a very strong word, Tani,' Tara lectured, even after realizing long ago that her words had no effect on Tanisha's practically non-existent filter.

'At one point, you ran out of species of insect to compare them to.'

'It was never hate...merely a very strong dislike.'

'I do have a theory as to why you've become so obsessed with helping them, though.'

'Two things—obsession is quite extreme. Spending a few hours teaching them history and maths in the morning does not qualify as obsession, just charity. Second, as much as I wouldn't like to hear this theory of yours, I don't assume I have a choice in the matter.'

'In any case, my speculation is that the entire situation with the suitors and the responsibility of the kingdom is bothering you.'

'That theory is, expectedly, utter rubbish.'

'Is it? The fact that you, Princess Tara, will never have any agency in the say of either the happenings of the kingdom or these children does not bother you in the slightest?'

'I believe it was you who told me that this was my "destiny". I agree with your sentiment, though. I know I won't be a princess forever. Let me have some semblance of this "agency" while I still can.'

Tara called for all the teachers to convene before lunch the next day—she had an important proposition for all of them.

'The children are involved in all kinds of activities but a few of them have expressed to me that these have started to become repetitive.' She figured this introduction would have enough of a shock factor to retain their attention for a few minutes. 'Our students have a particular penchant for the arts, as I myself have grown to discover. They could perhaps delve into some cultural aspects of both India and Poland and prepare a performance of sorts for the Maharaja…a play by some Indian playwright or perhaps an epic could provide them some exposure to our culture.'

A curly-haired science teacher with moon-shaped glasses and an unusually high-pitched voice piped up. 'Your Highness, the idea is wonderful, but the other teachers and I believe that completing the syllabus in time and formulating some tests for the children is our foremost priority. Rehearsing for a play would significantly eat into our teaching time. The idea would have been most delightful otherwise.'

The other teachers murmured softly in agreement. Luckily, Tara was never one to rely on a standalone plan. Her other suggestion was less grand but equally meaningful. 'Yes, that is our utmost priority. In that case, would you rather that the palace organizes entirely optional Indian classical music lessons for the children? Procuring the instruments and teachers will not be a problem—we have palace musicians willing to teach the children. They can learn to play the sitar, tabla, flute, et cetera.'

'Has the Maharaja given this initiative the go-ahead, if it were to be made possible?'

'He is the one who suggested it.'

More murmurs. It was as if Tara were in a room filled with baritone crickets.

'We will need at least 10–15 children who are interested for this to become a reality. Rafal and Valery will certainly participate and so will Silana—I'll ask the three of them to draft a list of prospective participants by the end of this week.'

After she had dismissed the teachers and concluded the meeting, Tara went to the girls' cabin, where Silana sat talking to a pale, freckled girl with a brunette bob. Of course, the princess could have made the announcement right there and then, but she didn't want the children to feel obligated to join in order to impress or satisfy her. She conveyed the same to Silana outside the trilling of the cabin's high-pitched occupants.

'It's a wonderful idea.'

Wonderful. Tara swore she would kill someone if she heard that descriptor one more time.

'Have you considered the idea of including vocalists?'

'Yes, of course. Vocalists, percussion players, strings—as diverse as you children get. Also, if it isn't too much to ask, does spearheading this initiative alongside me sound interesting to you?'

'Yes, yes absolutely. I'll start sending out feelers among all of the different groups right away.'

'Actually, what I would suggest is waiting a few days before informing them. My father and I are still trying to manage the logistics of instruments, teachers and the like.'

'Absolutely. I'm very thankful to be a part of this.'

'We have managed a time slot for you to practise in the hall tomorrow evening. The lesson books should arrive by then as well.'

Tara left the girl to return to the excited chatter emanating from the cabin after asking her to alert Valery. One guard, who had made a dash to the boys' cabin upon the princess' request, came back with Rafal just as Valery also joined them. She hugged Valery and Rafal, which was a remarkable feat. The two children, having been central in integrating Tara more firmly into the community of children, had her eternal gratitude and acted as her informants. Every week, Tara would pull them both aside to ascertain the needs of the children and what she could do to further help them. The two were always willing to help her, Valery usually rattling off as soon as she had the opportunity—'The girls have run out of yarn and we're quite short on needles, so a bit of sewing equipment is in order, if you please. And what's this about a new cabin? Are you making one for the girls as well? If so, we would be terribly grateful.'

Tara raised her hands in a mock demonstration of being overwhelmed, smiling to put the girl at ease. 'Slowly... carefully. My Polish is good but not as good as yours.'

Valery agreed to slow her pace, but only slightly.

'What is this about yarn, now?'

'The girls pass their free time knitting and we are quite short of the stuff.'

'Duly noted.'

'Oh, and these boys in our camp now have a penchant for rescuing injured birds. We've been building makeshift cages of grass and weeds, but the birds are clever and manage to find weak points from which they slip out and then die because they cannot fend for themselves. Could you organize a birdcage for us, preferably more than one?'

'I will run this by the Maharaja, but I see no reason for him to reply in the negative.'

Valery smiled, nudging Rafal, who smiled for the briefest of moments. The boy was seven, yet stoic as a fossil.

'Rafal, do you have anything to tell me regarding any concerns your camp-mates have?'

He didn't seem to be in a particularly talkative mood that day, as indicated by the slight lowering of his head. Tara took the hint, patted his back and thanked him for his input. Rafal nodded in thanks, locked eyes with her for the briefest second, before breaking away and gazing at the grass.

Tara then decided to tell Valery and Rafal of her plan. 'If you could ask the children, not outright, mind you, if they would be interested to form a music club and give me a list of names, I would be most grateful.'

'Rafal can play the harp! He told me so, just a week ago!'

Tara pondered for a minute. 'We don't have a harp here, but I could arrange for it to be brought here from Bramsadha. Would you play for us, Rafal? I will be most grateful.'

The boy nodded his head, still looking at the grass. The gratitude could not have been more implicit but Tara knew he truly meant it. Valery continued, 'I can play the flute, you know! I played it for three years before the war. I was quite good—my teacher said he'd never had a better student! I would be very excited to play for you!'

'I'm holding you both to this. Before the week is over, you shall have your instruments and I shall have my music.'

Silana

Silana had waited more than two weeks for her instrument to arrive, doing a not-quite-decent job of hiding her anxiety. Her mother's shadowy figure still hovered somewhere in the background of her consciousness, unsettled by the music's familiarity. Tara, 17 days after her initial proposition regarding the instruments—Silana had counted the days by marking her blue handkerchief with red stitches—approached her before classes to inform Silana that all of the instruments would be arriving by the afternoon.

'We're trying to schedule times when you children can group together and learn—I've organized a piano, harp, tabla and two flutes. The sitars we have will be played by the court musicians themselves.'

'Before we even think of practising together, we need to become familiar with our instruments. Since you've organized for five children to perform, could you perhaps devise a system so that we each can practise for an hour a day? The others have portable instruments so I'd imagine it would be easier for them to conceal them.'

'Yes. My father has proposed a wonderful idea—we can scrounge for a secluded room in the upper wing of the palace, small enough to soundproof quickly yet feasible enough for you to use for practising. The court musicians are willing to volunteer their time to teach you all.'

'I have a few concerns...the only one this endeavour actually benefits are the children directly involved and not those who didn't have access to instruments growing up or others who aren't musically inclined.'

'What are you suggesting?'

'That we don't stop at this initiative. It's beneficial for those taking part—don't get me wrong—but the rest of the children could feel a bit sidelined.' Silana wasn't sure of the reaction she was going to get as the princess squinted at her with no hint of a smile on her face. Perhaps Silana had indeed asked for too much this time around.

'That seems fair. Tani and I will brainstorm ideas, as should you too. You must be getting late for your class. Run along.'

Silana fled to the classroom, heart racing. Her first class was maths and their agenda for the day was to self-study. It took up 40 minutes of the hour-long session; Silana spent the remaining 20 minutes sharing her concerns about Sebastien with Levi. She discussed his catatonia and unwillingness to interact with either of his sisters, angry at the fact her brother was disobeying their mother's only wish to 'stick together, be a unit'.

Levi explained, 'Your brother managed to make a few friends at first, including me. But just as he began to settle into the camp and make viable friendships, he detached from everyone. It wasn't an overnight affair, though.'

That last part made Silana feel entirely selfish. 'I'm a terrible sister,' she groaned, burying her head further into the well of darkness and covering her ears. She had no idea what her brother was going through, but would have to figure out a way to resuscitate him from his apathy. Drawing from her own experience at the camp, she remembered what had brought her out of the same pit—music. Silana suddenly lifted her head, looking straight at Levi. 'I'll play him music!'

'Is that how you're planning to go about this?'

'Absolutely. I have full faith. Oh, speaking of music…' Silana stole a glance at the clock; three minutes remaining. She explained her plan of starting a music club to Levi, and the involvement of the members of the camp. 'We're seeing how this batch plays out. If all goes according to plan, perhaps we can recruit five more band members and practise in rotation.'

'The idea is heartening but the scope for it is so limited.'

'If you have any inspiring ideas that involve a lot more people, I'd like to be the first to hear them.'

'If I manage to get a word in edgewise next time.'

Silana rolled her eyes. 'Not that you have many interesting things to say.'

'I may not be a musician but that gives you no right to have a superiority complex.'

'Of course it does. Piano is an art—both performance and academic.'

'I could learn it if I really wanted to.'

'Note that I said "performance" art—as in you'll have to play for a crowd. With that haircut, they won't let you anywhere near a concert hall, let alone a piano.'

'You've been waiting all day to mock it, haven't you?'

'How could I not? It's somehow growing…upwards.'

As the class ended, Silana and Levi gathered their belongings and walked in the direction of the eating area together.

'I'm going to play the piano this afternoon. I'll take him with me. This idea is a reach but it's better than nothing.'

'I must hear you play one of these days.'

'I assume you have nothing better to do today.'

'Ah, but this is your moment with your brother. The last thing I'd want is to intrude. Perhaps next time.'

The pair broke off, diverging to head back to their cabins, as they always did, to deposit their books. Silana told a few girls and Sunne of her plan during lunchtime.

'I'd love to come. Being there might jog any memory he has left,' said Sunne.

'God, you're dramatic, Sunne. He's not that far gone.'

Silana tried not to pay much heed to her sister's words but she did indeed see some frightening truth embedded in them. Time couldn't have dragged out more; aeons of waiting and looking at the beige clock resulted in Sebastien's sisters practically dragging him inside the palace. Sebastien huffed all the way, only stopping his incessant groaning when they had reached their destination. A palace guard donning a voluminous red-plumed cap and a sparkling white uniform greeted them, informing them that he would be accompanying them to the hall. He escorted them through the back entrance of the palace into its west wing. Silana was quite familiar with the route now, telling her siblings that this was but the beginning of the grandeur. Even Sunne was spellbound by the palace's interior.

The guard allowed Sunne and Sebastien ample time to marvel at the opulence as they walked slowly towards the great hall.

Silana, meanwhile, was mentally preparing herself

for Sebastien's reaction. It was a good start, though—the architecture had evoked a dim flare of excitement in Sebastien, something his sisters had last seen in Poland. Upon reaching the hall, Sunne looked around, head tilted towards the ceiling, trying to take in all that the sweeping walls and beautiful engravings had to offer.

Silana's siblings sat not on the opulent couches 20 feet from the piano but cross-legged on the floor right in front of it. Silana began with the same passion she had channelled into her first rendition of 'Claire de Lune'. The music swelled once more in her mind as reality faded to black. Silana soon forgot who she was playing for, letting the music seep through her entire being and melt into the keys. Her applause was in the form of Sunne's widened eyes and a single tear that trailed down Sebastien's cheek. Silana had known not to expect a fairy-tale ending but was fortunate enough to be graced by it.

Tara

Of all the ways Tara thought her prospective husband may approach her, open threats were certainly not one she had considered.

The morning had been calm—she had taught only two classes and was quite looking forward to having the day to herself—it was entirely scheduled, of course. Allotted times for eating lunch, reading, painting, sleeping—the princess had her entire day planned out. Over the past few weeks, she had patiently taught the new cooks to make her lunches to perfection. They struggled to incorporate her many dietary requirements into her extravagant meal choices, but Tara personally overseeing their work indeed gave them some sort of incentive. She hadn't even gotten to the second bullet on her schedule—reading *Pride and Prejudice* for the 300th time—before Aarti skittered to her room to inform her of the arrival of her 'suitor'; he would be meeting her for the first time.

'I'll definitely need another few minutes to change my outfit. Can you stall?'

'Watch me.'

Tara didn't know what she would do without this woman's fierce devotion to her. Unfortunately for her, putting on an outfit while she was in a hurry proved to be quite difficult. Her limbs tangled in all sorts of places—the sleeves of the choli...the vast array of layers she was mandated to wear. Her hair was at the very least presentable, arranged in a bun that looked half decent when she placed a delicate tiara on her head. Seven minutes—that must be some sort of record.

Only her father was waiting inside the hall in the east wing when she arrived. The princess grinned as she sat down next to him; Aarti had pulled the same stunt that she did every time Tara needed time to get ready to meet visitors. The woman would take them to a wing opposite to the one they were actually supposed to go to, wander around with them for a bit and apologize for being too old to recall which wing was which before finally taking them to the right one. This strategy allowed Tara more than enough time to appear punctual.

'His portrait isn't quite as shabby as I expected. I do hope that this prince is more polite than the courtiers he keeps.'

'I hope so, too.'

The quiver in her father's voice betrayed him. She didn't have time to deduce what it may have meant before an entourage of about 15 people strode into the hall. Aarti was apologizing to one of them, who nodded dismissively. She looked at the princess, gave her a knowing wink and shuffled out of the hall as fast as she could. In the midst of this group, head sticking out above all the extravagant—and quite frankly, tacky—headpieces, was the tall prince whom Tara recognized from the portraits the palace had sent her. She got a better look at him as the prince and the minister sat down on the couch, with the rest of the troupe standing behind them. They were all unmoving, their eyes boring into her—Tara felt as though she was staring at an iteration of a royal painting come to life.

The Maharaja broke the ice-cold silence with an invitation to drink chai. No one even deigned to acknowledge the offer except the minister, who began, without any prompting, talking of marriage. Tara shifted her gaze towards her potential partner, who returned it. He was a carbon copy of the portrait…but his eyes…they were colder than those depicted in the rendering. They made all the difference to him, really. If only he had kinder eyes, maybe this would have been a bit easier. But that was hardly any valid reason to reject him.

'As we had previously discussed, a union between our kingdoms through matrimony would be quite crucial for both our kingdoms' futures. Historically, our administrations haven't always seen eye to eye, but—'

'Minister, it has been brought to my attention that your connections with the British are not as tight as you have made them out to be. The escalating riots and tension in your kingdom also, perhaps, may have slipped your mind while you were talking about your kingdom's vast array of wealth.'

'The riots have been adequately suppressed and our relations with the British can very well be proven to you,' the minister said through gritted teeth.

'And how exactly might you prove that, Minister?'

'Simple. Invasion.' The minister grinned, the five rotten teeth he had left on display, and continued, 'This union is our attempt at expansion, whether it be with your consent or without. Our kingdoms may be equal in power, but I'm certain you will not care to see which of us the British support in the event of an invasion—a kingdom with a male heir or a kingdom without.'

Tara had never been this aghast and humiliated in her entire life. Neither had her father, whose attempt at pacifism had taken an entirely wrong turn. 'We would like to be given some time to consider this...generous offer of yours.'

As if sarcasm would save her father now. Tara felt the temperature of the room rise as the groups sat stewing in the tension.

'You may have a week to consider.'

'A month seems much more feasible.'

'A fortnight, no more.'

'Minister, as fit as that may seem, isn't this negotiation customary for the prince to take part in?'

'I am speaking on his behalf, and at the behest of his father, the King. A fortnight, Your Majesty. That is all you will have to ensure the fate of your kingdom. I suggest you and the princess choose wisely. God forsakes kingdoms led by ineligible women.'

Tara wanted to fling the table decorations in front of her at the minister and bruise his painfully upturned nose. *The utter nerve of him to call her ineligible, the sack of old beans.* She had never felt so helpless as her father agreed to the duration of the decision-making. Peace was as much of a virtue as patience, she had learnt, and had to keep telling herself as she led the voiceless prince and his loquacious minister to the palace exit.

Ineligible. If only the meeting weren't classified secret, she would have shouted to the minister as he waddled alongside the prince how this 'ineligible' princess was managing multiple batches of children, teaching them by day and spending countless hours planning their activities by night. It was quite decidedly futile, though.

'Go get your sister and come to my room immediately.'

Tara hitched up her sari above her ankles and ran to the west wing to fetch her sister.

'Is this about the suitor? How was he? Decent-looking?'

'His only redeeming quality.'

'The situation must be grave if Father wants to talk to both of us.'

Their father was pacing in his private salon, his shoes crashing against the marble floor with each step he took towards the walls adorned with portraits of past maharajas. This room was reserved for discussions of catastrophic urgency and the Maharaja conveyed the same to his youngest daughter. 'The kingdom is threatening invasion if we do not marry Tara to their prince. They've given us a fortnight to mull things over.'

'A fortnight? That's hardly anything. And what of the children? We can't risk their discovery and we have no place to send them to. We cannot possibly abandon them and let those ghouls infiltrate our administration.'

'It seems as though we may not have much of a choice.'

'Papa, I love both you and my people, but I refuse to spend another hour in a room with anyone associated with that kingdom, let alone marry into it.'

'He may not be quite as bad as you think, Tara. Please,

we have no other option. I'll give you time to think about it. I...I need to be alone.' He walked out of the salon and into his bedroom, latched the door.

The Maharaja hiding from his duty to his daughter. Tara had now truly seen everything.

'Tani, it's no use. I'll have to wed that horrible prince.'

She spent the rest of the evening lying listlessly in the sari she had met her future groom in, surprised by how impassively she had reacted to the entire affair. She moved her elbow, crushing some paper next to her—Tara sighed as she lifted the now-wrinkled schedule. She had successfully completed three of the eleven activities planned for that day. Examining it, she noticed 'walk in the garden, 6.30 p.m. to 7.30 p.m.' *There was still time for that. As long as she put her ill-fated marriage out of her mind...who knows...she could maybe even enjoy this walk.*

The next thing Tara knew, she had stopped to admire freshly blooming roses and carnations, marvelling at how their auras were tinted golden, courtesy of the roseate dusk that evening. Just as she was leaving the rose shrubs to marvel at the growth of hydrangeas, she heard an unmistakably familiar voice.

'Right where Aarti said you would be. Something about the roses?'

Tara hadn't felt this relieved in a while. Colonel Vijay Singh beamed at the princess as she spun around, reciprocating his enthusiasm. 'I was beginning to think they'd sent you off to war.'

'They almost did but your father insisted I stay. Royal

intervention, divine intervention, they're the same. As a token of my gratitude, I stopped at a local craftsman's shop outside our barracks to get you something.'

He fished around in his pocket and pulled out a painted wooden carving of insect ladybird the size of Tara's thumb. She thanked him, turning it over and over in her fingers.

'You're not telling me something. God, do you not like the ladybird? They had butterflies too. I didn't know—'

'It's not the ladybird.' Tara didn't take her eyes off it as she spoke. 'Anshugava is forcing me to marry their prince and threatening invasion if we don't comply.'

'What has your father decided to do?'

'So far? Marry me off.'

'Not to him?'

'There's no suitor left from a neighbouring kingdom.'

'What if you married a prince from one a little farther? I know of another kingdom not too far away with a prince who has quite a good reputation. He's about your age, too.'

Tara was aghast at this proposal. 'So you agree, then, with this sentiment—this idea of a loveless, political marriage? Am I nothing more than a bargaining tool? Colonel Singh, I can't deny that I expected more from you.'

'Tara—'

'It's "Your Highness" to you.'

Colonel Singh recoiled, taking a step back. 'I'm sorry, Your Highness. It was not my place. I should be going; your father is expecting me.'

Silana was infuriated as he walked away. *The utter nerve of men.*

Silana

Three months later

Silana had just finished stitching a rose that she had seen in the palace gardens on a handkerchief. It was one of her best works yet, and she knew her instructor would be very proud. Creative avenues seemed to be panning out well for her. The five-odd hours of piano she was able to practise during the week had quite a therapeutic effect on her. The notes intertwined with her memories and helped her release negative thoughts. When she stopped playing, she noticed that the melodies had untangled her thoughts and taken away the fears she had been harbouring. And for that, she was so grateful.

The Maharaja had given her two more lesson books and used to listen to her play whenever he could before he had had to return to the main palace two months earlier. The kingdom was, according to the staff, embroiled in affairs concerning the British and their role in the country's administration. The Maharaja was required to run the kingdom and smooth things over but made a point to visit the camps every other weekend. Additionally, he had left the children in the capable hands of his daughters. Apparently the eldest princess was about to be betrothed to a different suitor than originally planned. By Tara's own admission, he was extraordinarily kind-hearted. However, their kingdoms, though close, weren't neighbours. According to Tara, a few ministers were working on the logistics before the union could be finalized.

Silana was quite pleased with how the music club was turning out. The first 'show' they performed had been a raging success with both the children and the royals, so much so that more musicians were recruited to play the instruments in rotation—two children each to an instrument, as the system dictated. Silana shared the piano with another girl, Maryla, a freckled, ox-eyed girl who had been learning the piano for almost as long as Silana. Both of them had become fast friends, sharing lesson books, notes, camp gossip and everything in between. What solidified their friendship was a mutual hatred of sheet music. When first introducing Maryla to the lesson books, Silana had told her, 'Here, in this margin, I've written an acronym for the notes of both the treble and bass clef. I despise sheet music, but it's been my saving grace. I suggest you not be too ambitious and at the beginning of the book so you can hone your sight reading.'

She brushed off Maryla's incessant thanks.

'These are just a few things I wish someone had told me when I first started out. I am readily available should you need any advice.'

Maryla was a fast learner and soon enough the girls were learning to play duets together while working on their individual pieces. They learnt Johann Pachelbel's 'Canon' in D major in three weeks and Beethoven's 'Moonlight Sonata', first movement, in around two. Much to Silana's delight, the other children were also progressing with their instruments quite wonderfully, having learnt enough of the same piece to be able to practise together, overseen by Silana. Though their first time playing together was a racket of mistimed notes and endless struggles tuning their respective instruments, Silana was steadily hearing less squeaky string instruments and had to cover her ears to drown out the noise less and less, the day before being a record of only once. Getting their instruments to harmonize in a coherent macédoine of rhythm was not for the faint-hearted but they managed it.

The piece the group had been practising was nearly performance-ready. Silana did miss out on the chaos of the group, the piano being more of a solo venture and not quite blending into the assortment of Indian instruments, but she was glad to at least be able to relate to Maryla on a musical level.

Sebastien, on the other hand, seemed almost fully cured of the depression that had been plaguing him. About three months ago, he had joined forces with Levi and some of the other boys in the camp to start an initiative. Silana wasn't certain whether he was prompted by her skill or by the primal urge to outdo his sibling, but she was never one to pry.

Until the Maharaja was able to procure actual equipment, the boys played football with a ball that had been made entirely of rolled up socks, some begged, most borrowed and a few stolen from unwitting girls. The army officials often spent their afternoon practising with the boys, and eventually the games became more and more interesting with their newfound capacity to practise almost daily. They had enough recruits to split their group into two and, in order to demonstrate the prowess of training, were now set to play against each other in a match that evening. The Maharaja would be coming to spend the night at the palace for the occasion and the entire camp was buzzing as children rushed around to decorate the outside of their cabins and some rushed to line the ground with chalk to act as markers for the game. It was quite an exciting affair.

Silana's music club would perform after the game, with the night set to culminate in a grand dinner at the palace. The Indian classical group were set to perform a piece, 'Winter's Breath', before the dinner, followed by Silana's and Maryla's piano renditions. The girls were to play Tchaikovsky's 'Dance of the Sugar Plum Fairy' and 'Moonlight Sonata' respectively. Silana had pushed for a duet but Maryla had advised her against it. 'We want to show variety. With solo pieces, we have two chances to impress them. With a duet, we have only one. If one of us fumbles, both of us will have to bear the consequences.'

'I suppose you're right.'

'Music is so much more exciting when you have more of it.'

Both girls were sitting side by side, mulling over the logistics of their performance, Silana a mess of nerves, trying to soothe her anxiety by engaging in friendly raillery. A red-faced Aneta ran up to the girls. 'The Maharaja! He's come early! We're...starting.' She bent forward, hands on her knees to support her weight. 'He's an hour early!'

The trio bolted to the pitch, where the first half of the match was just about to kick off. The royal family and officers were present as well, seated on one side of the pitch. The girls sat on makeshift bleachers, cheering Sebastien, who was the captain of Team Red. Levi was the captain of the opposition, Team Blue. The game went on for about an hour, the score tied at 2–2 during half-time, but Seb scoring the winning goal brought the score to 4–3 in the second half. Silana ran to hug her brother, who was sweating even in the tingling chill that accompanied the fast-approaching twilight.

The Maharaja and his daughters were swamped by children during their walk back to the palace, but Silana could only think of her upcoming performance, clutching Maryla's hand as the pair entered the great hall and readied their sheet music. The children sat in concentric circles around the piano, with the royal family sitting on the same couch they had sat on when they had first heard Silana play, while the officers and royal guards stood at ease. Maryla was up first, silencing the excited chatter with the first note of her piece. Silana had never before heard as beautiful a rendition of the 'Moonlight Sonata' as the one Maryla performed, deservedly receiving a standing ovation. Silana knew she couldn't compare, but sitting at the piano and organizing her sheet in front of her audience was not an ideal place to second-guess herself. Her fate was in the hands of God...and Tchaikovsky. She nervously cracked her knuckles, waiting for the audience to finish congratulating Maryla. She positioned her hands on the piano, knowing that once she started, this irrationality would dissipate. She almost backed out of her performance, but then she looked at Sebastien. He, to her frustration, looked on with the same hope he had had when she had first played for him in the great hall. Now, she had to play...for him...their mother...and her vandal of a sister. She pressed her fingers and began playing the piece andante, gradually increasing the tempo and volume until it completely filled the room. Silana let herself melt into its delicacy until all that remained was the echo of its final note and thunderous applause.

Tara

All the paper setting Tara had to do was slowly getting to her. It reminded her of the potent hatred she herself had had for exams under the tutelage of her demented 'royal tutors'. The past three months had been nothing short of a whirlwind. The Maharaja had come up with a viable solution to their suitor problem as well—forming a matrimonial alliance with the kingdom of Mavanagar. The combined might of their two kingdoms would pose more than a formidable front against the invasion threat of Anshugava. Prince Kush, Tara's suitor, sympathized with Tara the moment she told him of their peril. Sympathy was not a common trait in monarchs and the sentiment quickly transcended into an alliance. Anshugava eventually gave up their quest for territory and power, much to Tara's relief.

Tara had met Prince Kush a few times, agreeing that he was probably the best suitor she could have. With that constant heckling out of the way, Tara was able to focus more on her duties towards her kingdom and the children. But throwing herself into her work wasn't just a distraction from her mounting duties; it could also be attributed to a certain colonel who had been lurking around the palace.

Tara and Vijay had been extremely cold to each other ever since the princess' outburst, addressing each other by their formal titles and only speaking when it concerned the children. Despite their tiff, the princess still kept the small wooden ladybird on her dressing table. They had stolen a few glances at each other during the football match but Tara was swept up in the hurricane of the night during the music performances and had failed to notice that he had slipped out of the gathering shortly before the commencement of the grand dinner.

Drafting the exam papers was quite a tedious affair, especially after the night of her father's celebratory dinner. The Princess had miscalculated the energy needed to politely socialize since she hadn't done so in quite a while. Tara had endured an hour outdoors, the discomfort of the situation amplified by dirt being kicked up by these boys every other second, and the children's incessantly tumultuous applause. The climax of the children's performances was, of course, the demonstration of the success of the music club. Her father was pleasantly surprised by the children's devotion to mastering Indian classical instruments and the beautiful medley they were able to piece together. The piano pieces, though, were the pièce de résistance. Tara had even stood up to applaud the girls, revelling in the excitement of it all when her relief finally trumped her anxiety.

The Maharaja had congratulated both his daughters. *Not too shabby for such an 'ineligible' princess.* Tara ate half her weight in food that night, mystified how nine hours of sleep could still culminate in her feeling drowsy the next day. One of the teachers, a prissy blond Polish lady who had a steadily receding hairline as her hair was always in a tight bun, came up with the bright idea of setting tests for the children to gauge their learning progress.

'I speak for all of us when I argue the children spend a lot of time in their extracurricular pursuits. Now, under regular circumstances, it wouldn't be a bad thing at all—it would, in fact, be quite wonderful.'

What would be wonderful was if this teacher could experiment with other hairdos, for a change.

'We can give the children roughly three months' time to prepare. If they don't do as well as they should, perhaps they can devote more time to their learning.'

So here was Tara setting the mathematics papers and creating answer keys. Luckily for the princess, she had formed quite a close bond with the science teacher, Miss Lucille, who was the only one who recognized the genuine intentions of the princess, while the other teachers thought she looked down on them. They mocked Tara behind her back, critiquing her 'ploy' for charity. Miss Lucille had shown Tara the ropes in regard to paper setting, for which Tara was endlessly appreciative. She had to handwrite all of the question papers and would have to ask her father for another large supply of stationery for the second time this month. He was certainly not going to be pleased, but Tara knew exactly how to get what she wanted by pulling at his heartstrings. The masses would call it manipulation, but she didn't mind—it was for a good cause after all. Tara had grown to not completely despise most of the children, with Aarti mocking her about how she used to refer to them as insects.

The children had grown to love the princess and had accepted her for who she was. At least, according to her weekly digest from Rafal and Valery. 'Taking everyone to the stream was certainly got you points!'

Tara had taken the children to the stream a month ago when her father was absolutely certain of the safety measures. It was a much-needed respite that they all had needed. The princess couldn't help but reminisce a little as she finished with the first set of papers, sighing and acknowledging her desperate need to take a break. The endless lines she had written were still imprinted in her vision, lining it with dark streaks of blue until she drew open her curtains and blinked rapidly at the brilliance of the afternoon sun. It was nearly lunchtime, and that would indeed serve as a welcome hiatus from her toil.

During the meal, her father gloated extensively about the achievements of his two daughters. 'Spectacular, just spectacular. I couldn't be more proud.'

Tara was, quite uncharacteristically, sick of the praise by this point and tried to change the topic. 'How has the kingdom been faring? It mustn't be easy, handling the entire kingdom single-handedly.'

'It feels so very strange to have to live in the palace without you both around. Meals are such a lonely affair; I'm almost talking to the pictures on the walls. The entire palace misses you; the gardener told me that the roses have never looked so lonely. But I'm reminded of the reason you two are away from me in situations such as this.'

Her father leaned forward, an inch away from getting his kurta drenched in sambar. 'You princesses and future queens have responsibilities. I can fulfil them on your behalf for only so long.'

Tara turned to look at her sister, whose evident confusion reflected her own feelings. 'Papa, what has suddenly happened?'

The Maharaja shifted in his seat, staring at his half-eaten *puri*. 'The British are becoming even more difficult. The protests have begun to move into the borders of our kingdom and I am afraid we cannot stop their swell if these protesters decide to push this mission of theirs forward. The cause for which they are fighting is noble, but their methods are violent and obsolete.'

'What does that mean for the children? For us?' Tanisha's irritation had morphed into worry.

'So far, not anything to be concerned about. Our guards have held the protesters at the western border, where they first began trickling in. I only hope it does not have to get to the point of us declaring an emergency.'

'An emergency?' Tara nearly screamed.

'It has not reached that point, Tara.'

'And what exactly is the reassurance that it will not?'

Her father ignored the comment. 'You needn't worry. The children shall remain here, and you both can watch over them until the union between Tara and Prince Kush is finalized. But after that, you both must return to Bramsadha with me.'

Tara was beyond livid. She was just a vessel for his schemes. Though initially dealing with the children had been burdensome, she had eventually found solace in it. Now, just as suddenly, he was threatening to wrench it all from her grasp. Tara couldn't bear to be in his presence for even a second longer. She muttered some excuse under her breath and made her way to the garden, half running, ignoring the

Maharaja and Tanisha calling after her. Her eyes glazed and she had to stop to wipe them before reaching the garden and, plopping herself down on a bench, looking around to make sure she was indeed alone. She spent a few minutes in quiet solitude before she heard a soft sound behind her—blades of grass being quietly squashed under heavy boots. She had heard these footsteps enough times to recognize their source.

'I must offer you my heartiest congratulations, Your Highness. The performance was indeed commendable.'

'Colonel, my father is to separate me from these children soon. Apparently the protests are escalating.' She beckoned him towards the bench. 'You must tell me all that you know. Of these protests and what they mean for my kingdom.'

He nodded. 'I take it there is no animosity between us anymore?'

'I cannot possibly blame you for my fate and this helplessness that reminds me that very soon I won't be able to have a say in the matters concerning my *own* kingdom.'

He was silent.

'The prince I am betrothed to now is half-decent...the very least I could ask for, really. But I've only ever longed for freedom and the ability to rule this kingdom without the direction of some foreign leader. I know these people and I've trained all my life to serve them.'

'Who knows! Maybe he'll succumb to your sharp tongue.'

'If only! God, what would I not give to not be bargained off for the sake of my kingdom.'

'I must confess something to you, Tara.' Vijay sounded urgent. 'It was I who suggested the union with Prince Kush to the Maharaja.'

Tara nodded. 'Thank you. I couldn't have asked for a better suitor. But it's not the one I want.' Her eyes locked with the colonel's inquisitive ones. 'I'd rather live with no qualms, in no one's shadow...maybe not to live a life as a princess is how I can achieve that, Vijay.'

The colonel looked considerably alarmed. 'The mere idea of it seems far-fetched and entirely improbable.'

'I shall leave the kingdom to more capable and willing hands, and a fate that shall remain the same whether written in history with me as this kingdom's ruler or not. You can deny it all you want, Colonel—us queens have no say in who writes our story or how they do so.'

In his eyes she saw simmering the same curiosity and wonder that had first drawn her to lock eyes with him. 'I've had no one to confide in over these past few months and have thrown myself into this initiative as a result. I'm afraid I might have nearly worked myself to death.'

He clasped her hand, and the princess didn't pull it away. 'None of these princes, no matter how wealthy, attractive or grand, shall ever have my heart. A long unfulfilled dream of mine has not been being saved by a well-built prince in antiquated armour, but finding this valiant aspirant sitting under a tree, reading a book that is all too familiar or asleep in some backwater moat. All that mattered was my father was completely airbrushed from the story, and none involved this business of ruling.'

He edged closer to her with each word she spoke, the wooden frames of the bench rattling under their weight.

'Vijay, there is nothing left for me here except these children. Apparently, I am the only one who's realized that.

These three months away from you have been difficult to the point of suffocation, and I do not wish to spend the rest of my days entangled in some loveless political gamble. I must guide these children for a little while longer. Then I wish to leave with you and escape to somewhere far from here.'

Silana

Everything was steadily increasing for Silana—her commitments, her interactions and most notably, her workload. Shortly after the performance wave hit and left Silana in some distant land of euphoria, she had to buckle down to prepare for the upcoming exams. Many of the children, however, didn't seem to be taking their academic pursuits very seriously, given their situation. *To each their own.*

Silana wasn't unduly concerned by the chaos of the war and studying was the most viable option in her pursuit to ground herself in reality. She encouraged her siblings and close friends to do the same; most followed suit, but some didn't—one of them being the once-academically-motivated Levi. Silana used studying as a distraction from her past, while her friend saw it as a path that led back to it. When she confronted the boy regarding his lack of ambition, he had argued that the rigour of it all reminded him of the endless days he had spent cooped up in his room trying to reach an end that had been out of his grasp from the very beginning—higher education and career opportunities. Or perhaps he was too taken by the ambience of this novel place to focus too long on a textbook.

Silana and her companions used to settle under Aneta's tree—as it was now unanimously called—after their classes to study, and with preparations now in full swing, Silana had to make a conscious attempt to not neglect her piano playing, having significantly reduced her practice time. The exams began just as the monsoons had started to intensify, the children having to adjust to studying in the chaos of their dorms and running to and from classrooms, hiding books under their clothes so as not to spoil them. Luckily for the children, these tests lasted only for a week, but the dates fell right in the middle of what was one of the fiercest monsoons the kingdom had experienced in years.

The general sentiment in the camp regarding the incessant downpour was one of disdain, but Silana oddly revelled in the needless chaos and hauntingly pulchritudinous yet melancholic atmosphere. Not to mention her utter joy at the petrichor that pervaded every inch of the camp during the brief spells of dryness. What she disliked about the rain with a burning passion, though, were the pests that accompanied it. A great variety of insects including gargantuan flies, beetles, millipedes and spiders would crawl into the shadowy corners of their cabins. Both the princesses, after seeing the magnitude of the storm and the plight of the children struggling to brave it, had written to their father and expressed an urgent need to arrange some protection for the children. The Maharaja managed to organize a shipment of umbrellas that would satisfy the needs of half the students, the idea being for two children to share one. Silana shared hers with Maryla, considering that their routines were nearly identical. Exam season passed quicker than Silana had anticipated and she ended up scoring enough to secure her a close second position, bested by a mere three-marks difference some 17-year-old 'genius' had achieved.

The festivities after the exams increased, as did their scope. The children had almost entirely mapped out the surrounding forest, knowing just where they could gather discreetly, find baby parrots they would take back to camp to nurse and forage for berries that grew in scattered bunches in nearby bushes. The palace staff who tended to the children took care to ensure that they stayed as far away as possible from potential snake nests, warning them of the reptiles' fondness for the thicketed regions of the forest. Life had never been this verdant for Silana. Now, often finding herself either below Aneta's tree or exploring various mossy, forested trails with her companions, evenings seemed to transform quicker into night-time than they ever had before. However, since the day of the football match and the children's musical display, Tara, as they had begun to call her, had been growing steadily distant from the children. It was slight, but noticeable to the extent rumours swirled that the princess was tired of them. Bit by bit, she had begun withdrawing from the children—first, leaving her sister to organize most of the children's activities, and then ceasing to attend all the miscellaneous football matches and musical performances, finally extending into her not even meeting the children during her teaching hours.

The past few weeks had thus provided Silana and some other older members of the camp to step up and take the reins from Tara and teach their juniors. Silana and Maryla decided to utilize their musical escapades to the palace as an opportunity to probe further and uncover additional intricacies regarding the princess' peculiar behaviour. One staff member, a stout, friendly woman, seemed quite keen on giving them details. 'She hasn't left her room since that dinner you all had. Well, other than oscillating between her bedroom and "art" room. She's made more paintings than I've ever seen before.'

'She paints?'

'Only when unfathomably bored or embroiled in an internal conflict. The circumstances make us believe it to be the latter. But I doubt it is anything you children have a hand in. Perhaps she's just overwhelmed by this new marriage prospect.'

It wasn't much reassurance, but it would have to do. Clearly, this stout woman's ramblings were going to be the closest Silana would get to answers. Tanisha had tried to take up for her sister and facilitate events during the weeks, but morale was down, given the absence of the elder princess. Silana, Sanja, Levi and a few other children had met the other teachers who taught them how to draft lesson plans using textbooks. The children would fall asleep on stacks of handwritten textbooks and lesson plans, wondering whether this needless toiling had finally pushed the princess to her breaking point—it was certainly pushing them to theirs.

Silana urged Maryla to not give up playing piano in light of the situation, encouraging the girl to learn a few more duets with her. These medleys would constantly play in the corner of her psyche that was once occupied by her parents arguing over the smallest of inconveniences. These memories had been what made her, her very essence, but Silana had learnt to understand that they did not define her any more.

She neither resented them nor forgot them, simply referring to her past from time to time to use it as a yardstick. Often, though, her past would merge into her present. She often saw Anna's and Sigrid's faces in her new friends—in their eyes, their smiles, their mannerisms and their love for her. These observations would build a delicate bridge of thought that traced back to remembrances of fraternizing under a tree that belonged to Silana's past. She would also see the day her father burnt her journal in the small fires they lit on icy nights. She threw in many a drachma in order to see her mother, yet Iris' fountain of anamnesis had almost always been replaced by her father's inferno. Silana would look upon his twisted features with more courage than she ever had before, even as he continued to mutilate each page of her mind's transcript. He didn't seem to haunt her anymore, this vision steadily fading away into embers that transformed into her mother and Aunty Ilse, both expressing to Silana how proud they were of her and her siblings, and how eager they were to reunite with them.

All she saw in these golden embers were yesteryears. Yvonne, as useless as the four walls of the rooms her father used to reprimand the children in, her communication limited to inconspicuous gestures of affection—quick kisses and faint smiles with as little emotion in them as their father's tellings-off. If only Silana had known how much they meant to Yvonne. This realization had long been buried in Silana's own subjective view that love could only be conveyed through words. Her father would draw her back into his world of hurt using lies embellished with assertions of love—countless assertions that swirled to form a relentless hurricane of words. But Yvonne's silence in love spoke louder than Lukas Haydn ever would.

Silana thought of her father every time she copied a new book—all in an effort to educate Jewish children. Silana could only imagine what he may have done, considering the magnitude of these literary pursuits. She handed her father all of the books and left him in a dungeon to tear the pages of each one, too rapt in his own private storm to realize where he was, muttering curses with what breath he had left.

That afternoon, she reflected upon it all with Levi. 'I've been seeing my mother lately. I'm beginning to worry. Why would a person who's alive need to send us these many avenues of memory to seek her in?'

'That's quite a hypothesis.'

'You may think that…you may tell me that I'm reaching, but I know what I see.'

'And there is indeed no doubt about that. But don't you think you should find comfort in her presence than find reason to suspect it?'

'You somehow know just what to say.'

'It's a gift.'

'Don't overdo it.'

'I hate to be a damper, but we still have to finish drafting those new lesson plans.'

'We're a day or two behind schedule.'

'Three, actually.'

'You can ignore my oversights.'

Silana made her way back to the camp after her cloud-gazing excursion with Levi, having ruffled a few of her friend's feathers.

'Her duties had significantly increased but Silana derived great satisfaction from completing them. She herself was quite startled by the number of responsibilities she had taken, realizing she'd been using them as a distraction. 'I've come to enjoy it,' she had told Sebastien a few mornings ago. Whatever darkness had come upon her brother had thankfully long dissipated but it had taken with it some of his characteristic sense of responsibility.

'Me stepping back wasn't such a bad thing, was it?'

'Why did you step back?'

A silence she'd heard before filled the gap between sentences.

'What matters is I'm here now.'

It wasn't the answer that Silana wanted but one she had heard a million times before; not accepting it wouldn't do her much good either. Being a unit was not the easiest thing when thrown into a melting point of political villainy, abandonment and exile, but the siblings had stuck it out.

Sunne's change had been less noticeable than that in either of her siblings, only comprehensible to those who had known her prior to the entire situation. Life had forced Sunne into a world where her complaints wouldn't be entertained, but Silana supposed her sister had to learn to grow up somehow. Of course, she never lost her sense of wonder and optimism, but it had been diluted.

The evening sky was a swirl of colours. Silana was no longer bothered by the ants that occasionally crawled up her legs, instead helping them find their way back to earth. It was that evening, during an ordinary dinner, that the younger princess proposed the idea of a Polish Independence Day celebration to the children. 'The occasion is in two weeks. If you children have any suggestions, we would be more than happy to hear them.'

Silana could hardly ignore this godsend avenue to keep herself occupied. She approached Tanisha with some other girls as soon as their dinner concluded. She had been mulling over ideas at dinner and was bursting at the seams. 'We could organize a small parade and flag demonstration. Some of us can take white cloth and, uh, red paint and make flags and other decorations, and the rest can make a float. Oh, we could have a traditional dinner!'

Tanisha had to calm her down. 'I thought my Polish had improved, but you're making me doubt that now.'

Discussions regarding the preparations extended into the next few days, with a small committee of children, with Silana and Aneta at its head, being formed with the responsibility of executing the event. The two weeks seemed to slip by swiftly, Silana's anxiety warping her perception of the days. In around a week's time, the preparations were in place and the decorations were all but hung up, with the following week spent accomplishing just that. Tanisha had taken the liberty of organizing violins, brass and percussion instruments for the hour-long parade demonstration. Silana had asked the princess to set up a small podium for the speeches as the Maharaja would also be joining them in the celebration.

The night before the event, Silana couldn't help but feel a sense of loss. It wasn't necessarily about losing her life in Poland, brought upon by the Polish Independence Day celebration preparations, nor was it related to her parents. Silana stared at the familiar but now more corroded grooves in the wooden ceiling, their twisting becoming steadily more evident. The grooves predictably morphed into the faces of her parents. They didn't say anything this time but stared straight at her, though not unnervingly—they knew something she did not. She took her eyes off Lukas Haydn but not her mother, and Silana could have sworn she saw a hint of a smile before both of them melted back into the shadows.

She had kept her best outfit ready for the day—a snow-white dress paired with paler stockings and a Venetian red hat that sat atop two cascading French braids. Silana had worn the hat only twice—upon her arrival at the camp and on her birthday. Throughout the day, Silana was swarmed by both her friends and her duties, both irritating her equally. Her chores had left the girl nearly as red-faced as the flags beating in the wind, their scarlet and white hues a stark contrast to the camp's viridescence. The celebration was a hit—the floats and accompanying music a moving patriotic demonstration—at least from whatever little Silana could ascertain considering how overwhelmed she was with duties.

What frightened Silana most about the entire ordeal, however, was the fact that she was to give a speech at the end, after Aneta—both the girls had been persuaded by Tanisha. A proficient orator back home in Poland, she hadn't really had the time to look much into the speech.

'Speak from your heart,' the princess had advised. *Where else was she to speak from?*

The butterflies in Silana's stomach grew exceedingly

persistent as Aneta delivered her speech, believing that her own would not compare in the slightest. That was until Silana was called to the podium, and her glossophobia melted into the relief of seeing familiar faces in the eager crowd of children. She took a sharp breath. 'We, the children of Poland—'

She fumbled with her paper, nearly dropping it. 'We, the children of Poland, cast away from our homes, embody not just the blood of our nation, but its spirit.'

Her speech went only uphill from there, with bubbling pride emerging from a chrysalis of trepidation. Silana was a crescendo whirlwind of emotions as her mother, Sigrid, Anna and Aunty Ilse, all sitting in the audience, cheered her on.

'India shall always be dear to my heart, but I was born on Polish soil, and to Polish soil I shall return one day. The people, our families and friends who have loved us and died for us, are from Poland, and one day we will honour their lives by returning. Poland is our past, our present and our future. Our country has been forsaken, but one day the sun shall rise upon a free Poland to grant it a new light and a new hope. We shall be there for that rising—in person or spirit, for we are the future of Poland.'

Tara

The scythe-wielding reaper sat perched on Tara's bed that week. Tara let him perch on her shoulder as she painted; however, she shooed him away after seeing his spectral presence reflected in the features of all her characters. Most bore the same mask of disappointment, but what terrified her was the haunting acknowledgement in some of its gazes. *It's not related to him, it just cannot be.*

Tara's ornate hovel was adorned with all manner of paint tubes. She flitted between her unfinished projects, trying to find a spark of inspiration in any of them. Her artworks had steadily transformed from renderings of summer days glazed with a dreamy yellow to either ships ravaged by the torrents of the North Sea or autumn trees that managed to find themselves in the midst of raven woods. Tara's plan to elope with the colonel had been hatched a few weeks ago. It was the most bewildering one of her entire life, for the princess had never battled such a cocktail of guilt, worry and relief before and it made her feel dreadfully sick. She assured herself that these feelings would soon pass but she couldn't help but entertain thoughts of doubt. The tiara that she had set aside while painting glinted knowingly at her from the desk—another reminder that she would be stripped of her title, her duties and her very essence…everything she had worked so hard to build. The prospect of her talent going to waste due to some foreign prince or the agony of leadership being tantalizingly close yet out of reach left her in an existential turmoil. This inner conflict had kept her occupied, with Aarti's concerned attempts to motivate her to tidy up the hovel being unfruitful. 'Or let me do it instead!' This resulted in the princess trying to physically cordon off the room.

Aarti had served most of her meals in the privacy of the hovel, recognizing the girl's struggle, after making a last-ditch attempt by mentioning the children. 'They are wondering where you've been. They've missed so many classes already.'

'The older ones have been taught enough and more; they're well equipped to help their younger counterparts. And with Tanisha, they're in capable hands.'

'The question is, Your Highness, why aren't they in yours?'

The princess ventured outside for the first time in weeks for lunch that day, where she pensively mulled over her sister's potential reaction to her elopement. She'd always felt that Tanisha was more deserving of the throne than she was—her effortless connection with the people, prowess for taking initiative and lively spirit—Tani would be more suited than Tara could ever dream of. *Perhaps it was truly all preordained.*

Tara's mind was quickly mainlined elsewhere as a red-faced Aarti rushed towards her, nearly out of breath from the ardour of climbing the palace steps. 'Princess, it's that piano girl. She appears to be...sick...she's with the doctor now. According to the guards, she fainted in class today.'

Tara hastily changed her clothes and sprinted towards the infirmary. She didn't even have the time to wear decent jewellery. The princesses working together were much more efficient than the nurses in dispersing the small gathering of children next to Silana's bed, with the exception of her siblings, much to the gratefulness of the presiding doctor, Amrut Vohra.

'She's in a stable condition now, Princess. I imagine that it was simply dehydration. The girl has been under considerable stress and I suppose she also got a little too well acquainted with the afternoon sun. '

Tara mumbled in agreement as she scoped out the infirmary—the bluish walls so sick of their mundanity that they had begun to peel.

'I'm so glad you came, finally, Tara. Oh God, this has all gone so wrong.'

'How can you blame yourself for this? You're one of the most capable people here.'

Tanisha was too blinded by self-inflicted guilt to agree. Tara pulled up a chair beside Silana whose dark hair was spread out like a raven's wing beneath her. Dr Vohra conveyed the situation to the Princess.

Tara clutched Sunne's hand while tears streamed down the latter's face. They had gathered around Silana's bedside and Sunne's other hand gripped a corner of her sister's blanket, as though some unforeseen forces would steal her away.

'The dehydration is more intense than usual. A preliminary examination is turning up nothing significant. Silana is more or less in the clear,' continued Dr Vohra.

In the clear.

'She'll most likely be fine by tomorrow.'

Tara made a silent promise to Silana that she would stay with her in the infirmary. As the day turned into night, the Princess felt grateful to have the perpetual company of Tanisha, Sebastien and Sunne. She didn't even mind when they questioned her whereabouts.

'Suitor business.'

'You've finally chosen someone?' Tara couldn't tell if the look on Tanisha's face was curiosity or concern.

'Almost. I must apologize to you all for my absence.'

The younger princess gave her a slow nod in response, before turning her eyes to Silana. Concerns were eased when Silana finally opened her eyes. The children came in droves now to see her. Amongst them were Rafal and Valery, who admonished Tara for her extended hiatus from teaching.

Silana conveyed that she had 'never felt better' to Dr Vohra, who took her claim with a pinch of salt. The knowing smile she gave Tara was all the assurance the princess needed. The number of children began to steadily decrease as it neared dinnertime. The nurses also tried to reassure the princesses and Silana's siblings regarding Silana's condition in an attempt to persuade them to go for dinner and return afterwards.

'We're now checking her pulse every 20 minutes. Whatever may have happened seems to have cleared up; we're attributing it to exhaustion,' said one of the nurses.

'Starving yourselves won't do any good. Do you want a matching bed here as well?' commented another.

'You people are worried over nothing. You should go.

Even I should be out there enjoying dinner!'

'You can be in here with us instead! It's delightful!' Tanisha commented. 'After all, what did happen to you?'

'You see I was near Aneta's tree; I'd left some knitting there. I retrieved it, but on my way back I began feeling light-headed. I thought it might be because of the afternoon sun and convinced myself I just needed to sit down once I returned to the cabin. But I ended up collapsing some distance from the camp, near enough for some boys to find me a few minutes later and raise an alarm. I'm feeling better, though, if I could just—'

'Completing that sentence will not bode well for you, I promise.'

Silana huffed right back into the solace of the thin infirmary pillow, arms crossed across her chest. 'Well, when shall I be let off?'

'I suspect tomorrow; they can't seem to find much wrong with you. Although personally, I don't think they're looking hard enough,' quipped Sebastien.

'I would slap you if I had the strength,' she glowered at a chuckling Sebastien. 'Sunne, do the honours.'

Tara was quite perplexed that the siblings could ignore there was royalty sitting amongst them as they carried on with their petty fights. As the night grew darker, their conversations ranged from activities that were going to take place during the week to backburner chatter. Tara and Tanisha were fierce in their refusal to leave until Silana fell asleep; they didn't have to wait too long. After convincing the Haydn siblings to return to their bunks and rest with the promise of rousing them at dawn, the princesses decided to spend the night in each other's company. They would wake up before the first rooster cawed to visit the girl once again.

'I just can't stand it. She's going to be all alone until the morning...I wonder why such things always happen to the most decent people. Our mother, for example.'

'That's quite an unfair comparison...this is nothing like that. The girl has most likely suffered from a heatstroke as they are not used to our climate conditions, and there is nothing more to it,' Tanisha tried to convince herself and Tara.

'Have you informed our father about the situation yet?'

'I'm quite sure the staff or healthcare workers have informed the palace, but Papa is likely busy. I shall tell him again should he not contact by tomorrow.'

For the first time since she had made the decision to elope with Vijay, Tara's mind was occupied with something more pressing than thoughts of him. The first crow of the rooster came just as Tara's exhaustion was beginning to dissipate, much to her luck. She yawned and woke up Tanisha, and made their way back to a still-asleep Silana, after sending Aarti to fetch Sebastien and Sunne. The girls watched from the infirmary as the moon slowly morphed into the sun rising. The old-fangled clock mounted above the girl's bed read '6.24 a.m.'—or at least that's what her sister told her; Tara's vision was too blurry to tell.

As the Haydn siblings entered the infirmary, an amiable nurse briefed them. 'The girl is recovering well. The signs of illness she was showing earlier seem to have passed.'

Finally, something to keep the princess awake. Tara clasped the nurse's hands in delight, thanking her with all the profuseness that an overflow of the cocktail of relief and drowsiness would allow her to.

Silana

The shadows of the tall grass cast across their cabins melted into the moon as Silana stared silently. It had been three days since Silana had fainted and everyone she interacted with seemed to be worried about her. It was a terribly tiresome affair to have to quieten each demon pounding to be let out of her skull while pacifying a friend or acquaintance. Silana was convinced that she was overworked, and judging by how one day in the infirmary had rejuvenated her, even Dr Vohra seemed to agree. 'My advice is complete rest. I know that you aren't too overjoyed with the prospect of being confined to your cabin, thus I advise minimal activities as opposed to none.'

So merciful of him. Distracting herself through studies was hardly an option now—she was sick of the pitiful glances and incessant remarks about her health. Keeping her chin up became easier as the days passed and the rumour mill began churning out other tales. At least her piano required minimal physical exertion, the girl finding that element a constant in her now heavily scrutinized routine. Throughout, a steady pounding in Silana's head was a quiet score to her thoughts. *It's the stress.*

And for the most part, her days were distracting enough to avoid her persistent headache almost entirely. It seemed to be clearing up too, due to the medication Dr Vohra had prescribed her. The days, however, seemed to creep past her eerily, like they were anticipating something the girl was not aware of yet. Her homesickness was now more potent than ever.

'This would have never happened back in Poland.'
'This?'
'My episode, of course.'
'It's true that we don't often have such a harsh sun over there, but I thought you'd be used to it by now.'
'I did too, Seb.'
'Do you ever regret coming here?'
'Huh?'
'Do you regret it? Would you have rather remained in Poland?'
It took Silana a minute to process the question, the fault of those demons inside her skull. 'I have about as many regrets coming here as our father did when he signed that arrest warrant.'
'I've almost completely forgotten what he sounded like.'
'Have you, now?' Silana chuckled.
'It's not something I'll forget anytime soon, what with the book burning and all.'
'Ah, that was a fun day, was it not?'
Silence.
'Silana, enough time has passed for us to now look back at this with some objectivity. As much as I hate to say it, our life in Poland died the minute we set foot on that train.' Sebastien picked up a small, misshapen pebble and flung it at a nearby bush. 'I'm not indifferent to our reality. Trust

me, it's very much the opposite. But to what extent can you evade it?'

'The roles were quite different last time around, weren't they?'

'And we have you to thank for it. You and your unshakeable hope.'

'This is probably the kindest you've ever been to me... I'm not that far gone.'

'I'm so glad you agree.'

The next pebble the boy tossed was at his sister, who feigned disdain. 'Old habits die hard. Come, it's almost time for breakfast. I heard they have eggs today!'

Silana wrinkled her nose, preferring to walk back to the cabins while Sebastien sprinted across dew-speckled ferns and harmless fungi. *We cannot evade our reality.* This truth rang in her ears the entire day. She used to reiterate this statement with a frighteningly emotionless exterior while comforting Sunne on rough days, but its implications had never truly hit her the way they did today. Perhaps the devils, becoming more potent by the day, had chiselled a path into some abyss that this realization could seep through. It left a bitter taste in her mouth that only dissipated when she was around either her cabin-mates or her piano. The classroom failed to act as her escape any more. Even after persuading the elder princess to resume teaching, Silana could no longer derive joy from these small victories, feeling less and less competent with each passing day. But keeping appearances was of the utmost importance, should that overbearing doctor decide to put a stop to her activities. However, appearances were only skin-deep, and

Sunne knew Silana well enough to see beyond it.

'I'm worried about you, Sil.'

'It should be the other way around, firstly, and secondly, your worry is misplaced.' Silana hated (loved) how perceptive her sister was turning out to be. 'I'm just feeling a bit under the weather.' *Plausible.*

'You're a terrible liar.'

'Since when have you become so pushy?'

'I learnt from the best.'

'I beg your pardon, I'm not pushy!'

'So? Are you going to tell me?'

Silana suggested a walk in the woods and her sister agreed.

'For the first time since we came here, I'm worried about what will happen to us. We don't have a home to return to, certainly not one we shall be welcomed back into, and no inheritance to fall back on. It had somehow escaped me that we are well and truly alone.'

'Do you believe that? That we are well and truly alone?' asked Sunne.

Silana drew her lips in a tight line.

Sunne continued. 'Excluding the princess' support, the most important thing at this moment is that the three of us are able to rely on each other. You're refuting the most fundamental thing that Mama drilled into us when we were still staying with Aunty Ilse. We're a unit. That is enough reason for me to believe we're far from alone.'

'Something's certainly happened to this world after my episode, everything's become topsy-turvy. Sebastien was giving me a similar disquisition this morning.'

'The point of no return indeed. It's getting dark, we should head back.'

The sunset peeked through the canopy of the trees as the girls discussed their plans for the next day. They arrived just as dinner was being laid, settling into their respective seats with the princesses at either head of the table. Nothing about the night seemed especially extraordinary to Silana, and indeed, nothing was. Yet the small lanterns that the palace staff had hung across the branches of trees shone like stars. The conversations Silana had found to be crude and in sharp contrast to her meals in Poland now filled her with a strange sort of warmth, and for the first time, she glowed like the rest of the children at the camp did with a joy not even the night's darkest shadows could steal away from her.

Tara

A winded Aarti banged frantically on Tara's door just as she was about to settle in for the night. This was entirely inappropriate, and she planned to tell off Aarti about it, but the woman interjected, 'Your Highness, it's the piano girl again.'

Tara was in the infirmary and by Silana's bedside in no time. She hurriedly greeted her sister and asked to see Dr Vohra. Silana's ebony hair formed a halo around her head while resting on a pillow. Sunne looked as though she had been crying, sniffing loudly at intervals.

'She just...she just fainted after dinner and we had to carry her here.' Sebastien explained.

Tara felt her heart grow heavier, almost as if it were going to drop down to her feet.

'Dr Vohra?'

'Her pulse has been fluctuating. We've been taking readings at 60-second intervals.'

Silana was almost as pale as the bed sheet beneath her, her forehead soaked in sweat and her eyes squeezed shut. It was almost as if Tara were watching someone sleeping through a nightmare.

'Her other vitals have been normal and there are no injuries.'

Tara, though entirely flabbergasted, stayed by Silana's

side that entire night. Tanisha tried talking to her sister but gave up upon receiving only monosyllabic responses. Tara stayed by Silana's bed, going so far as to order her staff to bring in chairs from the palace itself for the other two Haydn siblings.

She clasped Silana's hand for hours on end, watching from the infirmary as the moon morphed into an aureate twin of itself and eventually disappeared into the western sky. Silana's siblings had been whispering words of comfort into the girl's ear, and her pulse had begun stabilizing over the course of the day. Tara and Tanisha were squished in one chair, and Sunne and Sebastien in another, with Levi sitting on a stool at the foot of Silana's bed. The nurses tried to lift their spirits and pacify them regarding Silana's condition in an attempt to coerce them to have their meal and return, but no one listened.

Silana was comatose the entire day and unresponsive to Tara's pleas. As day gave way to night, Tara stayed awake longer than any of the others did—until it was only the nurse who checked Silana's pulse every 15 minutes and the Princess herself who were awake. Tara fell asleep near dawn, clutching Silana's hand tightly—when a jolt and sudden separation of their physical bond woke her up just a few minutes later.

A nurse had severed Tara's grasp on Silana's now alarmingly cold hand, yelling something to a few doctors who came rushing from their dorms to gather around the girl. The nurse's urgency and the doctors' frantic movements snapped everyone out of their drowsiness as they realized the gravity of the situation. Sunne had burst into tears by this point, burying her head in her brother's embrace, and

Tara's heart dropped to her feet at the sight. She was on the verge of collapsing, clutching Tanisha for support as the doctors yelled to each other in an indecipherable language. There were nearly five doctors gathered around Silana's bed now and Tara was too dazed to focus on what each of them was doing individually. She fully snapped back into reality, however, when the chaos subsided into something entirely worse—an eerie silence. The yells had become murmurs and she followed the doctors' movements as each of them turned to look at the clock perched upon an adjacent wall.

No, no, no. Panic. Yell for medicines, do something, anything.

Dr Vohra looked at his clipboard, stopping for the briefest second before proclaiming in a shaky voice, 'Silana Haydn, 15 years. Time of death, 3.03 a.m.'

Silence hung heavy in the air for a few moments. It seemed as though time itself had been paused. The next thing Tara remembered was sobbing into Silana's cold, limp hand. She caressed her fingers and tried her best not to look at the girl's face, which was now a cold mask of placidity.

Sunne had collapsed on the floor and Sebastien held her as she rocked back and forth. All the emotions Tara had felt during her mother's passing, all which she had bottled deep inside her thus far, came spilling out as unrelenting as an avalanche. Silana's hand was wet with Tara's tears, the doctors looking on in pity, not having the heart to place the tell-tale white sheet over the girl and wheel her to the morgue.

There were so many things Tara had wished to say to the girl. Her attachment to Silana represented all the things the children had changed in the princess, for the better. She tried squeezing her eyes shut multiple times and opening them, hoping to find that it was just a nightmare.

Tanisha, her green eyes tinted red, tried to talk to Tara, kneeling to meet the eyes of the princess, who just stared back at her sister blankly. All her attempts proved to be of no avail—the princess was so entirely devastated that even though her sister was talking directly to her, her voice seemed to be distant and muffled. It was as if some unseen force had enveloped Tara and was holding her tightly in place—she couldn't move a muscle and was utterly paralysed.

The day was a blur for Tara and Tanisha had to arrange everything for Silana's last rites. News spread around the camp quickly and Tara felt as though she were walking in a dream.

The Maharaja was on his way back to the summer palace, the information having been conveyed to him. Tanisha spent the afternoon looking after the children, the grief as palpable as the fear regarding Silana's condition. The most likely explanation the doctors could give the persistent Maharaja upon his arrival was the possibility of a stroke—the result of some underlying condition the girl had possessed. Tara watched as the grief she had buried inside her resurfaced, more pervasive than ever, its monstrous presence darkening Tara's room. She threw open the curtains and turned on all the lights but still this cloud of darkness hovered.

The princess had an idea. She brought out her paints, the white tubes with coloured bands scattered across the floor as the princess searched for the correct shade. Titanium white, forest green and black. With no idea of what to paint, she decided to go with a half-eaten pear. The rendering was simple but her hands shook as she tried contouring the fruit to add elements of light and shadow. It took her hours but it was a shoddy work at best. Tara was exasperated, trying to salvage whatever little of the piece she could before a familiar knock at her door distracted her from her task. She unlocked her bedroom door for Aarti, who looked worse than Tara had ever seen her before. The housekeeper's normally slicked-back hair frizzed unpleasantly at the top of her head, her bindi was missing and the hem of her sari was caked in a dry layer of mud. 'Did you finish your breakfast?'

Tara lied that she had. Aarti looked past her towards the breakfast tray. 'No, you haven't. You painted instead. And look at this mess you've made. I have to clear it all up now. As it is there's been so much happening today.'

'I'll clean it, don't worry.'

Aarti resisted the princess' attempt to shut the door, squeezing her rotund frame through.

'That's not at all important right now.' The princess retreated as Aarti managed to enter the room. 'A child passed away today, and it's affected all of us, not just you.'

'You don't understand.'

'I never said I did. But your sister is out there, and your father, handling those children alone, while fighting back their own sorrow. Being lonely in your grief didn't work for you when the Maharani passed. It won't work now either. Tara,' Aarti's tone softened, 'if there's anything that girl has taught you...that I have taught you...it's that family is the most important thing you could ever have.

Hold on to it before it slowly depletes and all that is left to love are memories.'

The golden hues of the sun streamed through the open window.

'Where's Tani?'

Later that day, the princess channelled her numbness, for it helped her to aid the children without faltering herself. She took the reins from Tanisha, gathering the children to help them embrace their grief and encouraging them to share their experiences with Silana and never once letting either Sebastien or Sunne leave her side. The former of the two had been spending much of his time at the infirmary—Tara assumed this to be his version of a quest for answers. That evening, dinner was Silana's favourite—biryani. Large bowls of the dish adorned the dining table but the children seemed hesitant to eat. Most of them lit small diyas and ceramic lamps in Silana's memory, sharing moments of silence for her as they sang to the trees of their sorrow. The singing, initiated by Sunne, lasted through dinner and most of the night, slowly dispersing into the cabins with the children as they retired. They were Polish folk songs; Tara recognized one as 'Drugie przyjście'—the second coming—a theme of God's intervention and rebirth. But the songs talked of flowers, not of girls—

'A w ziemi było jej serce,
Jej płatki zwiędły i rozpadły się,

Ale jej dusza pozostała w gwiazdach,
Na które słonecznik patrzył jako dziecko...

(And in the ground was her heart,
Her petals withered and fell apart,
But her soul remained in the stars,
Which the Sunflower looked at as a child...)'

*E*pilogue

The Royal Palace
1st Jeval Road, Bramsadha
Gujarat, India

My dearest Tani,

I hope all is well with you, your husband and little Kirat in Bombay. I miss you every day and plan on visiting before the month ends.

Writing this letter felt more personal than a phone call today. Penning a letter is entirely unconventional for me, as you know, but it was as if the day itself called out to me. Most curiously, it happens to be the 25th anniversary of the passing of our dearest Silana. I've marked all my calendars with that date—I remember so vividly the state she left us all in. How could one ever forget?

It's been 20 years since we shut the camp after the end of the war—oh, how I miss it! I miss the screaming children and their love for dirt. I would give anything to experience those years again with you and Papa! It's nearing three years since his passing but it feels as if it were yesterday. Our daughter is fortunate to have met Papa before he left us. It's a shame Kirat never met Mama though; she would have loved her.

Our father was never the same after he lost his title—as

though a small part of him died when he was no longer the Maharaja of Bramsadha. It was but inevitable that the rest of him would soon follow. Despite our people's wish to elect me as head of the region instead of my husband, perhaps seeing a woman handle the affairs of the kingdom for the first time was a shock. We'll never know, will we?

The King and I often tell stories of the camp to our daughter—him of the few years he knew the children after our marriage, and me primarily of Valery, Rafal, Levi and Silana. I see that girl in so many places—in the notes Kirat plays on the very same piano Silana once sat at… she even looks a bit like her, too—the same round face and eyes brimming with curious wonder. I haven't seen that look in a long time—now that she's a teenager—but when I tell her about the children who had come to us and lived in the camps, I catch glimpses of it.

I take her to visit Silana's grave each time we go to the woods and she puts fresh flowers there. They're always a mix of white and pink cherry blossoms—the same ones Silana was buried with. I like to think that as they wither, their life seeps down to her and makes her eternal life ever more wondrous. She deserves it…all the children do.

Aarti is old and quite blind now. She keeps telling me that she's never seen anything as profound as the impact those children had on us. Even you were motivated to travel to Bombay and make use of your degree—to think that the most restless of us all is the most focussed!

I miss you terribly. My small haven here is full of love but its rooms are emptier than ever. I try to fill them with memories of the times we shared in these very halls. Though

I wish I had stored more of those seemingly unimportant whimsies, what Silana and the rest of the children taught me is far more precious and unforgettable.

Do reply to me at the earliest; I need a legitimate excuse to venture out to meet you. This husband and daughter of mine really do get on my last nerve sometimes.

Much love,
Tara

Vishwananda Building, 7th Floor
Apoorva Singh Road, Colaba
Bombay, India

Dear Sunne,

How have you been? Reaching out to you has been the most soothing yet bittersweet part of this entire day.

Sil's 25th death anniversary...she's been on my mind every moment and I know you miss her as much as I do.

It's been 20 years since you moved back to Poland...a long time to be away from you. My decision to stay here is not one I regret, but I do wish I could see you and Aunty Ilse more than a few times a year. Do convey my regards to her, as well as from Padma and Viraj. Aunty Ilse calls me often to ask how I am faring, living in Bombay with 'only' this new family of mine—my wife and son.

Please pass along my regards to Levi as well. His law firm has been the talk of the Polish community here. I hate to have lost touch with him, but our jobs have us quite occupied.

Viraj is on the cusp of entering secondary school and aspires to study medicine too, influenced by my vocation rather than any other reason. Silana is hidden in his passion though—she was the reason for mine. Becoming a neurologist here was the last thing I expected I would do, but it has made me realize this career is the one I was meant to pursue. My speciality in stroke research and my determination to study it are all attributed to our late sister.

My amazement shall never dwindle when comparing Papa and her. His trial after the war was one of the most distasteful things I'd ever seen. The evil finally caught up with him. His execution seemed fitting, especially with what he did to Mama... We never really did find out what happened to her.

Sunne, the past continues to cast a shadow of doubt but I look back at it with less fear now...more nostalgia—for the camp, the royals, the other children...but our sister especially. She wouldn't have wanted us to live the rest of our lives in sorrow—a life without happiness is hardly a life at all.

I am pleased you've started a job as the principal of our old school—quite a promotion from being a mere teacher. To think the number of tantrums you threw within those very walls. Aunty Ilse told me of your mission to educate the children about the good Maharaja. I wish you all the luck in the world...wherever Mama and Silana are, I have no doubt that they would be just as proud.

Your loving brother,
Sebastien

In Gratitude

To my brother and father, who add mischief to my life.

To Nanu, whose unbounded drive I hope to emulate one day.

To Sir Digvijaysinhji Ranjitsinhji Jadeja, whose unconditional goodness and love I hope to immortalize through my work.

To my publishing agent, Dipti Patel, who believed in me and without whom this book would have never been published.

To Dibakar Ghosh and everyone at Rupa Publications, who were so very crucial in facilitating this book. I am eternally in your debt.

To my editor at Rupa, Anupama Roy, whose invaluable advice and input helped this novel take shape.